A CHARLIE CHAN

E-GIRL
UNPLUGGED

ADI FLYNN

BAL
KON
media

E-GIRL UNPLUGGED

Published by Balkon Media

Paperback edition ISBN: 978-1-8384529-3-3
Hardcover edition ISBN: 978-1-8384529-7-1
Also available as an E-book and Audiobook

A CIP catalogue record for this title is available from the British Library.

Edited by Hanna Elizabeth

Paperback, E-book & Audiobook cover: GetCovers
Hardcover design: Particular

www.adiflynn.com
www.balkon.media

also by adi flynn:

CHARLIE CHAN CRIME THRILLERS

E-Girl Unplugged

#BookTok Made Me Do It

Catfish Unmasked

For Noel Smith —
exceptional carpenter, extraordinary uncle

Never one for the ol' books, but he crafted a mean bookcase

prologue

THE NIGHT WAS DARK, especially so through the tinted glass of the hired Range Rover Evoque, as it blazed past The Three Graces, some of Liverpool's most grand and recognisable Grade I listed buildings.

It was darker still within the cab of the car, where the driver sat behind the wheel in a fevered panic, tears streaking makeup down her face. The Evoque took the third exit off the roundabout and disappeared into a gaping tunnel entrance, leaving Liverpool behind and the clusterfuck that had been tonight.

Emefa—e-girl, pop diva, and addict—shivered from manicured fingernail to pedicured toe. No matter how fast she drove, it felt like she could not leave the event behind. It followed her, almost like the very burden she was trying to shed was holed up in the back of her car, adding a drag of weight to her escape. Her leg shook involuntarily against the pedal, forcing a thrumming rhythm out of the engine. She still didn't realise that the air con was on full blast.

Her phone rang—a distinctive ringtone. It startled her. Not her agent, or her mum, or any of her dealers. She scooped it off the passenger seat, tapped it onto the magnetic dash holster, and glanced at the screen. It was Marcus, her producer. She killed the call, then dragged the flat of her hand across her forehead, peeling away a layer of foundation that had come loose with her sweat.

The car exited the tunnel like a bullet and was suddenly illuminated from behind. High beams singed her rearview mirror. Someone was driving right up her arse. She pushed the accelerator and tried to put some distance between the vehicles. But her own headlights caught the glare from a red and white striped barricade. A hard stop made of admittedly flimsy plastic on a slow-moving hinge. The tunnel toll.

She slammed on the brakes. The car skidded itself to a stop, millimetres from the barrier. She reached across the passenger seat and dug through her handbag for her credit card. She pulled out a few, and finally selected the glitzy shimmering pink Monzo card usually reserved for hotel bars and late-night fast-food runs. It was her petty cash account. A bit of 'off-the-books' play money. It wouldn't get her far, but it wouldn't be disabled if her producer suspected that she'd gone missing for a quick fix. Again.

Stretching her arm, and some of her upper body through the window, she couldn't reach the card reader mounted on the wall of the tollbooth.

"Come on," she grunted.

Undoing her seatbelt, she leaned even farther out the window to tap. Still not close enough. Her arms weren't made for labour, they were made for taking selfies. She opened the door just a crack and edged herself off the seat to buy an extra few inches.

The car behind her was stopped, but she couldn't make out the face of the driver. She glared at the vehicle suspiciously. As if waiting for them to get out and charge her.

The card reader finally beeped. She threw herself back in the car, the car door slamming and knocking her card out of her hand, and onto the ground.

"Shit!"

The barrier rose. She had to choose between escape and entrapment. She sped forward and left her card on the tarmac. The barrier swung closed again, keeping her high-beam pursuer at bay as they paid their way through.

She forced herself to exhale slowly. It was fine; she was in control. She felt relieved, but not enough to slow down. A few minutes later she was out of the urban sprawl, lighting up the Wirral countryside with her headlights, on a mission to get away from everything and everyone.

Marcus called again. The screen buzzed and lit up the darkened car once more. She swiped to kill the call, missed, and swiped again, with a quick eye to the rear. The lights of the other car were long gone. Hands still shaking, she took the phone from the mount, and scrolled to find her favourite chill-out playlist. Her fingers and thumb weren't behaving, and her phone slipped through her fingers to clatter into the footwell, casting its light on the ceiling, the shadows shifting.

Looking back, her eyes locked onto a mound in her back-seat, a lump that rose as her rain jacket quietly slipped to the floor. It had the vague shape of a man.

She screamed.

The car mounted the kerb and hit dirt. She spun quickly to catch the wheel. She was driving over boggy mud, tearing up the soft earth, as her car ploughed through the unsettled field. The high-clearance wheel arches clogged with gunk and fertile muck as she bounced and shuddered her way to a sudden stop at the base of a tree. The front of the car was planted firmly in the trunk of a huge sycamore. The headlight that was still working hit a patch of fog beyond, which closed in all around her.

Everything hurt.

That was good. She knew she was still alive.

Some of her running mascara was mixed with blood and she felt it run down her cheek. She groaned as she tried to lift her head off the steering wheel, but she could only raise it enough to see that the windscreen was shattered, a mess of glass shards above the dashboard.

She heard the door open, and then sensed a figure standing next to her.

The man took a bracing breath and hauled her out through the bent doorframe.

"It's okay," he whispered, his voice as wispy and see-through as the fog. "I'll be taking care of you now…"

chapter
one

Eleven Months Later

LIVERPOOL. February. It was nippingly cold, but festivities kept the streets bright and warm all through the city centre. A crowd had come out, an army of scousers, to join in the celebrations. The city was in good spirits.

It was New Year for the Chinese population, most of whom were descendants of the tens of thousands of merchant sailors who'd, during the Second World War, once formed Europe's largest Chinatown—but for everyone else, it was another excuse for a party. St Luke's, more commonly known as the 'Bombed Out Church,' and the length of Leece Street were transformed into a pop-up festival ground celebrating all things East Asian.

Shoppers were out in droves. A traditional parade weaved its way along the normally busy dual carriageway. Firecrackers went off, tiny ones like popping chestnuts, while two tassel-lined and bedazzled lion mascots roamed the streets. One part dance and one part reverie of the spirits, it was a march of a creature who brought good luck and fortune for the New Year.

One of the dancers was well into it. She wore the lion's

head over her torso, working the blinking eyelashes with an accessible squeeze-grip and the mouth with her other hand. It was like manipulating a giant Muppet whilst dancing. She could see through the mouth. She wasn't exactly hiding, as she had to see where to go. Not that she'd get lost. Charlie had lived in Liverpool her whole life.

Charlotte Jane Chan was an English girl through and through, who just happened to have been born to parents who'd emigrated from Hong Kong. When people asked where she came from, *like, where she's really from*, she would put on an increasingly obnoxiously Scottish accent and riff about Edinburgh until they left her alone.

The Lunar New Year was one of the few times she felt the urge to really embrace her heritage. She was delighted to be finally given the chance to do what she'd always thought, growing up, must be the most fun thing the celebrations had to offer.

When she saw kids watching, she took a detour to give them a wink of her enormous eyelashes or jostle her felt-lined jaw at them to try and put a smile on their faces. Her co-dancer was mostly just following along for the ride, pushing the lion's back and rear-end up and down, sometimes adding an inauthentic twerk if it got a giggle from the teens in the crowd.

Charlie was unimpressed, but there wasn't much that could be done about changing partners at this stage.

The parade ahead of her was made up of students from a Cantonese language school, a Wushu academy, as well as representatives from various business associations and some canny restaurateurs, offering dim sum samples and menus. They handed out lucky golden cats, paper fans, lanterns, and origami—Asian stuff, not strictly Chinese. The band behind played fittingly traditional music on an array of instruments. It was lovely.

"There she is!" Charlie heard. It was a distinctly nasally

voice she could pick out from the whole crowd of scousers. It was the sound of Rebecca Jarvis' nose piercing, acting up in cold weather again as she whipped out a phone. Charlie turned to her friend and gave her a sassy wink and mouth flap. The perfect Insta moment.

Rebecca was a pale-skinned e-girl with a large side order of punk. Usually, she looked like she'd just stepped out of 80s-era Camden, except for the fact she was born twenty years after that look took off and subsequently disappeared in the UK.

She inherited her mother's love of the Ramones in the womb, and it influenced her to favour a rough-and-tumble appearance. She normally wore ripped jeans, some kind of cropped jacket, a T-shirt that looked stolen straight off the back of someone in a hit-and-run, and heavy boots. The ensemble was often topped off with either an electric blue or shocking pink wig.

Today, she'd toned it down for Charlie's benefit, and opted for full-on cultural appropriation with a silver qipao dress complete with mandarin collar. She wore her natural dark black locks tied up with an array of golden floral hair pins. She was a good enough friend to ditch her skateboarding plans to show up for Charlie's sake.

And so was her other friend, who Charlie spotted across the street.

"Ashley," Rebecca shouted. "You're going to miss it!"

Charlie saw Ashley Powell—a proud black man in a sea of white faces—doing his best to navigate through the crowd, talking animatedly into the ear of a young woman. Ashley was in good form. He'd also made an effort for the occasion.

He'd shaved to accentuate his chiselled features. His hair was freshly frosted, and he was wearing a sleek but warm velvet jacket with tailored trousers that drew attention to his shoes— two-tone Oxfords, polished to a mirror shine—which were the real appeal of his outfit. As usual. They cost more than the rest of the outfit put together.

The girl he was chatting up, however, didn't seem all that interested. Ashley rolled his head down, defeated, and walked through the crowd. On his own.

Rebecca held back laughter.

Charlie decided to play around. She got up close as he crossed the street and tried to startle him.

"Hey, Char—"

She tried to nip at his head.

"Hey—not the hair! Take the jacket, but not the hair. The jacket's out of season anyway."

He continued his strut across the street until he wound up beside Rebecca.

"This jacket," he complained, "is what's throwing me off."

"Why?" she asked. "It's dark, you're dark—it matches, yeah?"

"Fashion isn't about matching," he politely protested. "It's about a statement. If I blend in, my statement is"—he mumbled gibberish while barely moving his mouth—"and that's boring. Or creepy. I'm standing out, top-down my look is meant to be a beacon, you see?"

"This is my beacon," Rebecca said, flicking her nose ring and then running a finger down the five piercings in her left ear. "She'll always be the one that got away."

"At least," Ash said, "we can both take some solace that we aren't the worst-dressed people here." He turned to Charlie, who stood beside them with her lion head perked up like an attentive dog, listening.

"You're peacocking," Charlie mocked through the gaping mouth of the lion. "Bright colours, standing out, lots of movement—that's what animals do."

"Yeah, and it usually works," he said.

"I'm glad you're having fun, Charlie," Rebecca cut in. "But try not to overdo it. We've got work in the morning."

"I know," Charlie said, tilting her whole body to quirk the head as she spoke. "But come on—this might not be coming back next year. The committee really had to beg, borrow, and steal to get the funds for this last minute."

"You'd think the City Council would be all over this, lavishing you with funding. If nothing else just to show how woke they are," Ash said. "Look how many people are out and about. Spending their money, growing the economy."

"Chance would be a fine thing." Charlie shook her head and the lion's.

"I didn't know twerking dated back to the Ming dynasty," Ash observed as he watched the rear of Charlie's lion shake, rattle, and roll.

"It doesn't," she said pointedly, glancing back at her co-dancer with the sternest look she could manage through the grinning mouth of a red and yellow lion.

"Show us what it can do, then." Ash reached out to touch one of the lion's eyelids.

Charlie shook her head and rattled the tassels of the fake fur. Ash recoiled and brushed himself off pre-emptively, worried it would leave garish lint on his precious burgundy.

"That's overdoing it," he said.

"I am not," Charlie began, and then took to flapping the mouth open with each word, "overdoing it at all!"

"Go on, *git*," Rebecca said, snapping her finger like she was trying to scare her away. "Finish up so we can hit the pub."

Charlie gave the gathered crowds one last lion dance to rapturous applause and then crossed the road before removing the heavy lion head and stepping out of the tasselled costume, sauntering back to the muster station with the other dancers and musicians. The parade had been a success.

The street congestion tapered off as they left the trendy bars and restaurants of Bold Street behind and continued down past the chain stores—the regular pulse of life ever-changing—through the streets of Liverpool.

But some people just couldn't wait for the festivities to end before they went and ruined the fun of others. People who saw peace, not as a time for rest and preparation to accomplish distant goals, but as a weakness that had to be exploited for self-gain. Opportunists, when they followed the law. Criminals in any other case. In the case of what Charlie saw, it was the latter.

"Stop!"

The thinned-out crowd turned at the roar of an active, older gentleman in a security guard uniform. A younger bloke ran out ahead of him with a pile of clothes still on their hangers tucked under his arms. They came bounding around from Paradise Street, past the Wushu display team packing their props and costumes away in a shipping container. Charlie was just fifty yards away from hanging up the lion for another year.

"See ya, Granddad!" the scrote shouted. "If you had some new kicks, ya' might have stood a chance—"

Taunting was the last straw. That was what separated good criminals from bad criminals. Good criminals made detective work hard for Charlie and her crew. Braggarts and loudmouths were simple catches. She was off the clock, but made an exception.

She ran out in front of him and swung what she had in her hands, giving him a rearing headbutt with the lion's head. He got nutted by pure Chinese myth and stumbled into a bin on the kerb. The security guard caught up and applied a knee in his back and a solid arm lock on the bandit, to recover a whole rack of designer hoodies in the thief's possession.

"Got ya, sunshine," the guard grunted. He looked up at his apparent partner. Charlie was too busy looking over the crumpled remains of her lion head. One of the eyes was completely crushed, and the lip flap wouldn't open the whole way. It was ruined. But they still had a whole year to fix it, and it had been broken for a good cause.

"Happy New Year!" Charlie cheered, and ran over to join the rest of the troupe.

They all wondered what happened when she approached with the mangled prop, but no one said anything. Meanwhile, the security guard held down the shoplifter until the police showed up.

Liverpool was a melting pot. Asians, Afro-Caribbeans, Caucasians, Southerners, Northerners, and the occasional Everton fan to spice things up. Without them all, Charlie thought, the world would be a much less interesting place.

chapter
two

LIVERPOOL IS neither crime-free nor a wretched hive of scum and villainy, despite what Chelsea fans might sing on the terraces. It is, however, riding the perpetual wave of history that rose in the 60s when the Beatles forced the whole country —and then the world—to remember the name of a city on the British Isles other than London.

Steeped in maritime history, echoes of its former greatness and importance stand testament on every street corner. It's a fusion of cultures, people, politics, and football.

The city has its fair share of deprivation, desperation, and deterioration, but it also has an unrivalled sense of community, ambition, and humour. It is at this very intersection—of the newly minted, the old money stalwarts, and the middle- and working-class citizens—where the underworld exists, flourishes, and ensures mysteries always abound.

The local police cover the more immediate and violent crimes, which leaves a lot of lesser work to the private agencies like Charlie's. Whilst it was a day-in and day-out grind to grow her business, Charlie took solace in the fact that she knew she was doing good.

The world was only going to become more and more digital. People put so much of their private lives online that it ironically made her job harder, not easier, especially when clients demanded an immediate turnaround. It required extensive trawling to unearth scandal from all the mundane, making expectations of instant gratification difficult.

Charlie's job was fifty percent paperwork and fifty percent waiting to catch people committing a crime so she could audio-visually or manually record it for later. Not to stop them. That was what the police did. She was just a for-hire intermediary to help uncover wrongdoers at the request of clients. The reality of her business shook her foundation, but never sent a crack through her principles. If it was dangerous, or she felt that someone was in genuine danger, she felt compelled to act.

Charlie Chan & Co. Detective Agency was incorporated and had opened for business in Liverpool six months ago. It was the culmination of Charlie's personal drive and motivation, her life goal and passion project all rolled up into one. To be a private investigator, to right the wrongs, and to find answers to the secrets which held people down under the drowning waves of a constantly moving world. She was a crime solver, having served four years as an assistant investigator at Quinn Investigations before she felt ready to launch her own agency.

Her five-room corner office used to be a treatment spa on the ground floor of an old red brick building in the centre of the Baltic Triangle. Massages and meditation rooms and such. She kept the carpeting, since it was nice and soft, but changed everything else. There was still a massage table somewhere in their storage unit, but that was only for emergencies.

The office layout was pretty standard, a front desk that acted as a reception, an open-plan bullpen where the real work took place and, around the perimeter, a few private offices. Hers was the main one right by the door, and Rebecca worked out of the office in the back. When Ash wasn't working the front desk, the team took turns. Then there was a storage room brimming with an array of audio-visual equipment, props and wardrobe for undercover stings, a small meeting room and one office that remained unoccupied but ready to be activated when the agency expanded. The toilet didn't count as a room, as there was very little room for the toilet in the first place. It was a repurposed kitchenette with rattling pipes.

Their office space was very much function over form, but right now it was all that Charlie and the agency could afford.

In a way, it was the start of a new year of work too. The last six months went by in a breeze. Business was moderate, but the issues brought up were the definition of pedestrian. Charlie had budgeted for a quiet start, but she still wasn't breaking even, and her modest savings were quickly depleting. She needed a case. A big case, not just for the paycheck that would come with it, but for the reputational boost. She needed to get on the crime-fighting map.

Charlie arrived to find Rebecca and Ash mid-conversation in the bullpen. She was sore and slow and felt heavier than she did the day before. The thrill of the lion dance had worn off, along with the adrenalin that had kept her going. She massaged her left shoulder, which had been rubbed raw by the internal straps of the lion's head.

"Oh, morning boss," Ash said. "Look at you, all puffy eyes and pallid skin. Did you have a good New Year?"

"Uh, yeah," she said. "You saw me. I was having a great time."

"Yes, you were," Rebecca said. She picked up her phone and cycled through to the TikTok videos she'd posted. "I've sent it to a casting agent. If you're lucky, you might get to be the new live-action Mulan."

"Haaaah," Charlie groaned, an elongated sarcastic laugh. She dragged a chair from the wall and fell into it.

"I thought *I* was hungover," Ash said.

"I'm not hungover," Charlie protested. "I went straight

home and fell on my bed; I slept the wrong way, now my shoulder hurts."

"You know what else will do that?" Ash said. "Getting hammered."

"Never happened," she said.

"Come on. Admit it. You didn't want to ring in the new year all on your lonesome and you scored yourself a cheeky hookup on Tinder." Ash waved his finger at Charlie like he'd revealed her deepest, darkest secret.

"I don't do dating apps. Never have, never will."

"We all break eventually. Try it, you might like it. "

"How was your evening?" Charlie deflected. "If I get close enough, will I be able to guess the vintage of what you drank?"

"It was a twenty-five-year-old single malt and it wasn't worth it; had it with a friend. I had a study session when I got back. We... she and I"—he paused in mock sincerity—"took the edge off while we dove into chapters eleven and twelve of *The Theory and Practice of Change Management*."

Rebecca grimaced. It was the most establishment-sounding thing she'd heard all week. "Bet that's a real page-turner."

"Yeah," Ash agreed. "It's riveting. Really just... pounding at the skull with all the points it tries to make."

"Sounds like a blast," Charlie said. "And did you make any worthwhile progress in your studies?"

Ash gave a halted look, as he remembered how his night really transpired. Charlie and Rebecca could tell immediately how it went. And hopefully, the girl got something out of it, too.

"Oh, yeah," he said. "Very worth our while."

"She didn't scuff your makeup, did she?" Rebecca asked.

"She did not," he bragged. "She was very gentle. While we were reading."

Charlie rolled herself onto her feet and leaned against the

15

desk. "Are you having a *sex talk* while at work?" she said in mock disgust. "How crude!" She gasped at Rebecca, who gasped right back. "Dreadful!"

"Oh, the peril," Rebecca said in a posh lilt. "I'd've not come to work had I known I'd share my desk with a sloot!"

Ash rolled his eyes and held back a chuckle. For a group of strangers who had only met just six months ago, they were fast becoming close friends. Not that he would ever admit that out loud.

Charlie clapped her hands. "But for real—let's get to business. It's been a crap month. We need clients, ladies and gents. New billings, and we need to be hitting our growth expectations. I want this place sustaining itself off of the pulse of the neighbourhood. I want this city's mysteries to become our staple crop so we can feed the country with answers. That's my New Year's wish, and we're gonna make it happen. I'm manifesting."

"Your wish is our command," Ash said.

"How are our new leads?" Charlie asked.

Rebecca opened the lid of her laptop and tapped in her lock screen password. Her face went flat and emotionless, as if on a reflex, when she opened their social media page.

"Got five from the Facebook promotion," she said. "That's disregarding the spam. Good news, though, we've got over one thousand followers now."

"Great," Charlie said. "Followers don't pay the bills. Run me through the potential clients."

"Sure thing," Rebecca said. "Uh, one's here, actually."

"What?"

She pointed over her shoulder. "Well, not anymore. He was in the meeting room. Said he was looking for Charlotte Chan—whoever the hell that is—said he'd only speak to her."

"Ugh," Charlie grunted, quietly. "I wish you'd texted me; I could have been here sooner. Where is he now?"

"He popped out for some breakfast, said he'd come back,"

Rebecca said. "He was waiting for us at the door. Called himself Dave, said he was interested in working with you."

"Dave what?"

She shrugged. "Just said Dave."

Charlie nodded and shrugged.

"If we're all caught up, I'm going to crack on." Ash got up from the table.

He took his place at the front desk to start work in earnest, while Charlie got into the mood of a real private detective. "That's good. Someone's passionate about needing help; I'm passionate about helping. Perfect match. Let's hope he comes back. What else?"

"The Barrow," Rebecca continued, "Hall, Webbs, and the Keisha cases are still ongoing. Ash is doing up the report—we covered that off before you got here—he'll have it by lunch."

"Great," Charlie said. "I went ahead and shut down surveillance on Overt Designs. It's been four months now and we've got nothing. And today is our interview day for a new associate— Don't forget about that."

"Right, I'm the coffee boy," Rebecca said. "Need to get plenty of biscuits and pastries and whatever else the mainstream crowd likes. Is it tea? Do these people still do tea at midday?"

"I think so," Charlie said. "Just don't be too weird. I know you like to test people, but… well, let's try not to put them off."

"Do we even need an associate? Should we not cancel? I know you said I need to work on my listening skills, but I distinctly remember you saying something *just now* about us not having enough work—"

"Chicken and egg isn't it? Arguably, no, we don't. But if you and Ash are bogged down with admin, you're not out there solving crime. If I can free you up, we can find and close more cases. Ergo, we will need an associate, once the associate starts working."

"That made no sense."

"Not even in my head. But to answer your question. Don't cancel. Associate o'clock is on."

"Sure thing," Rebecca said, "but then again, if we keep doing off-the-clock work, we'll be out of help to give to people. Won't we?"

"Hmm?"

Rebecca nodded. "You fighting crime on the streets of Liverpool," she explained, "for free."

Charlie rubbed her forehead. "Yeah, and I broke my lion."

"Oh, love," Rebecca said, "they're not gonna let you be Chinese next year if you go around breaking their stuff."

Charlie smirked, but stopped herself from fully laughing. She looked at Rebecca with a much sterner disposition. "They let the little bastard go, too. Caught with about a grand's worth of Armani in front of hundreds of witnesses and not even a slap on the wrist. No space in the cells, so he was just told to go home and stop robbing. It's bloody embarrassing that's all the police can do now."

"It is," Rebecca said, agreeing with a totally different point. "Best we get to work on showing them who the real crime stoppers are in this city."

"Yep." Charlie straightened her back and cracked her knuckles. She had to take the good times as they came, because with work, she was mired in the worst kinds of cases.

She liked helping people, always had, but some people didn't always deserve it. Finding a missing teen to assist a father in need was all well and good, until the rest of the story came out about why the teen had decided to run away in the first place. Things like that kept cropping up. They had when she was still learning the ropes, but that misfortune followed her to her own agency as well.

For Charlie, there was only really one case that needed solving. The whereabouts of her own father. Everything else was part distraction and part training exercise, enabling her to get better and better at investigating. If the official records were to be believed—scant as they were—her father's disappearance had confounded the greatest minds across both sides of the Atlantic. MI5, NCA, CIA, FBI, every organisation with three initials for a name had tried and failed. Charlie had vowed she wouldn't.

She had a great team to help her. Rebecca did all things tech-related. Her e-girl exterior hid the true identity of a nerd who liked to talk about the positives of crypto and DeFi, whether or not someone asked. Ash was a bad boy on the rise to goodness, working on his MBA at night school while he worked off his self-laid burden to society from his early years as a lieutenant for a street gang. He knew the ins and outs of the criminal mind intimately, almost as well as he knew his designer clothing houses.

Their business was right on the cusp of achieving recognition. One more case would do it, and that case was about to walk in off the street and demand their help. Charlie was sure of it. Liverpool would have more than just a group of well-intended busybodies roaming the streets. With enough effort, her ambition could be realised.

Then her real work could begin.

chapter
three

DAVE DID COME BACK, and he brought sausage rolls for Ash and Rebecca, which they graciously accepted before showing him back into the meeting room.

He was in one of the chairs. Not the right one, but it didn't matter, since there were only two. Other chairs were wheeled as needed from throughout the office. Otherwise, meetings were held informally out in the bullpen when everyone was together and had the time. The meeting room doubled as an "interrogation" room, but only if they put in the plastic tarp and a few rolls of gaffer tape to make it look more brutal and dangerous. That alone was usually enough to unsettle the truth out of the suspects they invited in.

Dave was middle-aged, 40s or so. He looked haggard and upset. He was bald from crown to forehead, but kept a consistent pelt of hair all around his dome. He was utterly unremarkable in any other way. Not large enough to be overweight, nor tall enough to be notable. He just seemed to be a dude with a problem, and he came to what he assumed was the right place to deal with it.

"Hello, David?" Charlie asked as she entered the room.

"Oh, just Dave," he said. "Are you…Charlotte?"

"Short for Charlie," she greeted with a smile. He stood,

confused by her reply for a second, and they shook hands. Charlie took her seat across the table to start the deal. "My team said you'd only speak with me?"

"That's right," he said. "I was referred to you by Paul Wooton."

Charlie nodded, with a sideways glance. "Right. You're a friend of Paul's? Uh, how is he?"

"Surviving," he commented. "Six months in on an eighteen-month stretch."

One of her last cases working at Quinn Investigations, where she first got her legs wet in the swamp of private detective work. He'd been part of a drug bust. She'd overpowered him and his cronies when they attempted to flee with what could only be described as Charlie's very own unique interpretation of kung fu—unique in that no living (or dead) grandmaster would guess she'd had over eight years of formal training. In fact, the only thing that resembled traditional kung fu was that she'd used her hands and feet, everything else was very much made up on the spot. Provenance or not, it was explosive and effective and having overpowered the lot of them, she'd held them until Merseyside's finest arrived to wrangle them into custody. Paul Wooton started serving at His Majesty's pleasure, right around the time Charlie started up her own agency, almost like an accidental celebration of his incarceration.

"I'm surprised he referred me," she said. "I'd imagine there were some other choice words that went along with it?"

"He ain't like that," Dave explained. "He's a good guy... usually. Just got into a bad spot, like a lot of blokes have done. Desperate times, desperate measures. I'm sure he'll be right with the law once he's out. And, anyway, he was sure of it. If anyone could help, it would be you."

"So how can I help, Mr...?"

He nodded, as if giving up his name was somehow a hard

concession to surrender. "Phillips. For the last few years, my business has been struggling."

"I'm sorry to hear that," she said. And she was. As a business owner herself, she knew all too well that the business defines you. Its success is your success, and its shortcomings or failings... manifest as your own.

"What is it that you do?"

"Commercial property. Buying and selling. Made a bit with the boom, but it's been thin pickings recently. No one wants commercial premises anymore. Everyone's working from home these days, you know?"

"Sorry to hear that. And why do you think you need our services?"

"Thing is," he began, "it's a struggle, but I'm managing. It's just taken up all my time. I've got to be away more for longer, and that's taking time away from my home and my wife. And it's straining us. And now, I think she—Sophie, my wife—is having an affair."

Charlie could see the poor man was just about to burst out crying. He held himself back and stiffened his lip. This was a serious concern of his, not just a wayward or sudden misconception. He'd been dwelling on this for a while.

"What led you to believe this?" she asked. She didn't want to sound dismissive or assert some sort of bias. She was a woman, too. Not married, nor in a relationship, nor had any of hers in the past gone particularly well, still, her perspective was a rare one, worth leaning on.

"Little things here and there," he said. "She's going shopping all the time. Dresses different, putting on new perfumes and such. Does her hair and nails up more, even though we really can't afford it right now."

"Have you challenged Sophie about it?"

"The spending? Yeah. I thought, y'know, we had been doing ok. We've never been mega-rich, but up until a few years ago we were doing alright, got a nice house, could have a weekend in Ibiza once in a while.

"Why are you away so much?"

"I have investors that need placating. Family offices, mainly in Europe. They wanted in when all the cranes were filling the skyline, now they want out, but I can't shift the buildings for the price they want."

"Have you been transparent with her about your finances?"

"I showed her the books and told her that things are tight, but she says it's important to keep up appearances."

"What about your suspicions?"

"Oh, she hit the roof," he said. "Told me I was redirecting my frustrations on her. Projecting, apparently. I didn't know what that really meant. Said she isn't looking at other men. But there's something going on, I'm sure of it."

"Did you two have a strong, positive relationship until recently?"

He shrugged and nodded. "I guess."

"That's not a confident answer, Mr. Phillips," she said. "I need the kind of confidence from you that only honesty can bring about."

"We've had some rough patches," he said. "It's different when you get older. You're still in love, you just fight more because you want things to be like they used to be. And well… yeah. Actually, being honest, that was a while back."

"What happened?"

Dave swallowed, assessing Charlie and realising he was at the point of no return.

"I registered on one of those sugar daddy websites last year," he admitted.

Charlie gritted her teeth. Normally, outside of work or when not immersed in her duty, her reaction would be to laugh. She found no amusement in his circumstances. People went through all sorts of embarrassments and made bad decisions to hide the truth of their own failures. At least Dave was starting their negotiations on the right foot. With the truth.

Well, that, and laughing at a client was bad for business.

He went on, "Never met up with anyone. It was daft, really. One of the contractors I use had mentioned it, said flirting with strangers gives you a testosterone boost." He shook his head and wiped his palm over his scalp. He was showing off his biggest insecurities right there. Charlie picked him apart like a jigsaw puzzle. "I was careful, used a new email account and that, but some hackers put two and two together and when I didn't pay up, went and spread my profile to all my private contacts. It damn near ruined me."

"And your wife didn't take it well?"

"Understatement of the year there," he said. "Had to sleep on the sofa for the best part of nine months. Got a crick in my neck. Still have."

"How long ago was that?" she asked.

"The summer, two years ago," he said. "If I'd known—"

"And now," she said, "years later, you think her plot for revenge is having the affair you never did?"

"I wasn't even going to," he began.

"When you explained it was strictly for flirting to help with your own self-image and balance," she went on, "did she not believe you?"

"No, not at all," he said. "Oh sure, I'm doing all this for you—that's a hell of an excuse, innit?"

Charlie nodded. She understood his inner plight, but her own deductive mind ran a different scenario. She started to paint the tapestry of their relationship. Being the wife of a businessman, and someone privy to the company accounts of the business, it's possible Sophie would have the motivation to do critical research of her husband's interests to see if his reason was based in truth.

She would have likely found whatever profiles he'd looked at in the search history of his computer at home or at work—probably at work; he seemed like a man who filled his time rather than spent it—and see the connections. Even if she didn't fully believe his story, the premise would intrigue her, to flirt with the opposite sex for a boost in hormonally-driven personality alteration. She'd be more liberated and powerful, without having to deal with the tired old routine with her husband. Adultery wasn't necessarily the end game. Jealousy as a punishment also seemed likely. Nine months on sofa-jail was a long time, but if she really hated him why invite him back into the marital bed at all?

"Can you help me?" he asked. "It's driving me mad. The not knowing. Even if she is, at least then I'll know."

"If you're sure about that," she said, "then we can help."

He nodded firmly. He wasn't the bitter type. He seemed far more distressed to even be asking, like he already foresaw the worst-case scenario and accepted it in his heart. His mouth and face just had to catch up.

Charlie got out a standard agreement form, officialising their relationship as client and detective. She walked him through the paperwork in the near silence of the meeting room. Only nearly, as something was going on out in the bullpen that she'd need to inspect. She left Dave to fill out the last of the forms while she went to investigate.

Rebecca was listening to music. It sounded like a 2000s-era acoustic number with a psychedelic backing track and moody ballad lyrics sung by a sad-sounding woman.

"Hard at work?" Charlie asked.

"OMG," Rebecca said. "It's here! Seven million streams already and it just dropped, like, *now!*"

"Mr Phillips is just completing the paperwork. You can add him to the client list," Charlie said, but it didn't elicit the reaction she was hoping for. "We have a new client, Rebecca."

"It's Emefa!" Rebecca said, ignoring Charlie. "She's back!"

She pointed to the screen. The track, entitled *E-Girl Unplugged*, did, indeed, have seven million streams and counting, with a post date of under an hour. Comments locked, likes disabled.

Charlie raised her hands, begging for context and unclear of the significance. She glanced over to Ashley for some insight, or at least a pithy chastisement of how 'out of touch' she was, but he grinned back at her.

"It's Emefa. She's back." Ash helpfully repeated, and clapped like an excited seal. As if that explained everything.

chapter
four

Eleven Months Earlier

THERE CAME A TERRIBLE AWAKENING. Somewhere, in parts unknown, under the dimness of dark curtains and the shuttered veil of an oversized duvet cover, a girl stirred. Her life flashed before her eyes. She saw the well-laid foundation for her future that had been upended by an auspicious dream to be a singer, followed by all the favours and fortunes which had conspired to give rise to her dream. She remembered everything, up to the very last day when she thought she might have died. Everything, that is, but the face of the man in the backseat of her car.

Emefa blinked her eyes open. It was right after her crash, and she could very clearly feel it. She still had a bitter taste of iron in her mouth and her saliva felt tacky. Her pounding hangover and come down were overpowered by her whiplash and bone-deep bruises all over her body. She tried to move, risked getting up. The light hurt her eyes, but fortunately there was very little of it, allowing her to open them wide enough to see the room past the lacy fabric that hung from the four-poster frame.

"Good morning."

Emefa startled. There was a person at the foot of her bed, observing through the lace curtain. He was just a tall, man-like shape. The very same dark figure who'd frightened her off the road, and who had carried her to safety. His mouth and nose were hidden by a black fabric mask.

"Where am I?" she asked. "What happened?" Her voice turned into demands, strict ones. "Who are you?"

"You've been in the wars," he said with a lulling, almost sultry voice, trying too hard to keep her calm. "But it's okay now. Everything is okay."

"Did Marcus put you up to this? Is this an intervention?" she asked with a hint of disgust. "Is this rehab?"

"Marcus had nothing to do with this," he said reassuringly, which made her freeze up in fear. "Truth be told, Marcus doesn't know where you are. No one does."

Emefa nudged herself over to the edge of the bed and parted the curtains. "Yeah, right," she scoffed. "What time is it? I need to be at the airport." She patted her hip and her chest, then committed to a more thorough self-frisking. "Where's my phone?"

"I've taken it," he said. "You won't be needing it. Not for a while, anyway."

She gawked at him. "Uh, no, I need it. And I need to be in Prague for a gig. I don't know what you're playing at, but—"

She got up to scold him, but a sudden surge of pain hit her from the ankle up. Something went wrong in the crash. Naturally.

The man raced over, just a few long strides, and helped her back down onto the bed.

"Shh," he shushed. "Don't get yourself in a tizzy. I've decided you need a bit of space. A bit of time to get back to your roots. Rediscover your voice."

"This isn't funny," she said, smacking him away. She stood up anyway and winced through the agonising pain as she limped to the door. It was locked. She tried another door, which was an empty wardrobe. "Why's everything locked?" she asked. She limped over to the blackout curtains and pulled them open to discover the windows were barred and the frames were nailed shut. She spun round. "Open the door."

"That's not going to happen," he said. "You're here for your own good. You need to reassess some of your life choices."

Emefa looked furiously at the man, who was cloaked in shadows. More than the mock rage she put on for the show that her fans loved to see, the 'aggressively girly' off-kilter punk idol who had the prettiest snarl in the country. She marched up to her captor. Although he towered over her, she did not stutter or flinch. In her mind, she was still in control.

"Let me out right now!" she shouted.

He shook his head. "I'm very disappointed," he said. He reached up and gently grabbed her by the neck and handled her with a tender grip. Hard enough that she couldn't get away, but painless while she remained immobile. "We don't shout, and we don't scream. We're only going to use our inside voice. Think of your larynx."

Emefa tried to get her knee up between his legs but hit his thigh. "Unless you want your testicles to end up next to your larynx, I suggest—"

Emefa shuddered violently. Her whole body seized and shook and then fell limp to the floor. Her captor held a long-shafted stun baton in his left hand, obscured by his long coat, that left a pair of tiny burnt bug-like marks on her skin where it contacted.

"As I said," he explained to her fading consciousness, "you need some time to reconsider your life choices."

Emefa faded out, realising what she'd just experienced was not a dream. It was a living nightmare.

chapter
five

THE CLOCK STRUCK TWELVE. It was time to take interviews. Charlie had Ash sit in, while Rebecca worked the front desk. That was the plan, initially, but the first candidate got held up in the front lobby. Charlie could hear them through the door. Then the song replayed again. They were fan-girling over Emefa's new tune, *E-Girl Unplugged*. Apparently, it was just rare enough that another person with selectively poor taste would come to their office the very day that the artist's new song was released. In investigation, there were no coincidences, but in regular everyday life and business, they were the norm.

"So," Charlie said, with her phone in hand, "this Emefa—which is somehow short for *Esoteric motherfu*—"

"That was an older alter ego," Ash corrected. "I looked into this. She relapsed a few months before her last gig during what she called a girlcore circuit. Huge pink hair and crazy eyeliner, but also a little slut-chic with low-cut tops and petticoat skirts. She's got looks and talent, if you're into that. She's a style diva. If she tags an item of clothing on her socials, it's sold out in minutes. She's only twenty-two, but she's already had a couple of number ones and a clutch of BRIT Awards.

She's a big deal, whether you choose to acknowledge it or not."

"Yeah," Charlie said. "You should write those Wiki articles; the language is spot on."

"I'm not a fan," he said. "When I saw what she was wearing in her latest posts, no interest. Idol unfollowed; fascination deleted."

Charlie checked it out. The girl had almost daily postings, right up to the night of her last gig at the Liverpool Arena. A lot of behind-the-scenes photos of the green room and random bits of stage scenery interspersed with pictures of herself in wildly heavy makeup. After a gap of a few months, she put up a text-only post as a picture on Instagram, which confessed to a long break and rehabilitation. Her posts became much less frequent and more thoughtful and contemplative. The focus would be a flower, or a shape made from pebbles, accompanied by a life-affirming quote. Some would show an ear, or the side of her face in shadow—enough to know it was Emefa, but only just.

Until today. Her hair was down, long and wavy with bright tips but mostly dark from the roots out. You could see her whole face—thick eyeliner and lashes, her lips looked bigger with a dark shade of lipstick. She looked good. Contemplative. Sober. Clean. Her attire matched the mood of her song. It was kind of e-girl but toned down, like her nan was coming round to visit the family and she'd be told to dress normal. She'd put on some weight and was looking better for it—more rounded in the shoulders and hips in a way that kept her natural curves plain and simple.

"You wouldn't think Rebecca of all people would be into it," Charlie said as she continued to scroll through the feed.

"I think it's ironic actually," Ash said, "in that weird way where you say you actually don't like something but then talk about how much you love it non-stop, like you're telling yourself a joke all the time."

"I believe that," Charlie agreed. "Or maybe not. Her heyday was a bit before Rebecca got serious about her rebellious phase, wasn't it?"

"True," Ash said.

The conversation held no real weight, but the intrigue still tickled the little part of Charlie's brain that was quick to connect strange details into patterns. Her detective skills sounded a soft alarm to keep her aware that it was something to think on. A quick search showed Charlie that theory threads and subreddits had formed to talk up and shut down all manner of rumours over the embattled starlet. Celebrity gossip mining. Not her hobby.

Finally, their interviewee came in. It was a near-immediate rejection from the get-go. The girl, Lacy, was eighteen but acted much younger. She bounced her way into the interviewee seat and greeted her would-be bosses with a charming wave.

"Hiya!" she chirped.

"Hello," Charlie replied.

"Hello," Ash said, a bit more inviting.

"So Lacy, is it?" Charlie asked, scanning down the girl's very brief resume. "I have a few standard questions for you—about why you're applying and your skills—and then I have some challenges for you, to see how well you can think on your feet."

"Oh, so should I stand then?" she asked.

Ash chuckled and received a curious, determined look. She wasn't kidding. He stopped his laughter with a smile and turned to Charlie for help.

The interview session was simple. They wanted to know why she was interested in becoming a private detective and working for their agency. They needed to know what qualifications she had and what skills she could bring to the team. As for challenges, they were set up as illogical puzzles, methods which Charlie picked up from her time at the Quinn

Agency to test how fast, not how well, someone could think their way through an absurd situation. The goal was to test her reactions, even in a simple sit-down scenario, and her intuition as a detective.

Lacy failed at every point, but kept an upbeat attitude. She was a media student looking for part-time work in a socially friendly company so she could earn some spending money during term time. She didn't seem to understand what they did. Not the kind of help they were looking for.

The next candidate, Cameron, came in. He was a chubby man, mid-twenties, shaved head and bristly beard. He had a keen interest in all aspects of noir cinema and police thrillers, and had studied basic criminal psychology as an elective course at university so he could write his own graphic novel. His intuition was... interesting. He made extreme leaps of practical logic to arrive at a seemingly reasonable end point to solve the imaginary case. It was interesting, but not professional. His brand of logic was too special for their humdrum, real-life legal drudgery.

The third candidate, Martin, was a no-sale. He spoke exclusively in business school terminology, talking to them about their quarterly returns and investment opportunities, and balanced his whole routine on how he convinced a local web development company to outsource their work to India in a long-distance turnkey operation so the owners could make money doing nothing. When asked how that company was doing—or who they were—he quickly went on to talk about something else. Charlie felt like he was a man she would end up taking to jail eventually, and let him leave.

That was three in and three out, and by the feel of things, there was no real contender in the city looking to work for them. Which made sense. Anyone who wanted to fight crime would probably join the police. A humble little corner-shop start-up wasn't going to get perfect candidates. But they'd hoped they'd get someone decent at least.

"We've got one more," Rebecca said from the doorway, "and I'm done with my report."

"Great," Charlie said. "Put it on my desk and send them in."

"Which one where?" she asked.

Charlie hoisted her clipboard up and prepared to throw it. Rebecca ducked out and led the last candidate in. Charlie sat upright in surprise when she saw him. He was out of his normal security guard fatigues, but she recognised the jutting jaw and burning stare of the man from their shared moment the previous day. He was in a plain jacket and slacks, with a brown flat cap over his head. He took it off, revealing a salt and peppery field of short buzzed hair, and handed her his hand-written resume.

"Hello again," he greeted. "You look different without your costume on."

"Oh, it *is* you," she said. "With the wicked arm lock."

"You two know each other?" Ash asked.

"Somewhat," she said.

"Just briefly," the man mentioned. "Your boss took out a shoplifter I was chasing."

"Yes, indeed," Charlie glanced down at his resume. "Mr… Aston."

"Clive Aston at your service," he said. He rocked forward in his seat with a slight bow.

"And you're here," Ash said, "for the trainee associate position?"

"That's right, sir," Clive said.

Ash was taken aback a bit by the *sir*. He leaned forward and pressed to see just how much more he could get. "I'm not sure you would fit in with the sort of demographic we have here at the office. All things considered; this role is—"

"Open to the best candidate," Charlie interrupted. "Everyone deserves a chance, don't they, Ashley?" Ash closed his mouth and gave her a conciliatory nod. She went on with her first round of questions. "What drew you to seek a role with our private investigations agency?"

"A personal drive to see good deeds done at a decent price," he said. "It's a rare but noble thing you're doing. I'd like to be part of that."

"What skills would you bring to our current workforce?"

Clive pressed his back into the chair as he recounted his short resume. "I served in the Gulf War. The first one. It was before your time, I think, but afterwards, we weren't treated so well. I came back looking to serve out the rest of my years in the regiment, but government cuts and whatnot put me on a pension. I wasn't ready, or old enough to actually retire, so took a temporary role as a retail security guard. Temporary became permanent and I've been working the doors at JD Sports for twenty years now. It's mostly observation. You get to know people without ever talking to them, what they're like and how they act. It helps spot the bad eggs in the basket. But really, what brought me here"—He leaned forward—"was you. Running straight at a thief, bowling him over like that. How'd you feel?"

"Just another day on the mean streets," she said.

He smiled. "Makes you feel *alive*, eh?"

There was something comforting in Clive's honesty. He was a man with nothing to lose or gain. A 58-year-old veteran transferring his entire history from public service to private investigation, all so he could feel useful, not part of the backdrop anymore. It was straightforward and admirable. And most of all, as Charlie knew, it was the kind of personality that got results.

Charlie and Ash somehow made the interview last another twenty minutes, but they both knew they'd found their recruit. They offered on the spot.

chapter
six

CHARLIE SWIPED to accept the call from Ash, putting it on loudspeaker for Rebecca and Clive's benefit. They heard the rumble of a car engine. Ash was driving.

"…Two litres are wasted on you. The light's green. For the love of God…

"Hey, Ash. Any updates on the Phillips case?"

"Yep," he said. "His wife must've just got the memo that her husband was leaving town, because she's gone all out with the beauty treatments. Eyebrows, filler, mani-pedi, and hair."

"Reckon she's going out tonight?"

"Given that she also spent the last two hours choosing a new dress, I'd bet ten English pounds she is."

"Any idea where?"

"That, I don't know," he conceded.

"We'll have to follow her from home, then," she said. "I'll get ready at mine. Swing by at ten to pick you up."

"We're in luck if they go to the Condor Club," he said. "Bartender has a total crush on me. He might be able to get us into the VIP area. Downside is, I'll have to chat him up first."

"Not a bad trade," she said. "As long as you don't get hammered."

"I won't!" he said, insulted. "Never on the job."

Charlie ended the call. Everyone had their speciality. Hers wasn't blending in, or flirting, or coding, or delicate work with tracking and surveillance. She had to be the cold, stern leader of the group, the coordinator and director. And hopefully, that role was good enough. And she was good enough at the role.

The nine-to-five grind—or eight-to-four, or whenever the office got unlocked—ended. The time for office work and paper filing was close to over. Charlie spent the last of the afternoon arranging the electronic case files and reports she got from Rebecca and Ash into their respective client folders, and sifted through all the essential information so she had a handle on where they were on each of the investigations.

She was a meticulous, detail-driven note-taker, but she was also a child of the modern digital era. She didn't have the space for unlimited cork boards or whiteboards to stain with marker lines that crisscrossed until they looked like tartan fabric. She could do all of that on a laptop.

Once that was done, she had a solid setup of clues, persons of interest, and venues to have the team scope out. The long-running surveillance mission at a timber merchant over in Speke was called off early as the case attached to it entered the final phases of a wrap-up. They had their evidence, and the client would get it. What happened after that would be up to them. If a court case resulted, Charlie Chan & Co. would be on call as a representative witness for professional testimony. That was really the worst thing they had to do at any time, court duty. It was simple work, but banal to an irritating point.

When they weren't compiling reports, the team's time was spent on stakeouts. The usual crew consisted of Charlie and Ash. Rebecca provided backup from the office. She was the youngest of the agency staff, working instead of attending university.

Charlie had also chosen work over education and had foregone her unconditional place at St. Cath's, Oxford, to work for Michael Quinn following the disappearance of her father. Ash, however, had broken the mould and had recently enrolled on a distance-learning MBA programme. As long as he showed up online a few times a month for his tutor group and submitted his assignments, he was in the clear.

The stakeout method was always the same. They had a customised van and stick-on decals for various businesses that would fit in with whatever local environment they happened to be in. The van was gradient-shaded from one side to the other. The only difference was the shade of grey, but looking at it strictly from a street view gave off the illusion of two different vehicles depending on the angle of the viewer. That gave them minor deniability if it was ever pegged or described as a "suspicious" vehicle. They just had to show the other side in good light and hide how it faded from one side to another. It was Ashley's idea, and a brilliant one.

Charlie picked up Ash, and they drove in said van towards Seel Street just as the action heated up—in Liverpool city centre that meant all the boys wearing too-tight T-shirts and all the girls wearing too-big eyelashes.

She got a host of information from Rebecca's social media and online profile-skimming of Dave's wife. Sophie Phillips was a stern-looking older white woman. Her post history showed a swift change from a stiff upper-lipped middle-aged *Karen*, whinging about the poor customer service she'd received into a graceful, bright-haired gal looking for fun and friendship. It was a stark change, but given the marital relationship history, not an unusual one.

"This woman," Ash said, "is an old-school cougar. She's shopping a whole age bracket under her own demographic, not too far to be creepy, just close enough that she thinks she can pull it off."

"Can she?" Charlie asked.

"Hmm," Ash hesitated. He had to swipe through a few more pictures of Sophie taken off her Facebook and Instagram accounts. The Instagram was brand new, as new as her look was. Her total image makeover seemed to start from there, moving off of the Gen X network onto fresher pastures. "Maybe."

"How many?" Charlie asked.

"How many... drinks?"

"Yeah."

"For me, maybe four," he said. "Close to drunk, but not quite. Still in control, but really loosened up and maybe a little blurry. Also, she'd have to approach me *after* those drinks have done their magic. If we're together the whole evening, I'm not getting looser, I'm just getting uncomfortable."

"So, if I ever need you to do something," she said, "I shouldn't tell you to do it until after you're well and truly hammered."

"That's true of basically everyone," Ash said. "Might be her case, too. Flirting with boys, getting drinks for tables, going too far and feeling good about it. Maybe she's just coasting off a bad decision she knows she should regret."

"That's a pretty picture," Charlie said. "But we know how rare a pretty picture is. Life's art gallery is full of student art that doesn't quite pass the grade. And, like any art, a good masterpiece is only appreciated when the maker is dead."

"Je-zuss," Ash exclaimed. "Did you get Becca's eyeliner in your bloodstream? You're going goth all of a sudden."

"It wasn't that dark," she said. "It's just... what's simple is usually what's right. If she's simply cheating, then the simple answer is she's trying to hurt her husband."

"Right," he agreed. "If affairs were so easy to keep, you'd think there'd be a lot more of them."

"Oh, I'm sure there are," she said. "More than we'd expect. But if no one gets angry, then what should we care?"

"As long as somebody is having fun," he said.

They drove down the length of the street and slowed down when they passed The Ivory Staircase, the brainchild of a chic club designer who had one big idea and then never came back to Liverpool again.

"You sure they're heading here tonight?" Charlie asked.

"One hundred percent. She's said so on her 'gram. Look." Ash pushed his phone in front of Charlie's face, but she batted it away.

"OK, OK. Let's get in position."

Charlie and Ash circled the one-way system to find parking. It didn't matter how close they were, they just needed a window in sight of the entrance. They managed to squeeze the van into a spot on the corner of Suffolk Street. One window view was all they needed, and tonight it was all they had.

Once parked, they climbed into the back of the van, the left-hand rear window framing the club entrance. Ashley picked out a good angle and set up a camera on a swivel mount. That kept his hands free to shorthand any intel or observations, such as noting the time and place he saw the mark, as well as any activity. If something happened, he could snap away through voice activation.

Charlie, meanwhile, prepared her disguise. She was in an indigo-grey bodycon dress, down to her knees and hip-hugging, with short heels and a cropped jacket. She was ready to go clubbing.

"I'm heading in," she said.

"You'll try," Ash warned. "The queue is to the corner."

"I've got my phone on me."

"Nice. If you get bored, you can play 3D Carp."

"No, I won't be doing that. Call me if you spot anything."

40

"Right."

She stepped out and made her way to the club queue. It wasn't just to the corner, it snaked on up the side street. After about an hour, she was finally at least on the right road and just cleared a shutdown coffee shop two doors down from the club entrance. Then, she saw the target. Ash saw her as well. Sophie stepped out of an Uber. She'd travelled with another woman, and they cackled their way to the main entrance. Charlie watched them pass her by. She got a good look at Sophie's partner. Definitely not a man.

Ash got his own angle as they chatted and laughed their way past the queue. He clicked his tongue against his teeth and the camera snapped a shot. One after another. Sophie's wing-girl chatted up the man at the door, who then turned aside and made a call into a small mic clipped to his lapel. A few minutes later, a woman came to the door of the club and invited them both in with arms wide. He got solid pictures of all of them hugging and trading smiles like old friends. Then his phone buzzed. It startled him.

"Yeah?" he answered.

"Tell me you saw that," Charlie asked.

"I can see that you're not getting in anytime soon," he said. "But she did."

"They're gone now?"

"Long."

"I'll stay in queue," she said. "Try and find out who she was with. I'll find her when I'm in and buzz you as she's leaving."

"Don't get drunk and forget what we're doing," he warned.

"Chance would be a fine thing."

They hung up and commenced the plan. After another frustrating twenty minutes of waiting, Charlie finally entered and looked around the thumping club. She heard Emefa's new song come over the speakers, the opening lyrics were burned into her brain thanks to Becca playing the song nonstop in the office: *Unattached, unencumbered, unplugged, free from the apron strings that bind me. Now I play a symphony of my own choosing…* which was met with a ton of cheering, and a very small contingent of drunken booing. It didn't distract her from her main task for long.

She spotted the ladies on their night out and kept her eye on them from the bar. Her timing was poor. She got one very light drink down before the girls picked themselves up to leave. She texted Ashley before they got out the door. Charlie faked a selfie and snapped a shot of them over her shoulder, including the mystery proprietress—standing like Lady Muck at the railings of the VIP mezzanine level looking out over the peasants on the dance floor—who had let Sophie and her friend jump the queue.

It could have just been a coincidental night out with friends, but this club had a chequered history. Knowing someone like that was a point of interest on its own. It was a detail too significant to credit as sheer coincidence.

Charlie remained by the bar for the requisite ninety seconds to allow them time to clear the main entrance and then sauntered out herself.

"Night love." The bouncer opened the large glass doors for her, and she nodded her thanks, noticing the disappointment in the eyes of those still waiting in line behind the red ropes. Clearly, she wasn't a stag party of twenty off to their next venue and, based on a one-in, one-out policy, their long wait would continue.

The biting February air in the vestibule almost took her breath away. Her phone pinged with a new message: *When you exit, break right then turn around.*

Charlie didn't miss a stride and followed Ash's instructions. She saw immediately what had piqued his attention as she crossed over the road—Sophie and Anna were kissing in the street. Not your *mwah, mwah* ladies-that-lunch peck on the cheek, but hands clasped behind each other's heads coupled with furious tongue action. It was passionate, it was real and, at least in that moment, they didn't care who saw.

Sophie, it was now clear, was indeed playing away from home. Dave had been right to be suspicious.

chapter
seven

TIME MOVED ON. People forgot about the little things and held onto even smaller things that felt more personal in their lives. Disagreements evolved into rejection. Arguments escalated into fights. A fun night out transformed into a terrible morning in.

Charlie awoke face down in her pillow with a weighty pain in the back of her head that felt like it was pushing her upward. Like a magnet was tugging on a trapped ball in her skull. Alcohol wasn't what did it, she'd only had the one drink. Rather, it was the heady mix of colognes and perfumes and the general pulsating atmosphere of the club that had done her in.

Her normal life at home was far calmer and more controlled. She had a one-bedroom apartment in the Albert Dock. It was central, had great views out over the river Mersey and was secure enough, three floors up, to give her plenty of privacy and room for personal effects. She mostly kept old things from her childhood around, leaning up against walls or neatly piled on the coffee table. One day she'd get around to actually hanging some of it on the wall. Her family, specifically her mother, was steeped in tradition. She insisted that Charlie learn to appreciate and pass on her family history and culture despite growing up a first-generation immigrant.

Charlie was much more identity fluid. She still kept her culture alive in her heart, but she didn't live it day in and day out. She ate bread more often than she ate rice. She spoke English more fluently than the Cantonese her mother had taught her as a child. All the traditional instruments she failed to learn in her youth were now repurposed as decorations. Her wardrobe was brimming with T-shirts, hoodies and low-cut jeans, the only identifiably Chinese clothing was a thread-bare kung fu uniform.

She had a simple life at home, which made up for the adventurous life she planned to have at work. She wasn't quite there yet, which made the movement from one bland set of rooms to another still feel like a pinch on her soul, but it was fine. She was growing her business, which gave her a spring in her step. She rushed through her morning routine and showed up early, at 8:30, to find her newest employee standing outside, waiting to greet her.

"Morning," she said.

Clive folded his newspaper and stood to attention.

"Boss," he said, almost saluting, but thought better of it. "eight-thirty, eh? That's the start of your day?"

"Uh, well," she began, "I'm usually in closer to nine. Never later than half past but—"

"Well, that's good," he said. "The worst crooks tend to start their days at nine. But the serious professionals are usually early risers, they can be up and at 'em as early as seven. Helps them get a head start on the police, who only really begin firing on all cylinders after breakfast."

She could feel the condescension in his tone. It was colder than the winter air at her back. Not an ideal first impression on day one of a new job, but she got where he was coming from. It was the military mind in him speaking up. The get up, show up, and if you do nothing else today, at-least-

45

you've-made-your-bed mentality. Something worth listening to for experience alone.

Charlie opened the door and insisted Clive go first. Following a short but tense battle of "after you," "no, after you," they were in the relative warmth of the office and Charlie flicked on the lights. And the heating.

"I'll get you a set of keys so you can let yourself in, moving forwards.

"Thank you. Oh, we had a walk-in, would you believe," he said. "Old dear up the street thought her paper went missing. Turns out the newsagent no longer delivers. I cleared that up in about ten minutes, bought her a spare, and got back in time to read my copy."

"Wow," she said. "Well, we pay a fixed salary so…"

He smirked. "I've done some reading on you. Started this" —he indicated the office with his arms—"from scratch. Came from the Quinn Agency, a mutual departure. Wanted to show them up, or…?"

She pulled up a chair and sat down, part of her routine. Clive stayed standing at attention.

"Rebecca and Ashley already know this," she began, "but I started this agency to… gain the legitimacy I need within the policing system to requisition records from the UK Security Services on a missing person."

Clive hiked an eyebrow up. "You know what that reminds me of?" She shook her head. "One of the lads I served with. He joined the army so he could get free vacations and treat foreign lands as a gun range. Took one in the leg on a raid on Jalibah Airfield and left on the War Pension Scheme. Ten years ago, I caught up with him. He's on crutches, upgrade from a wheelchair, and writes tour guide brochures."

"Sounds like a happy ending?" Charlie said.

"If you want to do something," he said, "then do it. The side routes are more dangerous and often more circuitous than the direct ones."

"My case isn't so direct," she said. "It's… very complex. I just want the answers. Knowing what's happening is all I'm after at this point. Even if he's not coming back, I want to know why."

"Right." Clive nodded. He left the topic alone. He could tell what she had to say wasn't a business pleasantry any longer. She was there, he was there, the office was open—it was time for work. "Anyway, that morning chore aside, what am I meant to do?"

Charlie stood up and entered her business mode. "Right now," she said, "we're short on leads."

"For a case?"

"For clients. We rely mostly on word of mouth and social media marketing to bring in new work. Nearly all our clients are locals, callers from the city. We usually just mention we're next to the Baltic Hotel and they know how to find us. But we want to expand across the Northwest and beyond. We've got a van and a fuel card, we can travel if we need to. The problem is, I'm not even sure most people know there are private investigators in the UK. What you should do is look for opportunities and reach out on behalf of the agency."

He nodded along, slowly. "I can also keep the premises secure," he said. "It's not much, but it's padding for the rest of it."

"We need full-time connections," she said. "Someone in the community, constantly drumming up support for us. That's usually a job split between us, but well, we don't really reach out well to demographics beyond our own. We get lucky when someone… older comes to us with problems."

"Not skill-based work, that," he said, "but something that I can handle. Like I mentioned, I've met plenty of people, whether or not they knew it, while on guard duty. I can think of some connections right now, as long as you don't mind some work coming in that's more like a chore than a just cause."

"We'll take anything and everything," she confirmed. She motioned to the computer monitor in front of him, which she just noticed was still off. He'd been side-eyeing it the whole time, and never turned it on. It was a bit of a warning sign. Her intuition gave her an ill premonition, which she chose to shrug off. "This computer is on our local area network, so you just have to turn it on and you're good to go with the login credentials Becca's put on that sticky note. First thing you should do is change the password to one of your own choosing. Don't let clients use it, though. Mine and Ash's computers are on a locked-down intranet so we can only share files internally. It keeps our information secure. Once we train you—"

"About that," Clive finally interrupted. "How comprehensive will this computer training be?"

Charlie nodded. "We'll keep it quick and simple."

He nodded back and finally took a seat.

Right then the rest of the merry crew arrived. Ash slowed his approach when he entered. At first, he was wary of the stranger behind what was sometimes his desk, then remembered their new hire, and went to assess the man by his suit. Clive was 58, but his attire was even older. A waistcoat over a diamond-pattern smoke-coloured jumper with jeans. His shoes were thick and nicely polished. Best part of his outfit.

"Good morning to you," Ash said.

"Good afternoon," Clive said.

Ash smiled. "Oh, I hope we do this every day." He hauled in a heavy satchel and put it on the chair that Charlie abandoned. "I've got the shots from last night to upload."

"And IDs on the others?" she asked.

"The woman she was sucking face with is Anna Cartwright. That was easy enough. They're tagged in each other's Instas. The club owner is Leslie Redding. Commercial estate agent by day, Becca will be able to dig a little deeper." Ash paused when he noticed Clive was hanging on every word. "I was planning to pay a visit to the club later to see what the staff knows. I'll go on my own. I'm guessing Becca will be required to train our newbie here?"

"That's right," Charlie said. She opened the satchel and picked up the camera as Rebecca entered. She was also surprised to see the man behind the desk and his militant posture. It summoned a revulsion in her, a compulsion to *rebel*, but she stuffed it down.

"Hello, all," she said. "And to you as well, Mr. Aston."

"Ms. Jarvis," he nodded. "Excuse me, if you don't mind, but are you related to Sergeant—"

She raised her index finger up at him. She couldn't quell the rebel yell any longer.

"That is *my* desk," she insisted.

He nodded and got up. The newest member of the club already making friends.

"Let's all play nice, shall we?" Charlie said, hands full of equipment. "Save the angst for the baddies."

chapter
eight

Eleven Months Earlier

EMEFA AWOKE in the luxurious bed, her body still hurt from the crash. Her first attempt to escape had failed, and she felt her skin still tingling from the stun baton's charge. It drove home the point of just how helpless she was. Even worse, she had a headache. But it wasn't a normal headache. She knew what it was. It was the boring drill of withdrawal knocking against her skull. As with every one of her relapses, an occasional fix in the privacy of her own home had quickly escalated into a full blown heroin habit that would floor a rhino. Whether it was a natural tolerance or that her arena tours were so physically demanding, she found she needed a cocktail of uppers and downers, over the course of the day, before she was ready to come out of her hotel room and face her adoring audience night after night.

As she showered, her body, mind, and spirit were craving a dopamine rush. A little injection between the toes to take the edge off and combat the God-awful migraine that was gripping her brain like a vice. The water suddenly stopped flowing from the shower head. She fiddled with the chrome taps, but nothing happened. It must have been on a timer, or the masked man had decided that she'd used up her allowance for the day. She stepped out of the cubicle and towelled herself off before putting on the oversized cotton dressing gown.

When she exited her doorless en suite, she found her captor had returned with food. It was all soft and easy-to-swallow stuff, porridge and sliced banana and yogurt—nothing she could choke herself with—and a small bottle of water. Prison food, but lovingly cooked and plated. He stayed with her in the room while she ate.

He'd been in her room all night, even when she'd had to use the bathroom to pee, all just in case she tried to make a terrible decision without his consent. The darkest nightmare of her entire career was realised—she'd been singing of pain, loss, and despair for years. It has made her famous. Now, she realised, she was about to truly live it and she was both ill-equipped and ill-prepared.

She was in a conservatorship against her will. The kidnapping was just an extra flourish.

"I'd like to show you around," he said.

"Why?" she asked. "You've already made it clear, I'm stuck here. With you."

"Your road to recovery may be long," he said, "but we can shorten the distance with bridges of trust."

She looked at him in utter disbelief. Trust was not something she could give to a man who stowed away inside her car, caused her to crash, and then dragged her to an undisclosed address. He got up and moved toward the door, waiting for her to join him. She sat obstinately in her seat in front of the vanity mirror, which had become her dining table. A few minutes passed, yet her captor didn't move. He just waited. Watched her impassively and waited until her spirit broke. She got up and limped over to him.

"Don't hurt me," she whimpered.

"Of course not," he said.

He offered his hand, and she took it, cautiously. His heavy leather glove gripped her fragile skin with a gentle touch. He led her out of her room and down a flight of stairs into the rest of the building. It was an old Georgian house with a dozen or so rooms, enough space to require a maid. Every window was blacked out with drawn curtains. Light came only from energy-efficient lamps and wall sconces.

They arrived at what was once a very large dining room, now transformed into a purpose-built recording studio. It was as good as any professional room she'd recorded in. Sound-proof textured foam covered every wall. A microphone and music stand stood in the corner and faced a large mixing desk.

"We'll be working in here," he said. "No distractions, no deadlines. Just unadulterated creativity. You call the shots. The way it should be."

She scoffed. "But I'm clearly not calling the shots. You are."

"Think of me as your spirit guide," he said. "A mentor of sorts, getting you back on track."

Emefa glanced again at the studio. There was nothing dubious about it, which worried her the most. The sincerity in the man's attempts to *reform* her looked legitimate. They continued further along the hall into a kitchen with expansive cupboards and an immaculate granite worktop. She saw evidence of the breakfast preparation in the sink and dirty utensils sunken into the bottom of a soapy bowl. The rest of the area looked spotless.

"You'll write and record," he continued. "I'll produce and distribute. We'll cut out the middlemen and all of that nega-tive, unhelpful influence. Back to basics. Back to the sound of *Emo in C Minor*."

Emefa flushed with pride at the mention of her debut album. It was undoubtedly her favourite.

Then, to her surprise, he led her outside into a walled

garden. The rendered walls were about twelve feet high and enclosed manicured borders and planting troughs brimming with flowering bushes and thin-trunked trees. Planted to give the appearance of not planted, but not quite mature enough yet to pull it off. She had a view of the sky. It was nearly noon. Her time indoors, suppressed by heavy blackout curtains, had spun her sense of time and season all around. More importantly, she keened her ears to listen for the sounds of traffic or other houses, but heard nothing over the walls but birdsong.

"Here," he explained, "is where we'll take some selfies." He pulled out a phone from his long coat pocket. It was her phone, no mistake, with a hairline crack in the screen protector's surface. She reflexively stepped forward and reached out to grab it but held herself back once he pulled it away, showing that he was in unflinching control. She gritted her teeth and yanked a well-tended vine off the terraced wall.

"If you think I'm going to smile and go along with—"

He traded her phone in his pocket for the baton off his hip holster. "Just occasional posts," he said. "Ambiguous. Life-affirming quotes. Just enough to convince the world you're still alive." His words rang out with a degree of threat to them, but still in the ever-sincere and helpful tone. He wanted her to believe him. But it was clear she didn't *need* to for his plan to work.

chapter
nine

Come noon, assignments were allocated, and the group was into their work in earnest. Ashley headed for the club as promised, hoping to catch some talkative cleaning staff. Charlie was busy in her office, selecting the best of last night's photos and typing up their notes and observations. She had a library of names and titles, connections to make and assumptions to prove as she revved up her inspective instinct.

Charlie had left Rebecca to staff the front desk and to train Clive, which was going in a downward direction. The spiral started when she set Clive up at the desk, computer on, and tasked him with something very simple.

"We want to check in on our client's good word," she explained. "We found her estranged son the other week and brought him home. If she mentions us, we're square, but we did it gratis for a good word to her friend list. Go on Facebook and search for Ennis Tomberly."

Clive nodded and just kind of looked at the setup before him. He saw a keyboard and a mouse and realised that Rebecca was expecting him to act. Clive was not wholly tech-literate, which he seemed remiss to admit at first.

He went for the keyboard and started typing *F-A-C-E-B* – then looked up. Nothing happened. Which meant he had to do something else. He could feel Rebecca standing behind him, her back to the wall, judging him as he struggled. It was fine. It was just one pair of hateful eyes mocking his efforts. He'd felt worse in the army. He'd endured worse—twenty years on minimum pay chasing shoplifters through the town centre. He'd work it out in time. He thought the mouse might be his ticket to success. When he moved it, a pointer on the screen moved.

Rebecca stood by, dumbstruck. She was a child of the digital age, grown and raised on bits, bytes, and LED. Seeing an honest-to-God Boomer, a borderline pensioner, struggling with what she did as easily as she breathed, made her smirk. Clive finally managed to navigate the mouse over and figured out, through a process of elimination, a simple way to open programs. He clicked on it to highlight it, then logically, he pressed the Enter key. And opened the task manager, which he then looked through for Facebook.

Rebecca snorted.

"Yes, it's very funny," he said. "I've gone through training just like this in basic, young lady. I can endure."

"Yeah, okay," she said. "You just— I— I'm actually stunned you got far enough to figure out the Enter key. That's brilliant!"

He sighed and nodded along. At a certain point, she would have to teach him what to do. Or, better yet, he could show her up. He turned to his bag, a hardened rucksack with a canvas coating, stiffened by years of exposure to the elements, and pulled out a phonebook. "I noticed when I came to interview that you didn't have one of these around," he said.

"Why would we?" she asked, wiping a tear from her eye before it smudged her mascara.

"The name was Tomberly, was it? T-O-M-B and so on?"

"Yeah," she said. She held herself back as the man flipped instantly to the T section and walked himself page after page to the T and O, then to the O-M, and tapped his finger over three entries, one of which was initialled with E. He held his finger there and reached for the landline.

"What am I asking?" he said.

"You're not going to call her!" Rebecca said.

"Why wouldn't I?" he asked. "It's office hours, isn't it, and she's a client?"

"I just want to check if she posted about us online," she said. "It was our exchange."

"Now, Ms. Jarvis," he began, "you've seen me, a man of my age, which is admittedly past the middle, struggle against technology for a bit too long. How much older is this Mrs. Tomberly than I am?"

Rebecca deduced his point. It was unlikely Ennis Tomberly was online. She was impressed. It was the kind of passive-aggressive stunt she tended to pull herself. Using her weakness to make someone else look bad for believing in her. Proving someone right in the worst way and then celebrating it. She smiled.

"Here," she said. "For future reference, you want to click on the Chrome icon there. And you can double-click"—which she demonstrated—"to open things faster."

"Right," he said. "And I know what Facebook is."

"But you've never used it?"

"I've been asked if I'm on it," he said, "enough times to just tune the word out."

"Oh, same," she said.

"Hey, Becca," Charlie called. "I need you in here for a quick minute."

"Okay." She left Clive alone, stranded on the internet to fend for himself and produce some results. He wasn't a helpless man, just a bit behind the times. His resourcefulness, and his wit, were on par with the rest of the agency.

Rebecca joined Charlie in her office and circled around the desk to see what Charlie was working on. To a casual observer, Charlie could be mistaken for a crypto day trader, with a four-screen rig mounted above a very long curve-screen monitor. She had her usual charts and digital cork-boards open, which let her drag-and-drop files and folders around on condensed desktop-like interfaces. One screen was arranged with all the brand-new information that Ashley had collected from the night before. One of the photos, pulled from Instagram, had a line that reached off the chart and connected to a small node which was linked to another, far more complex-looking arrangement on her other monitor.

"This is the Phillips case," she said, pointing to the smaller arrangement. "What we have so far. I'll update it when Ash gets back but this"—she pointed to the top right monitor—"is what I've gathered so far on the Wedding Veil Killer."

"Ugh," Rebecca grunted. "That sicko?"

"Yes," Charlie said. "I found a possible link to our case. It's small, maybe negligible, but just last week there was another murder. The Echo printed what they'd gleaned before the police made an official statement and gagged them, but it's clear the MOs were too close to be a coincidence. As was the victim. White, early forties. Her name was Jennifer Bambridge. She was last seen at a nightclub flirting with a younger man who lacks identification from eyewitnesses. Apparently, the current profile of the killer has him being anywhere from Middle Eastern to pale as an Icelander."

"So, no one's talking," Rebecca said. "Loving that sense of civic duty."

"No one cares unless it affects them directly," Charlie lamented. "Some were club regulars, though. And that club is the same one where Sophie"—she pointed again—"met up with her friend Anna Cartwright, who both happen to know a local commercial property agent, Leslie Redding, who seems to specialise in properties in the L1 and L3 postcodes and seems to be a lot more successful at it than our client, and Sophie's husband, David Phillips.

"From what Ash has deduced, she gives selected friends and business associates a pre-listing heads-up when new premises come on the market. Leslie Redding is also the current license holder of the Ivory Staircase. She and Dave are basically each other's competition. A bit strange then that Leslie is mates with Sophie, no?"

"Who do I have to stalk?" Rebecca asked.

"No one," she said. "But all three women fit the same profile as the most recent victim of the Wedding Veil Killer. Same age and look, same venue, all older women with open date plans who like to unwind with a few drinks."

"Easy marks," Rebecca said. She edged herself in a bit closer.

Rebecca fancied herself a sort of expert on what made criminals tick. She had zero formal criminal psychology training but found it worryingly easy to get into the mindset of humanity's most disturbed souls. She was a regular buff of serial killer documentaries. The resident expert on sick psychopaths, nonces, and pervs.

"Yeah," she agreed, "that's danger."

"I think," Charlie said, "we could pass along a warning to Dave and try to keep Sophie out of town for a while. They used to go to Ibiza a lot when they first got married. Maybe he can suggest a fortnight break to rekindle the relationship, which should get her out of the city for a bit."

"But what about the other two?" Rebecca asked, "Same risk factor?"

Charlie shook her head. "Hard to tell. We've already got eyes on Sophie. By extension, we're going to be seeing a lot more of Anna, assuming last night wasn't just a one-off. Thankfully, Redding's high profile."

"Too big," Rebecca agreed. "Too loud of a kill. And at the same place—he'd never strike on the same ground twice, would he?"

"Unlikely. The first kill was from a club in Manchester—

The Lighthouse," Charlie clarified. "But the girl was from Liverpool. Local killings, local women, even if they're on an excursion out of the area."

"Out of bounds," Rebecca said. "Like… cheaters."

Charlie nodded. "Could be."

"Well, let's hope Ash comes back empty-handed," she said. "I don't think we're quite ready for a murder."

chapter
ten

CHARLIE DECIDED she was going to call Dave in for a meeting. It was time. They had the evidence he wanted; the truth that would set him free. The not knowing was more painful than knowing. Hopefully, he would leave with some sort of closure.

Ashley came in with some printed copies of the images he'd shot from the van—the deed itself, captured in crystal clear high definition along with some before and after shots, both for context and provenance. In a world of deep fake, generative AI and photo manipulation, it helped to have as many still and video images as possible, with an impeccable digital signature. Seeing the photos blown up and printed on quality photo paper felt a little voyeuristic. They were middle-aged ladies, in the throes of a passionate kiss, a private moment. But, Charlie figured, they had chosen a public location, and the agency was just doing what it was paid to do.

"Click on that file." Ash pointed to a MP3 icon on Charlie's desktop.

They all looked at the screen as the video footage expanded and began to play.

"In case there's any doubt."

"Just a reminder," Charlie said as she watched, "there is no casual surfing allowed on office computers."

"I can read all your histories from my phone," Rebecca said. "Don't tempt me to shame you."

Ashley had his arms crossed and leaned against the wall, continuously shaking his head like he had a loose ball bearing that was supposed to keep it steady. "That poor man."

"I'm surprised, mostly," Charlie said.

"Were you thinking she was just toying around?" Rebecca asked. "Playing tramp without putting out to make Dave jealous?"

"It was an assumption I made," Charlie admitted. "The wrong one. The worst case I imagined was her actually picking up fellas, hence my earlier concern. If she picked the wrong guy, she'd end up dead.

"You still trying to push the Wedding Veil Killer into all our work?" Ashley asked. "You think there's a connection here?"

"It's pretty tenuous," she admitted. "Not quite there yet. Thematic murder is— *Oh*, that's friendly."

Charlie was distracted by the video, which showed Anna gripping Anna's backside like she was kneading dough.

"That's a strong grip she's got," Rebecca said.

"She's grabbing more thigh than rear," Ashley criticised. "Can't say it's the smartest move in public. Wrinkled bum on a skirt is more forgivable than a laddered stocking."

"You made a copy of this, didn't you?" Rebecca asked. "For personal use."

"Not my thing," he said. "Anything without *me* in it feels worthless."

"Okay, we're done talking about that," Charlie said.

She stopped the video of two ladies making out and compressed it into a small thumbnail on her corkboard. The rest of Ashley's evidence was equally damning. Sophie was hooking up with Anna in a more-than-friendly manner almost daily. Her new clothes and the overspending on beauty therapies was to keep up appearances for her girl and her friends, so she was still cool to hang with them.

It was what Dave wanted to know, and that was what mattered. Charlie added this extra evidence to her client folder, transferred a copy onto a tablet, and placed the call for Dave to come in. He arrived about an hour later and sat down in the meeting room to receive the news.

"I'm afraid," Charlie began, "that we have some information. Some of it is good, but also some is bad."

Dave sighed. He failed to fully brace himself and held a quivering tone in his voice. "Uh—the good, first, then."

"Right," she said. "Your wife… is having an affair."

Dave sounded like he stepped on a nail. He held back a cry and choked it down into a wheeze of desperation. "That's the good news?!"

She nodded.

He slapped his forehead with his hat. "Well, what's the bad?"

Charlie took the envelope from the desk and pulled out the photos. The video she kept as backup, depending on Dave's reaction. "I'm afraid Sophie is having an affair. With Anna—"

"Cartwright?" he said, suddenly cheered up. He sighed with relief, even. Nearly chuckled. "Ha. That's not an affair. They're close, have been for years."

Charlie couldn't quite believe his acceptance after so much sincere suffering in the lead-up. She decided gratuity was necessary and queued up the video on a tablet. "Mr Phillips, I'm close with my girlfriends," she tapped play, "but we don't snog in public or muss up each other's hair for just under twelve minutes."

He glanced down with intrigue. He watched the video

and hid a smirk by pretending to clear his throat. "No," he said. "They've been doing that for years. It's fine, really."

She took the tablet back as he slid it over.

"So, you knew about Anna?"

"Sure," he said. "That's not the issue. She's seeing a fella; I'm convinced of it."

"So, with a woman," Charlie reiterated, "it's just— That doesn't count for the two of you?"

"Sophie is bisexual," he said. "She was curious when we met, and I indulged it. I... I'll spare you my thoughts on it, but suffice it to say, I approve of it. It is what it is, and it's always been. There's a risk with a man, right? A risk I don't want her taking. That she shouldn't take. That's a husband's role, and that husband is me. A girl can't do... that. So, it's not about that."

Charlie nodded along with his 'logic' until she understood it.

"So then," she said, "you want us to keep up surveillance?"

"Yes." He nodded. "Especially now. I'm going to Brussels for the weekend on business—"

"About that," Charlie interrupted. "Why not take her with you? A nice city break, chance to rekindle. Maybe bolt on a week or two afterwards? You mentioned you both used to enjoy holidays together."

"It's when I'm away she's most likely to cheat. No, she's staying here. You need to stick to her like glue while I'm gone. Follow Anna if you have to, day and night. If there's an extra fee, I'll come up with it."

"We'll maintain surveillance on the pair," she confirmed, "to see if any third party enters the fray, and capture evidence, if there is any."

"I trust Anna," he said. "I know her. Anybody else, I want the proof, just like this, if you can. Something I can show."

"Yes, we will do that," she confirmed.

He looked back at the tablet, just a glance. "Could you send me that as well? Just in case."

Charlie kept a straight face without an immediate response. He took that as a no and left. The job had changed past what was expected. Charlie had hoped to get Sophie out of town for a while. That clearly wasn't going to happen.

With Dave himself off on his travels, she would have to increase the hours they spent on surveillance. Charlie felt better knowing there would be eyes on Sophie, and Ash would be grateful for the overtime, but it seemed like an unnecessary use of resources. What seemed like a simple flirty affair with an unexpected partner turned into a bizarre game of cat and cuck. The complexity of their relationship daunted even Charlie's open mind. She went to gather Ash and Rebecca and set up a new plan of priorities.

"So?" Rebecca asked.

"Maintain surveillance," Charlie said. "Anna is a trusted, known party."

Ashley whistled. "My man's getting it done. Bloody proud of him."

"Shut up," Rebecca said, chiding him with an elbow.

"I can't hate," he said. "Although, I would have thought he'd be more broken up had he not known."

"How's that?" Rebecca asked.

"Think about it," Ash began. "If he lost his wife to a man like me—got age on him, style, grace, flair, *hair*, and the desperation and or jealousy factor. He'd be upset. That's a man losing to a man. It's a bad way to lose, because it makes him reflect on how he failed her in ways he can't improve. But losing a woman to another woman is like—his manhood isn't even real. It doesn't matter. The one thing he thought he had to give her, she can do without and still be happy. And worse, there's always self-blame. He'd be blaming himself for making his wife switch sides. How bad do you have to be to do that? It's the most damning of rejections."

"You're a Neanderthal." Rebecca shook her head in disgust.

"Elucidating," Charlie said sarcastically. "You'll make a top executive yet."

"I will," he said, "because looks are eighty percent of the game."

"Do they have CEOs at manwhore brothels?" Rebecca asked.

"I think those are all just local, union-run things," he said. "Where they're legal."

"Well," Charlie said, "at least he wasn't mad. Or he went mad and now he's in such a harsh denial we'll need iron gates to keep him from coming back when he decides to blame us." She clapped her hands to reset the room. "He's leaving town, which means the mice might well play. Keep a sharper eye on her. House, too."

"Within the law," Ashley said with a salute. He started out to gather up the van equipment and Rebecca nearly followed him.

"You," Charlie said, yanking Rebecca back by her distressed damaged T-shirt, "need to finish up the Alvarez case so we can close that and send it to the authorities."

"All right," she agreed. She turned around and went to Ashley's desk. She knew the password since they shared the terminal.

Charlie stopped by the front desk and checked on Clive before she went to her office.

"Feeling settled in yet?" she asked.

"Oh, sure," he said. "I've figured out this Google thing. You give it orders and it finds stuff for you. Video killed the radio star and you lot killed the encyclopaedias."

"We killed them," she said, "gutted them, and put their offal online for all."

"Lovely." He smirked. "You see what I mean, though? All

this spy business. You may yet have a career with the Intelligence Services."

"I'd have to do infiltration work to get that kind of rank," she said. "I'm not a good enough actor to lie my way into government."

chapter
eleven

WHAT BECAME VERY OBVIOUS, very quickly, was that Clive was still on the pre-foundation beginner's stage of computer literacy. He processed case notes, recorded expenses, and planned shift patterns on the stakeout missions, but did so by hand and slowly etched it into digital memory for hours afterwards. In the meantime, whenever Rebecca had to teach him something, she did so with a blithe attitude and a bit of a mean streak. Mainly with her music. She played Emefa's new track constantly, and it was driving the entire team mad.

She passed by the reception desk to the sound of the song being muffled and saw that Clive had squished Blu Tack into his laptop speakers and was navigating the keyboard blindly by trial and error. Her prank of turning on a hidden program to play the song on a loop had accidentally become a tutorial for Clive to learn touch typing.

"Computer's broken," he said.

"Not entirely," she remarked.

"You could've put on a classic for me," he said. "I'm not against hazing, but this is pretty middle ground of you."

"I got sick of hearing the Beatles when I was a kid," she said.

"What about 'Smith?"

"Who? The Smiths?"

"Aerosmith," he said. "Or some Van Halen."

"You're into metal?"

"Who wasn't in the 80s?"

"I thought old codgers like you only listened to what they still put on the AM radios."

"I'm fifty-eight, not seventy-eight," he said. "I was only a bit older than you now when Guns N' Roses was still touring, and I could drive myself over to the Manchester Academy to catch a gig whenever I wanted. I've seen Nirvana, The Prodigy, and the Chili Peppers. You're thinking of the pensioners who spend half their kids' inheritance on restoring classic cars and getting new hair grafted between the wrinkles in their head."

Rebecca was slightly stunned. Clive smirked and continued to slowly peck away at his research. She looked over his shoulder to see he was perusing a copy of the *Liverpool Echo* for minor stories as leads and tips.

"Can't believe people still buy printed newspapers," she said. "The news is a day old already. You know there's an online version, right?"

"I do," he said. "But some people still believe in print. One day all this"—he gestured to the computer—"might all go down. Run out of power, or the cables get snapped in a war. If that's all off, we've only got our mouths to tell stories with. Paper and print will only die if we lose our hands and our eyes."

"In a practical sense, yeah," she said, "but as a business, online is just cheaper, faster, and better."

"For now," he reiterated. "Anyway, it's been a laugh, but could you?" He pushed himself aside and allowed her to shut the music off. He tried to watch so he could figure out what to do, but the ritualistic sequence of events was completely arcane to him. She opened up one program, then another, the mouse cursor moving too fast for him to track. But the music shut off.

"Thank you," he said.

Memories, one two three, simple solid innervated— Rebecca mumbled along to where she'd stopped the song. She'd memorised the whole thing. Clive bobbed his head along to it. "Oh? Is it working? Am I inducting you?"

"I've heard worse," he said. "I don't get fussy over music. It's something that makes people happy. I have my likes and dislikes, but wouldn't mock someone for liking something I don't."

"I don't do blues," Rebecca commented. "Any song that's about a breakup, really. It's the wrong way to get over it. It's like telling a huge audience that you couldn't keep it together and asking for pity all the while."

"I see," he mused. "What's that song about, then? With those lyrics. I gagged the speakers when I thought I heard the word trout. Thought, no way, it couldn't be, girl's never seen a fishing rod in her life."

"It's deep," Rebecca said. "It's new, and it's darker and slower than her more recent stuff, which was just pure alt-pop. It's closer to her original sound. I guess that's why it's called *E-Girl Unplugged*. If you want to hear her good work, check out her debut album—" She leaned over to log in to Spotify, calling up a series of album playlists. "It's like she's going back to her roots, *Emo in C Minor*, her angsty *the-world's-not-fair* phase. This is like that, but better."

Rebecca clicked on Emefa's debut album, and it began to play.

"She's got a nice voice," Clive agreed. "People stick up their noses to pop music. They always have. I don't seek it out, not my style, but it never felt right to judge someone's work without actually working out what it means. I think music, like art, or art in music, only really functions if it has that direction. Like metal

Adi Flynn

—it's loud and it's completely aggressive, but most groups still sang ballads and love songs with those same sounds to get attention and to make it more exciting rather than sappy and sad."

"Really?" she said. "I mean, that's a… thing to think."

"You get bored when you're stationed," he said. "If someone has fun and you try to stop it, good luck getting them to save your life when bullets fly. You need to learn to have other people's fun. Enjoy the enjoyment. Happy handbag house music, trance, Rick Astley, death metal—or whatever, I've listened and enjoyed it all."

"Yeah, *happy handbag house music,* not a phrase I thought I'd ever hear anyone say, let alone you," Becca conceded. "So, really, what do you make of her new song?"

"Catchy, but weird," he said. "I swear, one of the words is trout, and she says it a couple of times. It's odd, a hangnail kind of thought. Put it on, I'll show you what I mean."

Rebecca smirked and clicked on the new track. "See, you love it!"

"Can you fast forward, about forty seconds in?"

"No. But you can. See that bar at the bottom? It's a timeline. Click where you want to the bit you want."

Clive hesitated and then gripped the mouse and guided the cursor about twenty percent into the song. He clicked. "Yeah, this next bit. Listen."

—*You're my rock, my guide in the dark, tears like glass splinter trout spark.*

He clicked stop. "Definitely trout. If her intention was to confuse people, then she succeeded."

Becca put a lot more value on what Clive was saying than he did himself. Clive was onto something that she had somehow ignored. People sang ballads to communicate their pain to others, same with sappy breakup songs, as pathetic as she thought them. Emefa was no random starlet or upsold vocalist. She wrote all her own songs, and they got more aggressive and poignant and considered as she grew as an artist. Her lyrics were part of the two-part play. They weren't always subtle—"*crash your private helicopter*" was the clearest dig against her producer that existed—but they were there.

Becca had to step back and wonder what was in her new song. She'd been on an approval-only streak listening to it, just grateful to hear the voice. It may as well have been in another language for as much as it made sense to her. She was so wrapped up in the backstage action of Emefa's career and blinded by the aesthetic she disguised herself with, that she missed what was being put right in front of her.

"Becca?" Charlie called as she entered the office. "Oh good, you're here. I have something for you. It's a shake-down. You like those, right?"

"A what now?" Clive asked.

"Oh, sorry," Charlie said. "Not a real one. She's acting as an in-between for an estranged couple who are going through a very hard time and won't talk to each other."

"A facilitator," Becca said, "is the official term. I *facil-i-tate* their arguments like I'm passing around notes in class while the teacher isn't looking."

"And this is a particularly nasty little letter?" Clive said. "A warning?"

"Yes," Charlie said. "They are constantly drawing new boundaries regarding their properties that have to take into consideration their mutual restraining orders. We have to keep both parties informed because they refuse to hire lawyers to settle their dispute."

"So, they hire private investigators?"

"We're much cheaper," Becca said. "We don't expense our morning coffees and we always answer the phone."

"They were one of our first repeat clients," Charlie said, a little proud. "And they are the type of people who talk about the services they hire to their upper-crust friends, so…"

"A little easy cash," Clive agreed, "and a little networking. But will it bring in good customers or more of the same?"

"Every drop fills a bucket," Charlie said.

"Well, I'll go and drop a whole load into the bucket," Becca said. "What time's the meet?"

"Be at her house at five," Charlie confirmed.

Becca nodded and turned back to Clive. "That gives us an hour to work on your IT skills."

Becca looked with both disdain and pity at the scraps of paper scattered over the desk that Clive had been using to jot down schedules and record phone numbers. She nodded towards the mouse and Clive reluctantly took it in hand.

"Today, grasshopper, you're going to learn the dark art of spreadsheets."

chapter
twelve

Saturday morning, and although the staff should be enjoying their weekend pursuits, it was team meeting time at the agency. A lot of good work got done, and there was still far more to do, yet it all felt like the whole crew was working towards a net zero of nothing.

Charlie brought Clive, Rebecca, and Ashley into her office to mull over the connection board she had for the Phillips case, with one stray thread that led to another board, which was much more involved and incomplete.

"All right," Charlie said, clapping her hands. She ran out of words. "So… how is everyone?"

"Oh, dandy," Ash said. "Thirteenth day on the trot. I've been working so many lates, I've forgotten what it is to sleep in my bed at night."

"From the stories you tell, I thought *not sleeping* in your bed was your goal," Rebecca quipped.

"I don't know what you may have heard, or assumed, but I'm a big believer in getting a solid eight hours," Ash said. "Sorry if that doesn't fit with the image you had of me stored in your wankbank."

"Ewww." Charlie recoiled.

"I'm weird," Becca said in answer to Charlie's question, almost like an awkward admission and a welcome segue.

"Oh, honey," Ash said, placing a gentle hand on her shoulder. "We know. It's called goth-chic. It's been a style since the 90s."

"No," Becca protested, pushing his wrist away. "About Emefa."

"Over her comeback?" Charlie asked. "What's weird about it?"

"Almost everything," Becca began. "First was the, just, total shutdown of her social media accounts. Completely out of left field. And her producers didn't say anything about the disastrous Liverpool gig, or about her taking some time out, until about two weeks later. They normally have a PR statement drummed up and released online within an hour of any incident. When she said a naughty word at a gig in Glasgow last year, twenty minutes later they were apologising for her —she hadn't even left the venue yet and was getting drunk in the green room while someone wrote a whole heavy-handed statement about responsibility and being a positive female icon and such."

"What'd she say?" Ash asked.

"Slag," Becca recalled. "A girl in the audience yelled up, 'You're my favourite whore' and Emefa was just correcting her—which leads me to this abrupt mood shift she's undergone."

"You'd know about mood shifts, wouldn't you?" Ash said. "You have one every time you talk about her."

"Yeah, and?" Becca said. "This is some real deep mind shit that's showing up, is what I'm saying. Like she got a brand-new publicist, but instead of following in *her* wake, they've forced Emefa to follow behind them and are artificially rebuilding her image out of the remains of what she left behind."

"She's a pop star," Ash said, swaying his head at the label

like it didn't quite fit but was good enough. "That's what they do. That's K-pop. Those aren't boys dancing, they're precious, beautiful slabs of tissue and fibre moulded to stimulate all the most expensive senses of a viewing demographic."

"But Emefa isn't like that," Becca protested.

Ash gave her a *oh yes, she is* look.

"She's no—" Becca said. "This isn't me being a moody hipster, for once. Look at her whole rise. This new page she's turning or whatever just doesn't make sense."

"How much sense does it not make?" Charlie asked.

Becca looked at her like she had accidentally lapsed into her mother's Cantonese.

Charlie blinked and rubbed her head. "I mean, how suspicious is it really?"

"More than not at all," Becca said.

"Go on." Charlie encouraged, "give us something."

"So, I've been trying to glean a location from the images on social, but all the metadata has been scrambled. It's not that hard to do, but it's deliberate. That's what's weird. The lat/long on one was made to look like it was taken in the middle of the Pacific Ocean. Another on the outskirts of Istanbul."

"Could it have been?" Clive challenged.

"Possibly, but why strip out the details about the type of camera used to take the shot and leave the location in? It just doesn't make sense."

Charlie finally sat up with intrigue. "In terms of percent, what's the over-under on this being a case?"

"Honestly?" Becca said. She leaned forward to engage even further, while Ash sat back and entertained himself by trying to spot dust mites and spiders in the untouched corners of the office walls. "Firstly, her producer, Marcus Durg, used to be big on preluding events and appearances. He'd give a week's notice or more when Emefa was scheduled to appear somewhere. He likes to play it safe, which is why juggling Emefa was supposed to be a sort of challenge. She'd be late or not show up, or show up early, surly and drunk. Basically, he couldn't plan for her, despite trying, yet he always played it around as a sort of publicity stunt."

"Could she," Charlie asked, "have been threatened with termination, forced into rehab, recovered and is now refocused sincerely on her art and craft?"

"No," Becca said.

"That— that seems like what she should have done," Charlie said.

"That was all part of her rise to popularity," Becca explained. "It was the artist versus system spectacle that got fans—like me—invested. We knew how the game worked. We watched documentaries about how hard it is to raise rock stars and their strange, quirky needs. She's no exception, far from it. But it's always well-produced. Steven Tyler does eight tons of blow but then always has something eloquent to say about the state of the world or endorses some kind of hair gel. It's manufactured. Emefa was like a rogue employee on the factory line throwing spanners around and pissing on the conveyor belt."

"Ugh," Ash grunted.

"She's so much more than just the e-girl aesthetic. She's full-on punk," Becca said. "But instead of making noise outside the building looking cute in pink, she got in, and is a bug in the system making a mess. That drew a crowd, so Durg decided to step in as a more active promoter. He's never done as much for a talent as he has for Emefa. He became her foil, her nemesis in a way. A designated enemy that turned all her fans against him, while he sold out arena tours and branded T-shirts and wigs and raked in all the profits."

"That's unique," Charlie said. "He took advantage of the open secret of pop idols being fake and played up the fakeness as part of the action."

"Like American wrestling," Clive noted. "The owner of

the whole corporation used to go into the ring and throw punches against men who could deadlift his limousine."

"Let's step back," Charlie said. "Do you think that her producer, Mr. Durg, may have been more involved in her disappearance than might be legal?"

"No," Becca said, building up a more conspiratorial and serious tone in her voice. "Why would he stop the golden goose from laying? I think he honestly has no clue where Emefa is."

Charlie's eyebrows peaked.

"He's not in control," Becca explained. "And he can't break that illusion now that he's settled into it. All that work he used to do? He hasn't done it since. After the first post appeared after the Liverpool gig, they went back on the defensive and claimed support for Emefa's period of recovery. There was no victory lap or public spectacle. And this isn't a situation where they'd cover for her going through something like an unplanned pregnancy or a terrible injury."

"You know that?" Charlie asked.

"Celebrities get followed into hospitals," Becca said. "It's grim, and a terrible practice, but it happens. Her agent has been followed—stalked, almost. Her security team, her roadies, even her backing dancers have been pestered by the press, and starting from last year a lot of those interviews were touched-up by her production company and all but redacted. Because all of them shared the same story—that they had no bloody clue where she was."

"So, they let the big secret slip," Charlie said, "that their biggest star ran wild and got off the leash, and now they can't track her down. Even after she revived her social media accounts?"

"If you read through the reams of recent subreddits and superfan blogs," Becca said, now heady with strange and circuitous claims, "the consensus is she might not be making her comeback willingly. I'm inclined to agree."

Charlie sat back. As far as she knew, there were no cases of a pop star being forced to produce music and provide a public image against their will. None that were so hidden and confused. Of course, that happened, but it was always covered up. The lack of cover-up did seem suspicious. It was looking less and less like a case of talent mismanagement, and more like a case of talent misplacement.

"If that is the situation," Charlie said, "and the police haven't made any headway at all in finding her—"

"Why would the producers notify the police?" Becca asked. "It just makes the whole thing look worse. The police haven't made any headway, because the police aren't looking for her."

"And if they can't go public," Ash added, "but still want to find her?"

"That's the question, isn't it?" Charlie said. "If they want her found, they'll need someone discreet, knowledgeable, and capable of the task." The four nodded to each other. "I'll get in touch with this Durg fella. If this works out, it'll be a high-stakes gig worth taking. *But*," she emphasised, "if it doesn't pan out, then it's back to prioritising the infidelity of Mrs Sophie Phillips, full time."

Ash clapped. "I've just got a new pickup line."

"Please don't make more cheating wife cases," Charlie said. "If we have to start cases just to solve them, we're no better than a mafia."

"More like a Triad, no?" Becca said.

Charlie rolled her eyes.

The rest of the morning was a bit of a write-off. With Emefa back on the scene, for whatever reason, Rebecca was committed to drilling it into everyone's minds as often as she could. She dubbed it method-investigating. There was an awful lot resting on her gut instinct, not least her reputation amongst the rest of the team.

Charlie couldn't deny that something was fishy about the

pop star's resurrection. She just hoped that the producer was willing to tell the truth. She put a call into his office and left a vague but teasing message. Twenty minutes later, she got a call back from Marcus Durg's PA—he'd meet her on his return from South Africa. An appointment was set for Tuesday at eleven. The fact that she got a response, and so quickly, was confirmation enough that this was a conversation definitely worth having.

chapter
thirteen

Eleven Months Earlier

NIGHT FELL. Or so Emefa believed. She was sent back to her room by her self-imposed caretaker to rest up for their upcoming activities. She would live on his healthy meals, his inflexible timetable, by his rules and his laws, or suffer by his hand. And assumedly they would keep the farce up under the same roof until he was satisfied with her growth and development enough to let her return to the world under the sunlight. She just had to comply and be the best idol he imagined her to be.

Or she could escape, which she tried. Her bedroom door was left open, and her captor retired for the night. He seemingly placed a lot of trust in her to not just wander off or hide somewhere else in the house to make him paranoid. She crept out of her room and, in bare feet, padded out onto the landing as silently as possible. She only knew what was behind a couple of doors and did not yet know where he slept.

The stairs were a challenge. They were nearly guaranteed to be creaky in a house as old as this. But Emefa knew how to handle old wooden stairs. She'd lived in a run-down home before. She sat down and very slowly lowered herself, feet then bottom, one step at a time. It was slow and grating work on her arms and calves, but it worked.

She was heading for the kitchen to get out to the patio garden. The front door would definitely be locked, and although the garden looked properly enclosed, she had a will and a wild streak that made even a tall wall seem like a short climb if it brought her to freedom.

She paused occasionally to listen for sounds of movement. There was a ticking clock, somewhere, but her internal rhythm told her it wasn't counting by the second and couldn't be trusted. She passed by the studio. It looked professional, but lifeless. Just like any other studio she'd recorded in. She didn't want to use it, not even legitimately. She halted when she saw some movement and waited to see what it was. It was just an LED light blinking under the mixing desk, casting an intermittent blood-red hue across the room. Off, on. Off, on. Just her and the light. Nothing else.

She was nearly free. Just one door between her and the open air. She reached up and gently, carefully attempted to lower the handle.

It didn't move.

It was locked.

She looked around for another exit, like the window. It was bolted shut, impossible to open. Same with every other window, even the one over the sink, and the windows in the adjoining room. Emefa crouched on her haunches and curled up. Her shoulders shook and tears flowed down her face.

Then the lights went on, blinding her.

"There is no escape," he said, as if he'd been watching all along. "I've planned your rebirth meticulously."

Emefa turned with a spiteful look. She saw her captor still wearing the cotton mask across his nose and mouth, sitting in a small armchair, his hand on the lamp switch. He wasn't important. He was a faceless, nameless producer. To put the idol first ahead of all branding. Sincere to the fault of madness.

He stood and reached out for her. Emefa had no fight left in her for the night. She accepted his hand in help and walked with him up the silent staircase, and back to her room.

"You need to get with the programme, little miss," he said.

"What if I refuse?" she asked. "No new lyrics, no new music."

He stopped.

"Then the coroner will report death by misadventure, or suicide," he explained. "There will be an avalanche of obituaries waxing lyrical about a talent wasted…" He turned to her fretful eyes with a complacent tone. "You'll be in good company. Joplin, Hendrix, Cobain, Winehouse—all taken before their time."

"I'm not twenty-seven yet," she retorted.

"The question is, do you want to be?"

He thumbed a tear away from her face as she shook with sobs. She had to accept her fate—one or the other. A captive diva or a grim reminder of the cruel realities of the entertainment industry. Either way, the tabloids would flow like gushing blood from a punctured neck. Emefa chose to live the story out, at least for a time, and see where her strange, twisted fate would take her as a singer. As far as contracts or restrictions went, it wasn't that much worse than when she was starting out. Just with lots more tasing and far fewer carbs.

chapter
fourteen

THERE WERE no days off for a working detective. As long as a case remained active and the clients kept asking questions, Charlie was on call to do first-rate solving of any situation that came up. Except for when more pressing matters surfaced. There were few emergencies that could deter her from her main agenda. One of those was her mum.

Leaving Ashley in charge at the office, Charlie drove over to Knotty Ash for the day. He was the most senior member before Rebecca, and the most active in the field. She felt much safer leaving the office now that Clive was there to cast his avuncular eye over proceedings. He was like a loyal, slightly judgemental guard dog who always kept the door open but never let the wrong people in. And he was getting better at using the computer. But he still instinctively took out a pen and paper when someone arrived to explain a situation.

Everything was coming together. Charlie Chan & Co. Detective Agency had a complete complement of staff and was fully functional. They'd just solved another infidelity case in a matter of days and Charlie was chomping at the bit to go stratospheric with her agency. But right now, her main problem to solve was helping her mum move out of the old family house.

It was a long time coming. The place was just too big for her, and the loneliness crept up on her unexpectedly. She was finally downsizing, where all her stuff would be easier to consolidate.

Charlie's mum took a pause in their packing upstairs to hold up a long qipao to her body in the mirror to see how well it still fit. It didn't.

"Mum!" Charlie exclaimed.

"Okay, okay," her mother said in her heavily accented but grammatically perfect English.

She carefully, and quickly, folded the dress up and placed it in an open box. Charlie helped by fastening all the box lids and taping them up as a final sure-fire seal. Everything stayed inside, no chance of letting their hard work go to waste.

Her mum, the one who drilled a sense of fastidiousness and discipline into her since she was a child, was acting a bit lazier than usual. She sat on the edge of the bed, which still needed to be brought down to the moving truck, and looked at the naked walls. The outlines of where all her pictures and ornaments had hung were still barely visible.

"I should dust these down," she said, "before we go. Did you already pack up the duster?"

"You don't have to do that," Charlie said. "The movers have to give the whole house a scrub down regardless of how clean you leave it."

"Well," she said, tapping her lips with her fingers, "I don't want them to think I was a pig, you know?"

"This, without doubt, is one of the nicer houses they'll clean this month," Charlie said as she taped up another box. "We don't have time for second guesses right now."

Her mom sighed. "I know, but… This is my home, Charlotte. It's the only one I can call my own. It's hard to hand over the keys. They're more than just keys. These unlock the memories we had in this place. Of you…." She choked up. "Of Lee."

His name was enough to send her into sobs in an instant.

Charlie sat down and hugged her mother around the shoulders. "I know, Mum," she said. "It'll be better when you're closer. We can go to lunch in town, go for walks—"

She sniffled. "That won't bring him back," her mother said. She pulled away and straightened herself up in the mirror.

Her breakdowns were never for long. The longest Charlie remembered seeing her mom cry was for ten minutes. When she was done, it was back to the basics, disciplined and ready. She still hurt inside, it was easy to see, but she could put on a strong face when it was needed. She moved the mirror aside and picked up one of the boxes it rested against. Charlie lifted a wide box in the corner.

"Not that one," her mom said. "That's for the charity shop."

Charlie took a look inside to see what her mother had deemed expendable. She was shocked to see just how valuable all the junk was. "Dad's old clothes?"

Her mum nodded. "I've held onto them long enough," she said.

Charlie pulled a grey suit jacket out of the box and held it up. Seeing it made her see her dad. She remembered him wearing it, looking up at him fine and fancy. And then looking down to see his pineapple pattern swimming trunks. It had been a cold day in Blackpool that year, and he hadn't wanted to go to the beach at all. Naïve to the fact that wearing a pineapple motif was code for being a swinger, he spent the holiday understandably perplexed when a number of older couples kept approaching him to ask what hotel room he was staying in. Just a happy little memory from Charlie's youth she couldn't let go of.

She was always looking up to him. Not literally, but all her memories of her father came from when she was small. Even when she was grown up, her dad just seemed bigger than her.

He was always in charge, making decisions that made her happy. While her mum always stressed her to find something she should improve about herself, her dad let her know there was always something to smile about. And now he was gone.

It still felt the same as when she'd grabbed his sleeve to walk along with him, and it sent her back to her childhood for a moment.

"It's a *new* chapter." She stressed the new, and nodded to the box. Memories of the old chapter filled it. Things she wanted to move away from. The house wasn't what she was leaving behind.

Mum left the room with two boxes and headed out to the front drive where the movers were loading things onto their truck. Charlie stayed behind to dwell on her dad's old suit jacket. She sniffed it to find some lost, nostalgic scent, but there was nothing.

She couldn't let it go. Not the jacket, not her father. She knew enough to know that there was so much more left to learn. She slipped the jacket on. She expected somehow it would make her feel taller, more in control. It was saggy on her shoulders and wide around the waist. She inherited her mother's figure, not his, which was a bonus. She patted it down to see how much she might have to tailor it. The tweed was all frayed and itchy. The lining was smooth and staticky.

She felt something hard beneath one of the pockets. Probably the spare button. Curious, her fingers searched it and found it was squarer and thicker than any button could have been. She reached down into the pocket and found a small opening between the layers that poked into the inner lining. She worked the jacket around a bit until she pulled out the contents.

Two silver and jade earrings, simple clips patterned almost like round latch hinges, and an ornate mahjong tile. His killer vice, and perhaps a passing gift for mom. Maybe something he won in a bet, or something he was too proud to lose in the final call.

"If you want something to wear," her mum called out, "you should try on one of my qipao. You'd look so much better—"

"Are these yours?" Charlie asked. She held up the earrings.

Her mum poked her head in the room and could tell, at a distance, that they weren't. She sneered, instantly forgetting about the fond memories of the house and her husband.

"No," she said. "Police must have been right. He ran off with another woman. Leave that jacket in the box. It's not worth saving."

"No, mum," Charlie insisted, "that's not what happened. You know it's not. He loved you and you loved him. There was something else. There was—"

"Stop!" she commanded. "Stop it! This is not a game! Or one of your goose-chasing cases. Your father is not coming back."

Charlie clutched the items in her hand. She was old enough to stand up for herself, but still felt too weak to stand up to her mother. Between her conviction and her mother's disapproval, she had the strength to stay standing but not to speak out. Her phone did the talking for her. It buzzed in her pocket. She exchanged it for the trinkets, stealing them away, and checked her text with a sigh.

"Okay," she said. "I've got to get back."

She threw off the jacket and left it splayed out over the rest of the charity items. She picked up a few boxes on her way out and headed her mom off at the stairs. The rest of the house was empty. The rest of her memories were gone, packed up in a van or stuffed deep into cardboard to have a chance at a second life. Her childhood home was clean and bare, a case fully closed. All she had to remember was the bitterness of not knowing for sure what had happened to her father, and now, a pair of earrings and a mahjong tile.

She offloaded the boxes with the rest and the movers handled the stacking and arrangement in the van.

"You know how to get there?" Charlie asked her mother.

"Yes," she said. "I have to meet the estate agent first, get the new keys, then buy these men coffee and sandwiches—"

"Okay," Charlie said. "Love you." She gave her mum a kiss on the cheek as she ran past. She had work to do. Progress to make. New memories to make, and old mysteries to solve.

chapter
fifteen

CHARLIE RETURNED to the office car park to find her usual spot already occupied by a police car. She squeezed her scooter into the compact space behind it and strode into the office building to greet her guest in the lobby. A squad car meant one of two things: a friendly visit from a local police officer to congratulate them on jobs well done and a reputation well earned, or a ticking off for overextending their limits as a civilian information firm. Again.

Seeing as it was Sarge at the office door, she knew it was much closer to the former.

"Sergeant Jarvis," she greeted. "Sir."

"Detective," he replied.

Jarvis was Rebecca's father. A career officer with just over twenty years on the force—almost as long as she'd been alive. He had a thick brown moustache that threatened to cover his entire mouth without daily primping. He was a polite, pleasant man who wore a distinct slouch to his brow, grown from a life of frequently frowning. Despite that feature, he never sounded distressed, or he hid it very well.

"To what do I owe the pleasure?" she asked.

They shook hands, and she awaited the sigh and turn of

phrase to make his pleasantries all seem like a cover for a more sinister approach.

"I was informed," he said, "that you had something to do with a recent shoplifting arrest."

"I may have," she said. "It wasn't a case or anything, though, it was more of an in-the-moment citizen's arrest sort of… thing."

"You'll be pleased to hear that serial shoplifter Patrick McKay is most likely going to do some actual time inside," he said. "He tried to do over a bookie this morning with a toy gun. I was at the custody suite when they brought him in. He'll be spending the night in the cells and is up in court tomorrow. Said he'd felt worse, I asked where, and got told about a Chinese lion—figured it was you."

"Well, circumstances have led you to the right place," she said. "I'm afraid I don't know if Becca is in at the moment."

The mention of her name made his pronounced brow furrow even more.

"Yes, she wasn't in when I got here," he said. "Ashley was on the front desk. He excused himself, said something about making preparations for a rendezvous tonight. Nothing too clandestine, I hope?"

"All within the law," she said firmly. "You have my word."

"Glad to hear it," he said. He drew closer, as if hiding his voice from anyone who might be hiding in the lobby. "I've heard your name going round certain circles at the nick. You're making coppers work hard to look good while you're out doing their jobs at a fairer price than free."

"I'm glad to hear that," she said. "I hope it hasn't inconvenienced you."

"Oh, not at all," he said.

A toilet flushed and the bathroom door opened. Clive walked over to the reception desk and eyed the policeman.

"Afternoon, sir," he greeted. "It'd be an honour of ours to help you if we can."

"Oh, hello," Sarge said. "No, nothing like that. I'm a friend and relative of the agency, Sergeant Jarvis, at *your* service, sir."

Clive snapped his finger and held it up at the lightbulb over his head. "Right! Of course! You're related to Rebecca?"

He rocked on his feet. "I am, yes. Her father."

"I worked at JD Sports until last week, as security," Clive said. "We met once when you came in to make an arrest."

"Ah, yes," Sarge said. "Fastidious notes, I recall. Well, then!" He turned to Charlie. "You're sniping up all the good talent already!"

"He is our newest hire," Charlie said. "Clive Aston, veteran and our local outreach coordinator, trainee detective."

The two men shook hands firmly.

"All right, then," Sarge said, a bit more serious. "Couple of things. I came to give you the heads-up that our IT guys are coming out to check your data processing procedures. GDPR and all that. I'll let them know you plan on passing like usual. It's happening on the 26th of this month."

"Thanks, Sarge. And the other thing?" Charlie offered Sarge a seat, but he declined.

"I," Sarge began, "am making the rounds informing private investigators about a potential threat to the community and its citizens."

"Is this a current threat or a future threat?" she asked.

"Current," he said. "You have heard, I am sure, of the Wedding Veil Killer?"

Charlie audibly sighed with relief before catching herself. She was glad it wasn't anything to do with her, just a standard serial killer roaming the area. She cleared her throat, feeling relief over news that grim looked downright suspicious.

"I have, yes. I've done some research as well, in an attempt to create a case and produce leads."

"I'd expect as much," he said, "but I am meant to warn you, not embolden you, in this pursuit. Merseyside CID has compiled what they believe to be the complete profile of the Wedding Veil Killer, including an official designation for reporting. They're to be referred to as the 'February 18th Murderer' in order to dissuade continued use of the moniker the Wedding Veil Killer. We don't want to celebrate his actions, nor do we want copycats getting any ideas."

"That's sensible," she agreed. "Will you share what you know?"

Sarge pulled out his notebook and continued. "The profile is as follows. The killer is believed to be a young man in his early- to mid-20s with access to undisclosed wealth and a white-collar job. Someone who works within the community and is noticeably present within faculties and functions where communications are frequent. In other words—"

"Like most serial killers," she interrupted, "he could be anyone, just a regular bloke with a regular job and a nice flat."

"Unfortunately," he said, "that is the best estimation. Race or background are unknown. His victims, beyond being white, have not shown a pattern nor signs of racially motivated hatred, nor religious—not strictly, anyway. The ceremonial touches indicated by the murder scenes so far indicate a fixation with which he chooses his targets."

"He?" she asked.

"Yes, ma'am," he confirmed. "Authorities are positive about that. Seeing as, well… It's hard to get into without the pictures. Things we can't share with you, understand."

"Crime scene photos," she surmised.

"Yes, ma'am, severe bruising around the neck with focus placed upon the trachea, leading to strangulation, and additional intended pressure on the right side of the neck over the carotid artery and jugular vein. Intense strength is applied to the point of causing bruising. This happens pre-coitus in a state of undress, and this itself is done without duress or violence.

"Toxicology reports on all of the victims show abnormally high levels of diazepam. Even if they were taking Valium or similar to get to sleep, these levels are way beyond that.

"In other words, he lures the woman to bed with him, waits for them to present themselves, then drugs them intravenously and immediately manoeuvres himself to kill them. Finally, once dead, he places the wedding veil used to murder them over the face. In two of the three cases, he retrieved a veil from the woman's own wedding dress ensemble, which she had nearby. In one case, he came prepared with one."

"Wait. What? Three? I thought there'd been two."

"There was another on Saturday night, or early hours Sunday morning."

"There's been no public statement about that."

"As I said, CID is all over this. Gagged the press."

"Can you tell me about it?"

"Officially, no."

"And unofficially?"

"Also no." Sergeant Jarvis shook his head. "Look, it's the same MO, same bored housewife victim profiles."

"Have the police traced the source of those veils back to any specific manufacturer, designer, rental shop, anything like that?"

"Afraid not," he said. "The manpower that requires, we don't have it. A load of seconded Met officers are moving in to take over the case. They want an arrest soon, before they start locking places down."

"And they've given this warning," she surmised, "because they don't want any of us to help catch him...."

He smirked. "I think it's more they don't want you to

inadvertently get in the way of the formal investigation and mess things up. I know you run a tight ship, Charlie, but give this one a wide berth. You're not his type anyway. His targets up to now have been married, white women. Not entirely faithful ones, mind, but it shouldn't end in murder."

"Understood," she said.

"Now, officially," he added as he got up, "I am to inform you not to pursue, track, or attempt to make a citizen's arrest on any individual who you believe could be the culprit, nor to engage directly if you believe a crime is, or is about to, take place. They're asking that you contact the police immediately with a positive description or photo image of the suspect and let the professionals deal with it."

"To give him a good head start."

"Look," he finished, ignoring the jibe, "just be careful, you and Rebecca both."

Sarge let his encouragement, officially, go unsaid. He wasn't allowed to tell anyone to be their own police, or it'd put him out of a job. But he knew Charlie, and she respected him. If anyone could put down such a terrible criminal, and that person was not in the police, it may as well be her. She just had to get married, change her ethnicity, and cheat before she could be the perfect prey…

"Be good," Sarge said as he waved and showed himself out of the office.

Clive rolled his seat closer to Charlie.

"Do the police often warn you off investigations?" he asked.

"No, and that's what's strange about it. It's had the opposite effect—I've been monitoring the case but wasn't thinking about investigating it. Now I am."

"Mobilising every private investigator, ex-cop, and amateur sleuth might help solve the case quicker. More eyes, more thinking power, more lines of inquiry…"

"Except it doesn't. It often complicates matters, leads to

false alarms, false arrests, and worse, potential contamination of crime scenes. Sometimes, we have to stay in our lane."

The Wedding Veil Killer murders had been gnawing away at Charlie's keen and personal sense of justice since the first murder. Or rather, it was that no one had been caught or, to her knowledge, even questioned that offended Charlie to her core. Justice had not been served and that niggled.

"Penny for your thoughts?"

"What do you know about the Wedding Veil Killer?"

"You mean the February 18th Murderer?"

Charlie smirked. "That too."

"Only what I read in the Echo. The first victim was found dead in Crosby, Ellie Scott, early thirties. She was strangled with a wedding veil in her home. Her body was found by the husband. She'd been laid out in bed and the veil had been placed over her face."

"Good memory. The killer struck again in December. Same MO. Victim was Sarah Croft, early 40s, post-grad student at John Moores. Drugged and strangled."

"Those deaths remain unsolved months later, and now there's another," Clive said. "A holy grail of modern criminal investigation. Whoever can obtain a positive witness ID, DNA proof that tied the owner to the scene—anything substantial —would receive accolades such that they couldn't build a big enough room to house the trophies. Or a positive news story, at least. Always a good thing."

Charlie nodded, ever more impressed with how Clive seemed to be fitting in.

"So, you want to take it on? The case?" he asked.

"We've been told not to."

Charlie winked and logged on to the computer in front of her.

"I hate to pry," he said. "I hate to notice things—but things aren't quite right between him and Rebecca, are they?"

Charlie nodded. "They're not talking at the moment.

Nothing hateful or serious. But she's been sofa surfing with friends for the past few weeks."

"Bit of a pastor's daughter, is she?" he said.

"She's literally a policeman's daughter," Charlie said. "And Ash is a former gang member who is on the long path of reform."

His eyebrows rose. "What other characters are you planning to bring in? If you hear that a copper gets fired for breaking a car apart with his bare fists, will you give him a corner desk, or is he going to work up the same path as me?"

"It hasn't escaped me," she said, "that I tend to gather people with spotty pasts to my side. But their skills are irreplaceable. Ash is responsible for all our clandestine monitoring. The van is his, and so is the equipment, all legit. He's a fine-tuner of pictures and audio, able to gather proof from single pixel-wide granules or corrupted MP3s. And Rebecca, as well as being a dab hand at some ethical hacking, keeps our computers running smooth and secretive. She uses military-grade encoding and encryptions on our cloud storage servers to keep our information hidden from prying eyes."

Clive blinked in a hollow reaction. "I thought she did the social media stuff."

"That too," she said, "anything online basically, and she's good at it. That's what matters."

"A good squad," he said, "covers for faults in one another. They utilise their strengths which are missing from each member."

"Good? That's… almost encouraging," she said. "Do you think we're a good squad?"

"Good enough," he said. "None of you are dead or have been arrested yet. That's probably where this all falls apart."

"True," she said.

She heard Ash enter the main door and moments later felt the cold blast of air he'd brought in with him. Ash approached, brushing imaginary lint from a lapel. He was dressed to impress with a fitted blazer, a crisp white shirt open at the neck, and some flattering jeans.

"Did I just miss a visit from our favourite law man?" he asked.

"Indeed," she confirmed. "Sarge wanted to give us the heads up on an IT audit, and they're very jealous of us at HQ. He also said, under no circumstances are we to investigate the Wedding Veil Killer."

"The February 18th Murderer," Clive corrected.

"He's killed again. It's all hush-hush."

"Send over what you have. I'll start with the bridal shops." Ash grinned.

Charlie nodded and immediately began transferring files to Ash's phone.

"Charlie informed me that you used to be a bit of a troublemaker in your past," Clive said.

"Did she now." Ash glanced at Charlie.

"What were you busted for?"

"Attempted robbery," Ash explained casually, as he'd explained so many times before. "I rolled with the Tocky Boys for a while. Right knob, I was. We were, all of us, collectively, a bunch of dickheads. Petty crimes, really, sold a bit of gear, vandalism, anti-social shit, but one day Scotty—he was one of the older lads in charge—dared us to help him rob an off-licence. We had to do it to prove ourselves. So me and two others caused a distraction while he held up a place in Cressington. No security grille or Perspex bars like the shops in Toxteth, just branded bags-for-life, vanilla diffusers, and alarms. We thought we could beat the alarms. Not a chance. By the time we got outside, there were six armed-response coppers waiting for us. My dad, he's a minister, talked to the Chief Super to get me off with some conditions. So, I got a suspended sentence and did three hundred hours of community service and decided, you know, living and being free really beats having twat mates."

"Nice," Clive said.

"But now I work here with Becca," he said. "Not sure it's a huge improvement."

"Mm-hmm," Clive grunted, recalling her *sledgehammer with a side order of sarcasm* approach to teaching.

chapter
sixteen

EVENING CAME. Friday night. When the lights went down, the lives went wild. Liverpool was a party-loving city. The locals, the students, and the hordes of out-of-town hen and stag parties all looking for a good night, poured into Liverpool's relatively compact city centre to get the party started. There were modern clubs, old-school pubs, chain bars, student dives, even sleek Insta-perfect cocktail bars that only opened once in a blue moon, if that.

Charlie and Ashley waited in the van with eyes on a well-appointed detached house, and watched as the Uber came to collect Sophie and Anna at exactly 11 PM. Once they confirmed no other suitors or third parties would be joining the two women, they pursued them to the town centre, parked when they saw the Uber pull up, and followed the women on foot.

As they turned onto Wood Street, Ashley and Charlie knew where they would be spending their early hours. A brightly coloured place where the strobe of the stagelights, which matched the beat of the songs inside, shone through the old warehouse glazing and could be seen up and down the street. A club which catered to any and all. Literally a floor for all seasons, ranging from ground floor drum and bass, first floor 70s and 80s, second floor Electropop, and a basement pumping out happy hardcore. Noise & Friction was the place. It was there Sophie and Anna had settled for the night, so it was where Ashley and Charlie would be too. As with every club on a Friday night, they couldn't walk straight in. They had to wait in line. A small group came in between their arrivals, which separated them by about six people, all of whom were loud talkers.

The women waited patiently. They occasionally laughed about something, but that was it. They weren't making conversation with the other people in line. Sophie was lost in her own little world with Anna.

"I'm almost glad," Charlie said, "that this seems to be going nowhere."

"Yeah?" he said. "You're not worried about the contract going bad?"

"I mean," she said, "It's just... It could've been so much worse. Right now, we're basically just following two people on a date, and no one is upset about it."

"True. I thought Dave would go berserk when he found out."

There was nothing to see through, no deeper mystery. But she could feel a pull of intrigue. Her intuition was never wrong. It meandered a bit, but it always led her to something. There was something pulling her towards Sophie. A suspicion that surmounted the presented evidence. Something else was going on. The surface level of crime was rarely the end. Small dealers worked for bigger enterprises. Loyal thugs had secret agendas. Crime lords always found a way to evade the law in purely legal ways. She started to suspect that Dave was right. The tragedy there was that Sophie was cheating on Anna, too.

The line moved at a decent pace. Groups of revellers came in and out. There was clearly special treatment being given to the larger groups. Singles or pairs could only make the club look so good mixed together. And groups, especially stags and hens this early in the night, usually bought way more drinks. As artsy or free-spirited as any club got, they still had to pay bills, just like the agency did.

The girls went inside. The wait suddenly felt so much longer than it was. Charlie took long, measured breaths to try and control the time and remain warm. Ashley primped himself on his phone using the camera.

"Chill, girl," he said, catching sight of her steely focus in the corner of his shot. "You're gonna shrivel with all that stress creasing your temples."

"I'll be all right," she said. "Do you have it?"

"I do," he said. Ash opened his palm to reveal a tiny microphone with a small battery no bigger than a fingernail. "Exactly one of *it*."

"That should be fine," she said. "Hopefully I can get close enough to deploy."

"How close *I can get*," he said. "She's bi, remember? I can easily flip her for an evening."

"Ash," Charlie said, "if we collect proof that Sophie is cheating by getting her to cheat with one of us, I can't in good conscience collect any payment from our client and will dock your pay the respective amount."

"Worth it," he said. "You know she'd bring her plus one with her... I'm so ready for this assignment."

Charlie rolled her eyes so hard Ash could feel it. Finally, it was their turn. They were let in, no issue, when another pair came out. From there, the hunt was on. They entered the pulsing neon-coloured club where the air smelled like liquorice and vodka to find their targets dancing to dubstep, perfect for some up-close staking-out. There was nothing suspicious about two young 20-odds taking a load off at the club for fun. Nothing wrong with two older ladies renewing their youth together in good company who passed no judgement upon their views of love. It was a safe space for sharing, which made it an ideal place to spy.

Ashley double-checked his device. He just had to stay in range, and it would live-feed all audio for about fifty minutes. If discovered, it was just a piece of plastic with slots, like a stray shirt tag or spare button. Even if it broke, the audio was always running while in Bluetooth range. He just needed his phone to stay alive to stream the whole thing.

"I'll try first," he said. The girls were at the bar, wearing low-back dresses with sequined sparkles that ran all the way down their legs. Ashley got within reaching distance of the women, and a man closed in on Charlie to fill the gap.

"Hello there," a deep, humming voice sounded in her ear. Charlie turned and met eyes with a tall, dark, and handsome stranger. Despite being in the technicolour kaleidoscope of a club, when she looked at him, things turned black and white. He had a charming smile and was dressed well. "I couldn't help but notice you."

"Well thank you," Charlie said. "It's always nice to be noticed."

"I'm Dion," he said, leaning close to her ear to be heard.

"Charlie," she said.

He cocked his eyebrow, uncertain he heard her correctly.

"Charlotte."

"Ah, I see," he said. "I thought I heard you right the first time. Such a rare name. It's valuable."

"Thank you," she said. "Dion is pretty rare as well."

"And valuable," he agreed. "I saw you come in with a brother. You think he'd mind if I borrowed you for a bit?"

She looked over. Ashley was leaned in and in full flirt. The bug was ripe for planting and his job was next to done. Sophie seemed disinterested. Anna was being more of a flirt for fun, a cougar batting a toy around with no intention of making it her meal.

"Probably not," she said.

"How about a step onto the floor?" he said.

She nodded, took his hand, and followed him out. It was

good cover, and it gave her a chance to see just how people were supposed to dance. There was a lot of bumping and grinding, stuff she interpreted as a series of challenges. Her martial arts training instilled in her a visceral reaction to getting held and then bumped from the side. It was usually answered in a snap kick or straight punch to the solar plexus. She wasn't used to just touching people for fun.

Dion guided her smoothly to the beat. Once the song changed, things got easier. It was an upbeat, psytrance song that inspired a lot of flailing and gyrating. The lights were loud, and the music was bright. It was a full sensory experience, yet Dion kept her grounded like a cool shadow in the blazing light. They danced for a while until he led her away to one of the vacant booths that lined the dance floor. She was panting. He tugged at his collar and shook his head.

"What a set," he said. "Can hardly breathe out there."

"It's nuts," she agreed. "Are you from around here?"

"Nah," he said. "Well, I settled here. I'm from London. Never thought I'd find so many good clubs up north."

"No raves at the palace for locals, eh?" she said. They shared a short laugh. Charlie decided, if nothing else, she could try her hand at making a move. "So, you're living here. Have you been here long?" She moved her hand closer to his. He read through her intentions, but instead of leaning in to turn small talk into short flirts, he grinned at her in a more friendly way.

"Sorry," he said. "I'm really only looking to chat."

Charlie sat up straighter. She pulled her hand back in embarrassment.

"Not that you've got nothing going on," he clarified. "I'm just into… more vintage wines, if you get me."

"Uh-huh," she said. "I'm sor—"

"Hey," he said, still smooth and in control. "Don't apologise."

She sucked in her shame and folded her hands to regain

her centre. Over Dion's head she saw Ashley giving her the signal. The bug was on, and their cover was solid. He was turned away as a harmless flirt by the two older ladies, who Dion would surely go to check out next. He'd have a better shot.

That was the whole point, Charlie realised. As if sensing the crystallisation of her knowledge, Dion got up and walked past Ashley as if he wasn't there. He was just waiting him out to get his chance, knowing he'd fail, and wanted to keep Ashley's plus-one trapped and too tired to stop him. He played her to get to Sophie. Or Anna.

"Mission accomplished," he said. "We're running audio now."

"Good," she said. "Let's listen in the van."

"We're not staying?" he asked. "I like to play a full game. One knock back is not enough. They deserve a second shot."

"Sorry, Ash," she said. "This isn't for fun anymore."

She got up and left, with just a wayward glance in Dion's direction. The ladies were laughing with him, loving him. It wasn't jealousy she was feeling, but danger. Like she'd just loosed a wild animal into the room.

chapter
seventeen

CHARLIE, Ash, Clive, and Rebecca reconvened at their appointed time in the late afternoon in the car park of Dog's Hind Leg Records, a formerly unassuming independent label based in Spinningfields, Manchester. The label gained popularity in the early 2000s with a few big hitters, expanded nationally, then commercially, and experienced significant growth when their main acts achieved international recognition. Emefa was one of their many major talents thanks mostly to her blazing charm and raucous attitude, and partly due to the swift forethought of producer Marcus Durg.

Ash ran back from the entrance and produced a pink permission slip. "We need to put this on the car, so it doesn't get towed."

"Nice of them," Charlie said. "On the inside or the outside?"

Ash shrugged.

Charlie placed the pass on the dashboard and checked that the registration and time were visible through the windshield.

"So," Rebecca said. Ash turned to her with a mild expression. She shrugged more aggressively at him. "Can we go in?"

"Wha— Yeah," Ash said. "Reception's open. It's quite nice in there, actually. Looks like a good place for parties."

"And our meeting?" Charlie asked.

"Yeah, we're on," Ash said. "He's, uh, not here yet."

"Is he going to be here at all?" Rebecca asked.

"The lady at the desk said so," Ash said. "She didn't say… much else. 'Put the parking pass in your car, he'll be in in a bit, coffee's cold and we're not making more.' Lovely eyes, though."

"Right," Charlie said, clapping her hands. "We've gone over our plan of attack already."

"I go for the legs," Ash said.

"And I'll grab his snout," Becca said.

"What?"

"Dog reference," Becca said. "It's not— I know we're not—"

"We're not violently attacking."

"Yeah, we got that, Charlie," Ash said. "We're just loosening up before talking to a man worth gazillions."

"Who, despite that," Becca added, "hasn't seen a living hair off the head of his biggest earner in almost a full year."

"Now," Charlie said sternly, "we can't let him know how far onto him we are. No accusations and no judgement. We happen to be private investigators with a fangirl so brilliant and deductive—" she gave Becca a moment to fan her face with her hand as she took in the excessive compliment, "that she was able to deduce that Emefa is in fact missing, and that we can help locate her on the q.t."

"Right," Ash nodded. "We lie."

"We *upsell*," Charlie corrected. "And we can find her, if indeed she's missing."

With that settled, she led her team, reunited under her steady leadership, into the building, past the receptionist, and up to the designated waiting room. They were told Mr. Durg was soon to arrive and would join them within the hour, if traffic allowed. They each picked seats in the executive board-room and kicked their feet to wheel them around. Charlie stood by the window and paced, like a flustered CEO, with an overview of much of the city's west side.

"What's the point in all this?" Becca asked.

"Of coming here?" Charlie asked.

"Of this," she motioned to the room. "They can do all this on Zoom now, yeah?"

"It's for appearance," Ash said. "Which I approve of."

"Who wants to be here?" Becca continued. "You could be in your own private penthouse lounge, trousers forgotten, wearing a robe and sipping wine, and contribute exactly as much business advice as if you were here, in a suit, hours out from a place you care about."

"Not everyone's a recovering shut-in," Ash said. "Some people like going outside and talking in the real world."

Becca grimaced. "Weird."

"That must be him," Charlie noted. A sleek, shimmering S-Class Mercedes rolled up the street and turned into the parking garage, out of sight. The three settled themselves back into place to wait like proper guests. It took at least fifteen minutes from the time the car drove in, to the time when their host showed up.

Marcus Durg was a man who was past his heyday, but still dressed and acted like he was in its heady midst. Middle-aged, no longer the slick young executive who managed the talents whose music guided the younger generation, but still energetic and charismatic to boot. His hair was slicked back and tied in a tail, his suit was chocolaty brown, and he wore leather driving gloves. Ash could tell the man spared no expense on his appearance, and the girls could smell his branded cologne from across the room. It was a very mild and not unpleasant tonic-like mixture, like he'd just been drinking at a very fancy bar.

"Mr. Burg," Charlie began. "We're private investigators."

He nodded to her. "I looked you up. Liverpool's finest, yeah?" He had more of a Home Counties accent, slightly diminished from what sounded like a lifetime talking to people from the States. "Nice to meet you. I'd say under better circumstances, but what are the good ways to meet a private detective?"

"Yes," Charlie said. "I suppose we ought to get straight to the point. We wanted to meet with you… because we can find Emefa."

He shrugged, a plastic grin on his face. "You can find her online whenever you want! She's active on her socials, she's making wonderful progress in her recovery; we couldn't be prouder of her. But, in the interest of her health, we are asking the public, and private investigators, to respect her privacy and not leak any information on her whereabouts to the public. Her fans… It's embarrassing for her to admit, but she needed a break from them, too."

"Sir," Charlie began, "that is not what we mean."

"Well, that's what I mean," he said.

"We have deduced," Charlie said, "through acute investigative work, that she is missing, and has been missing—out of your control—for about a year. Not as a stunt, and not for her own good. It's an unintended absence. And for the sake of her reputation, you've covered for this disappearance rather than involve the police. But I think you do want her found, otherwise why agree to this meeting?"

Marcus scoffed, "I'll need more than that."

"We have a contact," Ash continued, as he went for the legs, "within Merseyside Police, who informed us that no report of a missing person was ever filed, despite it being twelve months since her last public appearance."

"She's not missing. She's recovering," Marcus countered.

"Add to it," Becca joined in, "the shift in character, when her discordant attitude was the most profitable it had ever been at the time she vanished. This was not a planned stunt or an intervention, because none of the rehab clinics which provide discreet care for high-risk celebrities have taken her in, privately or not, in the last two years. We checked."

"Mr Durg," Ash came in with his best good-cop voice. "How would you describe Emefa's performance in Liverpool?"

"It's fair to say there were some… issues with the sound quality and—"

Ash tutted. "We've seen the videos online."

"OK." Marcus raised his hands in defeat. "It was a complete shit show. She could barely stand up straight. She hit the rider a bit too hard. It's happened to all the greats. Bowie, Winehouse, the Stones, Zeppelin—"

"I think we both know it was a little more than that. Not only was the rest of the tour in jeopardy, another performance like that and even the most diehard fans would have begun to turn on her, and that would have had significant repercussions for her reputation."

"I know. That's why I pulled her offstage and brought the warmup act back out. We were going to cancel the central European leg, give her three weeks off, and start fresh in the USA."

Ash nodded sympathetically. "Except when you went to explain all this to her—"

"She'd disappeared." Becca tapped each syllable on the expansive boardroom desk.

The combined assault of evidence, conjectural or otherwise, seemed to open Durg up. His smile faded. He checked the door behind him and immediately reached into his jacket. There was a sudden, tense moment where the detectives thought they were about to get shot to death, then he pulled out a letter.

"Alright. Come here," he said, "away from the windows, please."

Charlie led them around the table, where he placed the envelope and slowly opened it.

"What do you make of this?"

Inside the envelope was a letter. Written in curvy but very clear handwriting. It read:

> Marcus. I can see that the new single has gone down very well. I think this is evidence that my current situation should be sustained. It's good for me here, and I'm happier now. I've got a team helping me and we're making a lot of progress on the new album. I feel inspired ~~out~~ here. It is very calm and peaceful.
>
> When I am ready, I will send a new song soon. I'll also fire over a new photo as well. You should use it to update your website. I'll get it all over to you once it's <u>perfect.</u>
>
> Love and cuddles,
>
> E xx

"This," Marcus said, "is the last letter I got from her. Just yesterday."

"The last?" Charlie asked. "There's more—?"

"I've got them all," Marcus said, in a hushed voice. "Letters. Written in her handwriting—it used to be chicken scrawl, but I had her trained to correct it. I know it's her, but something's all wrong about it. All wrong. She disappeared without a trace and then, the next day, I got an email instructing us not to call the police. If we did, she would cease all contact." He tapped his finger on the table, hard, to drive the point in.

"I knew it," Becca whispered.

"I'll bring you the rest of the letters," he said. "Scans over email. Will that work?"

"It will," Charlie said.

She studied the letter intensely, down to every little mistake that was made. The crossed-out word seemed like an innocuous error, but it was no different from the replacement. The difference between saying "out" and "here" struck a chord in Charlie's head. Almost as if Emefa was trying to give a subtle hint, although a hint of what was unclear. Something she would only have to do if she was being forced to write. And forced to sing...

The meeting concluded soon after with fees and Heads of Agreement between the companies discussed. There were promises from both sides that they'd stay in touch and keep each other informed of any and all developments, no matter how seemingly inconsequential.

Charlie had set up the meeting up with Marcus Durg on little more than blind faith in Rebecca's instinct that all was not right with the Emefa narrative. She'd been right to question the official story, and now Charlie and the team had landed their biggest case ever.

chapter
eighteen

BECCA HAD A JOB. More than that, she had a calling. The most significant case of her entire life was unfolding before her. Years of research and dedication to the finer arts of fem-punk and counter-culture idols brought her to the highest grade of fandom: the benevolent stalker. She was hot on the last listed trail of Emefa's location prior to her strange disappearance. All she had to do was to trace the nearly year-old path that was taken under the cover of night. And of which there were no records.

Rebecca was grateful Charlie had enough faith in her to put in the call to the label. Her instinct had been proven right, but now they'd actually been hired to find Emefa, the reality and scale of the case was beginning to hit home. They needed to come up with some evidence, they needed to find out who she was with, and most importantly, where Emefa was.

Becca had reached a bit of a dead-end, having followed up on each of the supposed sightings that Emefa's fans had posted online.

Ash, when he cared to, made conversation with the record label staff who were free to talk about Emefa as she was and leading up to her "retreat," but all quoted the same management-approved narrative regarding her choice to take time out away from the world. It was completely hidden knowledge that she went missing, privy only to Charlie's team, Emefa's producer, and of course, her kidnapper.

Dog's Hind Leg Records was now a paying client, and that meant the pressure would be on Charlie and the team to produce something a bit more concrete than conjecture and gut feelings. Rebecca knew the best place to start was at the beginning, and that meant trying to make sense of what happened immediately after Emefa's last gig.

Marcus had sent through the CCTV footage of Emefa leaving the arena. She'd been alone and, based on the way she'd acted on stage and how she'd stormed past the backstage crew, not in a fit state to drive. The grey Range Rover Evoque was then captured on the car park cameras driving through the barriers. That's where the trail went cold. Since Marcus hadn't reported her missing, and the police hadn't been informed, if there was any more footage of Emefa driving in Liverpool, it was long gone by now.

Armed with little more than a registration number, Rebecca had begun her search. A caffeine-fuelled night later, she had a lead and every intention of acting on it.

Rebecca started the engine and edged the van out of its tight parking space so Clive could get in the passenger side. She switched the heating dial to max and blew cloudy breaths on her gloved hands.

Clive jumped in and put on his seatbelt.

"Where are we going?" he asked cheerily, apparently immune to the cold.

"It's a field trip to the great British countryside."

"Anything more specific? I like to be prepared."

"Crash site," Rebecca said as she reluctantly removed one glove with her teeth, pulled out her phone and snapped to a saved web page mentioning a crash the previous March, where a vehicle left the road and planted bonnet-first into a tree. "Found this last night. Unsolved case of a crashed Range

Rover on the night Emefa was last seen by her team and crew."

"There was an article about it?"

"Not relating to Emefa, it's an article in the *Liverpool Echo* last April about the blight of top-end vehicle thefts and how a tiny minority of scallies are perpetuating the tired stereotype that all scousers are car thieves. The journo interviewed Mike Daly, a farmer in the Wirral, who was furious the police hadn't removed a crashed vehicle from his land. Given the date, the vehicle type, and the location being possibly *en route* to Hawarden Airport, I think it was Emefa's car."

Rebecca pulled up behind a large green tractor. Clive and Rebecca hopped out. Rebecca immediately pulled her hat lower on her head and stuffed her gloved hands in her pockets. Exposed to the elements, the wind was biting at their faces.

"Are you crying?" Clive asked, concerned.

"Yes. There's a tiny bit of minus five wind chill factor stuck in my eye."

The cab of the tractor swung open and, like a scene from *Withnail and I*, a man with his right leg bound in polythene eased himself down to the ground.

"Don't you dare ask if he's the farmer," Clive warned.

"Hadn't even crossed my mind," Rebecca smiled back.

Rebecca approached the man, arm out, ready to shake hands.

"Are you the—" Becca side-eyed Clive. "*Gentleman* I spoke to yesterday? Mr Daly?"

"Mike, yeah."

"Thanks for agreeing to meet us. I'm Rebecca and this is Clive."

"Alright?" Mike asked.

"Good thanks, Mike." Clive shook his hand. "Don't want to take up too much of your time. Can you show us where the crash occurred?"

Mike quirked his head, beckoning them to follow, and traipsed across the field, dragging his lame leg. They walked about thirty metres until they arrived at a small copse of trees.

"It came off the road about where you're parked. You can still see the tracts it left in the earth."

Despite the long grass that had grown since, nature hadn't quite managed to eradicate the scars left on the frozen ground. Looking back the way they'd come, Clive had a clear view of two parallel gullies leading from the verge next to their van, all the way to where Rebecca was standing.

"It hit that tree hard. Engine block was all smashed up. It was a right mess. Total write off."

"No note on the windscreen, phone number to call?" Clive rubbed his hand along the trunk of the tree, which, although missing a large chunk of bark, was well underway with its own recovery process.

"What windscreen? Glass was all gone."

"What sort of car was it?"

"Range Rover. Nice one. Pretty new too."

"What do you think happened, Mike?" Clive continued, crouching down onto his haunches as he swept away the tufts of grass to see if there was anything of interest on the ground.

"I figured it had been stolen, the little shites wrapped it round the tree, and then done a runner. Real owners would report it missing and get the insurance payout. Everyone happy, except me, because I had to actually deal with it. As per usual."

Rebecca cocked her head. "Is it something that happens often?"

"Every now and again. Mostly in the summer, though. I've had a few crashes over the years, but they're usually back up that way, just after the Willaston turn-off. People take the corner too fast and come begging at the house to be towed out."

"How come they've crashed here?"

115

"No idea. The road's straight, so they either fell asleep or got startled and swerved to avoid an animal. Dog or something."

"You said on the phone that the car had been abandoned. What happened then?" Rebecca asked.

"I didn't do anything for a few days, expected a knock on the door. When that didn't happen, I called the Old Bill. They said they would inform the owner, and I thought whoever it was would organise a recovery. A week later it was still there, so I dragged it to the road with the tractor and had it towed. That's when I phoned the papers. Don't see why I should be out of pocket."

"Were there any personal effects in the car? A handbag? A coat? Anything that might identify the driver?"

"I didn't find anything, but I wasn't really looking. When I first saw the car, I was worried there'd be bodies lying dead inside. It was a bad smash and the door frame was crumpled. When I got closer, I saw that they'd both managed to get out. Guess they just wandered off and flagged someone down or called an Uber."

"Wait," Clive said, "*both* managed to get out? You think there were multiple occupants in the vehicle?"

"Yeah, that's why I thought it was stolen. Front and back doors were open and there were two sets of footprints. It had been raining for days, so the ground was really boggy. Large and small. Probably a teen and a younger mate, or girlfriend."

"You're sure? Two different sets?"

Mike nodded. "Plain as day. All sorts of stomping around next to the car and then side-by-side tracks leading back onto the road. Just by that hedge."

"Do you remember who you used to recover the vehicle?"

"Sure, Pritchard's over in Ellesmere Port. Ask for Steve."

Clive extended his hand to Mike. "Thanks for making the time for us today."

―――――

The fenced compound of Pritchard's Recovery & Scrap was remarkably neat, tidy, and well-swept. Rebecca pulled up outside the main reception and the proprietor came out to greet them both warmly. Steve was a businessman who may have provided end-of-life care for damaged, elderly, and unloved vehicles, but he did it with utmost professionalism.

"You looking to scrap that?" he asked, casting a well-tuned eye over Ash's van, totting up the value in parts and spares. "Engine sounds good. How many miles on the clock?"

"Oh, no," Rebecca clarified. "She isn't for sale. We were hoping to ask you a few questions about a vehicle you recovered last year if that's ok."

"Pfft. I can try, but we process hundreds of vehicles here."

"It was a grey Range Rover Evoque," Clive said. "Recovered from Mike Daly's land last March. Ring any bells?"

"That, I do remember. Mike was fuming about it. What do you wanna know?"

"Whatever you can remember. The damage to the vehicle, how it might have crashed—"

"I can just show you, if you'd like?"

"Wait? What? It's here?"

Steve pointed over to the neat rows of vehicles in the scrap yard, some piled on top of others, all in various stages of undress. "Sure. It's over there. Come on."

Rebecca and Clive followed Steve to a section of the scrapyard that housed the prestige brands. All of which had been stripped of doors, bumpers, headlights, spoilers, and grilles.

"There's not much left, to be honest." Steve indicated what could be kindly described as a hunk of metal that bore little resemblance to a fashionable SUV. Just a mangled chassis, the remnants of an engine, the outer frame, rear seats, and the damaged driver's door.

"Looks like there's been a few people before us."

"They go quick, these. Manufacturer parts cost an arm and a leg. So, owners always try us first. I was able to flog the offside wing mirror while it was still chained on the back of the truck."

"And no one claimed it? It was worth nearly a hundred grand."

Steve reached in through the gap that used to be the passenger door and took out a Perspex folder from the glove compartment.

"That's the logbook there. We contacted the registered keeper, a—" Steve ran his finger along the page, "Prestige Executive, they're a luxury leasing firm in Manchester. When I told them the chassis was fractured, they decided to scrap it."

"Did you find anything in the car? Something that might indicate who was driving it when it crashed?"

"No, nothing. Sorry. Apart from the broken glass, it was empty. Look, maybe if you could tell me what it is you're looking for, I might be able to help."

"We're looking for someone," Rebecca said. "She's gone missing. We think she was last seen driving this vehicle. But I guess too much time has passed to know for sure."

"Well, if it helps, it was definitely a woman driving when it crashed," Mike said.

"How can you be sure?" Clive asked.

"Front seat was as far forward as it could go. Practically next to the steering column, and it was stuck in place. We had to angle grind it to get it out."

Rebecca looked over at Clive with a grin. As far as field trips went, this had been very educational.

chapter
nineteen

Nine Months Earlier

ANOTHER LONG DAY in the studio. Emefa rubbed at the tension that had built in her neck and tried to remember how long she had been stuck there with her freaky Stan. The days blurred together. She was woken up in the dead of night to go into the garden and find inspiration in the darkness, then dragged back inside to detoxify her body and mind in a rickety sauna. And all the while, she knew she was being watched.

Every.

Single.

Second.

She'd been ogled in dressing rooms before by assistants and backstage staff who she was assured were all professionals and not in the industry just to sneak peeks at her naked body while changing costumes. With so many costume changes in her live sets, she'd become mostly desensitised to stripping down in front of wardrobe assistants and makeup artists, but remained passively disgusted and afraid when it came to her kidnapper. Mostly afraid. If she acted out or refused to follow his instructions, she got tasered. She'd been tamed, in a sense. All she could do was her job.

Life with her captor had its benefits. There was nothing to think about. All she had to do was the thing she supposedly liked best: create music. Everything else fell to the wayside. She didn't have to worry about her calories or her figure because no one would ever see her again, normally a frightening thing, but it meant not wearing makeup every day or avoiding carbs to keep a ragged and frail look for fashion's sake. She was starting to thicken up from healthy vegan meals that he prepared and ate with her, and truth be told, she was impressed with his seemingly endless repertoire of recipes.

She even started to feel a wavering of affection for him, being so doting and caring like an ideal boyfriend would be. It was an idea that made her a little sick at times, which he, of course, picked up on—not the reason behind it—and rushed to keep her well. She got sick once and was over it immediately after he brought her a host of unlabelled medicines.

But she was still a captive. And conscious that she was experiencing Stockholm Syndrome—if not falling in love with her captor, at least beginning to forget why she was angry with him. It was not an ideal setting to work in.

He informed her that it had been three months since they started seeking inspiration and it was time to update her social media for the first time since the car crash. He took her out to the garden to pick a flower she wanted to take a picture of. It had to be a good one. It would be her only message to the world for who knew how long.

At first, Emefa tried to get more of the wall or the house in frame so someone could try to identify it. Even just the shape of the clouds that day would be enough for some dedicated weather fanatic to recognise them and somehow deduce her location. She just needed to get a hint out as to where she might be, slightly south of Liverpool, slightly east of North Wales, a big house in a small village in the wasted countryside.

"Here," he said.

When he grew impatient, he did so either with care or with a stun baton. She froze up when he approached, expecting a shock. He pointed down to one of the flowers and held her camera over it. "Crouch down next to it. Like you're in conversation with it. You know what this flower is?"

"No." She lied.

"It's a daffodil," he said. "It symbolises rebirth. This is a perennial variety, which means it blooms throughout the year, then wilts, then blooms again and regrows over and over. Like you."

"It has to die to do that," she said. "If I die, I don't come back."

"But you did," he said. "From the car crash. I was there when you died and plucked you out to root you in better soil. A renaissance, if you will."

"Y—yeah. Uh… well, how long can this flower last without… good soil?"

"Not long," he said. "Every plot of this garden has custom-adjusted soil with an exact pH blend and nutrient balance to support different flowers. Some of the plants are for filler and soil stability, and to foster a natural competition where one flower is set to win out from as early as the seeding phase. It's all artificial, but the results are real. That realness is more valuable than the effort put into it—that's why people grow flowers, you know? We're not imitating nature and its wildness; we cultivate so we can *perfect* the things we think are beautiful."

She nodded politely. Really, she was hoping he'd give her some estimate of the distance she'd been dragged from the car crash. She'd been in and out of consciousness and her mind hadn't exactly been narcotic-free in the first place, but she was sure they hadn't travelled far. Once her *saviour* got poetic, he got a bit lost in his own head. She took the picture, and he immediately snatched the phone away from her to tag and post it. It was a wordless, sudden message of her life and renewal to the world.

"Stay out here for a moment," he said. "I need to moderate the comments for the first hour to weed out the bad sprouts. Remember, rebirth. New life. New thoughts. New feelings." He left her to that work and locked her out in the garden.

Emefa looked around at the building. It was definitely Victorian, possibly older. An established mansion with wooden shades and ceramic tiles and clashing fixtures like gutters or windows that looked forced to fit into the old frame. It didn't tell her where she was at all, and the windows were all tinted so they couldn't reflect the imagery from above the garden wall.

That wall was all that separated her from her freedom. It was too high and too sheer to climb, brickwork left smooth with mortar and stucco-style weatherproofing. There was a tree in the garden as well, a long and narrow-trimmed Baker Cypress too flimsy to hold her weight without bending.

But she tried it anyway. She was a few legs up when she found herself slipping through the felt-brush bristles and fell back down to the ground. She lay under the tree for a while, too tired to even weep, and looked at the grey sky.

Then, finally, Emefa found inspiration. She remembered the last time she hung out under the sky, lying prone on the ground, yet still sober. It had been a lazy afternoon reclining on a hillside overlooking Edinburgh the day after the final night of her first arena tour. She felt a sense of freedom then, that she could go anywhere as long as she sang when she landed. Singing was the way she explored the world; it was what set her free from the confines of her country.

She smiled for the first time in a long time.

She got up and waited by the back door. Her new producer came by and let her in like a pet.

"I got an idea," she said, almost excitedly, "for a new song."

chapter
twenty

It was Charlie's turn to tail Sophie Phillips for the day. She passed Clive, who was sporting a fancy pair of noise-cancelling headphones that were plugged into his laptop, and noticed he was working away at a text file. His typing was still slow, but showed improvement. It was his wording that seemed to take a step back. She tapped him on the shoulder. She heard Emefa's new hit single as he peeled the big stadium-quality headphones back.

"Out for a job, boss?" Clive asked.

"Are you still listening to that song?" she asked.

"I'm on a roll here," he said. He pointed to his screen. "I'm processing the words, see? Look at this." He looked down and configured his fingers to hit Control and F at the same time, then typed in *trout*. "Six times, this whole song, she says the word trout. Always in nonsense sentences—like *trout closes rooms too dark to venture* and *you are at most trout flesh* — only once with any reference to an actual body of water."

"Uh-huh." Charlie nodded.

"At the surface level, it seems random, but I'm sure it's not," he said. "Like how the Germans combine words haphazardly to forge new meanings out of them. Or the Welsh— I'm telling you, there's something here."

"Right." Charlie nodded. "You know it's ok to just admit you're an Emefa fan and that you like the song." She patted him on the shoulder and left him to his mad ramblings.

The song was dangerous; it seemed to have not one but two members of staff obsessing, and she made a mental note to ban it when she got back. Until then, it was back to stalking.

Stakeouts were very much Ashley's speciality, but Charlie was conscious that she'd been relying on him an awful lot these past few weeks. He had an assignment he needed to finish for university, so Charlie had insisted he take the afternoon off, and she'd take over surveillance. Despite her distinct style, Charlie blended into the city fairly well. Liverpool didn't exactly have a huge East Asian population. It used to, and it was certainly growing again, but her distinctness could look conspicuous depending which area of the city she ended up.

Sophie's days out of the house seemed to differ when her husband wasn't out of town. Previous ventures saw her doing everything possible to avoid her home and the areas where Dave might go for lunch or meetings. With him gone from the picture, at least for a short time, she actually went to the building where he had his office to dine at Ends Meat, the tenant on the ground floor, and enjoyed the privilege of shared ownership. She got to eat for free and even went back to the kitchen to chastise some of the young workers.

Charlie went in and ordered something quick so she could split as soon as she needed to. The restaurant specialised in the cheaper cuts of meat and offal, making use of what other restaurants shunned—a unique concept. Charlie understood the pressures Dave had been under to stay afloat during the past few years and it was impossible not to notice the glut of vacant commercial properties in the city, particularly office spaces.

Charlie enjoyed her chicken liver open sandwich and

paid cash as soon as she could. Once Sophie left, she followed suit and finished her purchase on the way. Sophie was a very self-involved woman. She was confident and in control. Years of getting her own way while Dave looked in another direction seemed to fit her into a divisive personality. Whatever obligation he expected of her, if it wasn't already in her plans, then it likely wouldn't happen at all. That attitude carried through to the salon where she got her hair touched up.

Inside was a treasure trove of gossip. However, it was hard to enter without seeming totally conspicuous. Hairdressers and barbers were, at least temporarily, their client's best friends. They'd just as soon rise to the defence of a patron against a stranger, and seeing Charlie hovering at the door with no appointment, and no desire to have one, would turn the rich den of shared secrets silent.

With that in mind, Charlie slipped into a coffee shop across the road and waited it out. She made a note of the time and day Sophie got her hair done and made a note to cross-reference it with previous appointments to see if she had a schedule that could be exploited.

Hair done, Sophie stepped out of the salon, hopped into her car, and sped off. Charlie, likewise, pursued on her scooter. As long as Sophie stayed in the city, she could keep up. If she went onto the motorway, then it would get complicated. Thankfully, Sophie's next trip was to a bar in Walton where she met up with what seemed to be an old friend of hers.

Every person Charlie had seen her interact with throughout the day had been a woman. She didn't even give men a passing glance. It really seemed like she just had no interest whatsoever, which didn't bode well for Dave's theory that another fella was hiding in the proverbial wardrobe, about to pop out.

Charlie managed to get a seat in an adjoining booth and,

after setting her phone to record, listened in to Sophie's conversation with her gal pal, Natalie.

"He's been sending me texts," Sophie said, "about all the places he's visiting in Brussels. As if he's bragging."

"As if it's something to brag about," Natalie added. "What's he talking up, exactly?"

"I don't know. I don't get him." She sighed. "You know, when we first met, he sold it as we'd be managing the portfolio together, and that would give us a stronger bond. It's all work with him. His whole life revolves around his work. He doesn't let me get involved, save to sign a few documents now and again."

"That's a rarity now, you know. A man who *wants* to work. Even with all the hardship that brings."

"He even talked about our kids," she went on. "God forbid I make that mistake with him. He's got this image of us all working on the business. A family office. And he's proud of that."

"It doesn't sound so bad. You're pushing it, but it's not too late, you know?"

"I thought it was romantic, really. At first, I did. Having a man who's got his whole life planned out with these grand ideas and was actually moving on them. That's what I liked. I was attracted to that, I think. The man himself behind it— Maybe it's just regret sinking in."

"You're not gonna split with him, are you?"

Sophie's silence spoke of her uncertainty. "I mean, it's not too late for us. I think. I don't want to give up on him. It's just this stupid flirting game he pulled; I don't know what he was thinking."

"Well, you've had your way, haven't you?"

"Huh?"

"You've gone with a man to get back at him, yeah?"

"God, no. Men are too needy. One's enough. I just wanted to scare him a bit. Get him desperate. If he comes to me asking for a chance or to start a family and is willing to actually take time off from the business, I'll soften up."

Charlie instinctively looked across the table hoping to be able to high-five Ash or Becca. Her theory was correct. But she was left hanging, continuing to listen in, feeling quite smug.

"You can't let him get off that easily."

"That's the other thing—aside from being too busy, when we do, you know, do it. It's rubbish."

Natalie grabbed the bottle of wine and went to top up Sophie's glass.

"No, thanks, I'm driving. You know, if he worked as hard at that as he did to secure financing from all these random investors in Europe, I think I wouldn't have any complaints at all. Maybe we'd have a smaller house, but at least we'd be happy."

"You'd miss that pool, though."

"You're right there."

The girls laughed. The evidence mounted even further against Dave's insistent worries. Sophie, for her failings, remained loyal to him. Not perfectly loyal, but there was no evidence that she'd strayed outside of their predetermined limits. And of course, she never would have told Dave of her stipulation to make amends, because why should she? It was clear there was a simple solution to fix their broken situation, and he was spending that precious time courting investors abroad.

Charlie finished off her notes. If there was any opportunity for Sophie to cheat, she would have taken it. Charlie decided that it wouldn't be in her client's best interest to continue this investigation. She'd report back to Dave ASAP, give him some advice on how to resolve his marital issues, and lose one of her few paying clients as a consequence. She was on her way out when she ended up running into Sophie at the door.

"Oh, apologies," Sophie said.

"Sorry," Charlie uttered.

"Hold up," Sophie called out. Charlie froze. The worst possible outcome of her stalking gambit was being recognised from across town. There were only so many coincidences she could write off, but a whole day of seeing the same person was too suspicious to ignore. "I think I saw you… at the club, did I?"

"The club?" Charlie asked.

"The Ivory. Yes, it was you," she said. "Chatting up that sweet Dion, yes?" Charlie's eyes went wide. Sophie tittered at her surprise. "He's a charmer. Too bad you let him slip the line."

Charlie nodded vacantly. "Well, he said he prefers more… refined vintages. He's really not my type."

"Hmm." Sophie smirked. "Better luck next time. Or perhaps if you strike out too often, you can swap to *another team* and see how they play." Sophie winked at her. It was a bad sign. It wasn't just a passing remark or action. She'd been made.

Sophie had committed Charlie to memory and her fidelity with Dave was clearly guaranteed all but for one man, Dion… He was the exception to prove the rule. The tailing missions she had just decided were no longer necessary, had to continue. And Charlie now had to bench herself.

chapter
twenty-one

CHARLIE WAS proud of her team and the passion all of them were showing for solving their open cases. She liked that they brought their own unique skill sets to the group, and that they were comfortable speaking the truth, even when the truth sometimes hurt.

"We need to establish a timeline," Becca said excitedly. "While you were blowing our cover with Sophie Phillips yesterday, I set up a meeting at the airport."

Charlie let the little dig slide, she was still furious with herself for allowing herself to be spotted. Rebecca was right. She was good, but not infallible. Reality checks like this were important to keep her on her toes and keep practising her field craft, but the net result was it now meant the team would have to pitch in on surveillance missions regarding Sophie.

Which was why Clive and Ash were working shifts monitoring Mrs Philipps, and Charlie and Rebecca were back on the road, trying to piece together Emefa's movements following her last gig.

At the Aircraft Handling building, Rebecca and Charlie introduced themselves. They spoke with the local agent who was the contact for Dog's Hind Leg Records, and who had managed the skies that fateful night.

"She never arrived," he said. "We called her production office a couple of hours after the scheduled departure and they requested the flight be rerouted to Marseille and off it went, empty."

"She just never showed up?" Becca said. "Do you know— did she register a car with you?"

"A car?"

"Like to arrive, so you knew it was her—is that what you do? If she arrived by car, what would have happened to it?"

"Oh, of course her car would be taken care of, the label had booked a space. They would collect the following day," the concierge said. "I believe—" He clicked on his laptop and scanned down a spreadsheet with his finger. "Yes, it was a '23 plate Range Rover that she was set to arrive in. But that never showed up either. I was on that night. Remember keeping an eye out so I could personally introduce her to the flight team."

"Does that happen a lot?" Charlie asked.

"No shows? Not really. We get time changes or even delays by a day or two. But they usually always show up eventually. It's not cheap chartering a flight, every minute it's fuelled and ready to go is costing, big time."

"What's the protocol when there's a no-show?"

"We invoice whether or not they arrive. We had front-of-house staff on duty for the meet and greet, the pilot and stewardess were booked, and the ground crew did their bit."

"So, nothing suspicious."

"As I say, it happens. Rich people, innit? Need to be somewhere so urgently they charter their own bloody plane. And then they don't. Change of plan. I wouldn't mind, but they even phoned that afternoon to check the departure time and if we'd received the email to make sure there would only be soft drinks available on board."

"Who's *they*?" Charlie asked.

"The bloke from the record label."

"You're sure it was a man who called?"

"Positive." The agent checked his spreadsheet again. "Durg. Marcus Durg. Eleven thirty-four am. He's a producer—"

Charlie practically pulled Rebecca out of the office to the privacy of the van, before dialling Marcus and putting the phone on speaker.

He picked up after the second ring. "Tell me some good news."

"Did you call Hawarden Airport the afternoon of Emefa's disappearance?"

"No? Erica, my PA, deals with travel arrangements for the talent. We keep the details hush-hush to avoid any scenes. But the logistics for Emefa's Legacy tour were booked months in advance. Anyway, she wouldn't call. Everything's email, so there's a trail. Why do you ask?"

"Someone called, pretending to be from your label. Pretending to be you. We think that's how they found out what vehicle Emefa would be driving and her itinerary."

"Do they know who?"

"No. They thought it was you."

"Can I suggest," Rebecca interrupted, "you use a code word or challenge and response with suppliers to validate that they're talking to the right person in the future?"

"I will, yes, of course. So, does that mean you know where she is?"

"Not yet," Charlie admitted. "But we will."

Charlie ended the call and sat back in the driver's seat. She turned to Rebecca. "I can almost hear those cogs ticking. Hit me."

"At the crash site," Rebecca said, still formulating her thoughts. "I was hoping to find out how or why she'd crashed."

"And did you?"

Rebecca shook her head. "It was inconclusive."

"Can we say if it was on purpose or an accident?"

"There are only three scenarios that make sense. One"—Rebecca stuck out her thumb—"given reports of her state of mind on the night in question, is that she was off her tits and totalled the car. That could have been because an animal ran out and she swerved, or she just managed to crash headfirst into a tree all by herself. Unfortunate, but very punk."

"Or?"

"Or…" Rebecca stuck out her index finger. "Two, an over-zealous pap gets too close, she freaks, and it turns into a bit of a high-speed chase and she loses control."

"Which leaves?"

Rebecca straightened her middle finger. "Three. It was a deliberate attempt to run her off the road. But the bigger question is, what happened next?"

"Easy. If she crashed by herself or was being chased by the paparazzi, whether they stopped to help or sped off, Emefa would have found help eventually and she'd be living her best life right now," Charlie said, continuing the line of thinking.

"Exactly, so that only leaves third-party involvement with malicious intent."

"A two-for-the-price-of-one kidnapper and rescuer combo," Charlie concluded. "Whoever engineered the crash, also took care of the rescue."

"There's panic at the arena, and the production team is having kittens they've misplaced their cash cow. The PR team's already drafting excuses why the performance that night was subpar, citing a change to her prescribed medication, the pressures of a world tour, etc.," Rebecca said, filling in the blanks.

Charlie nodded. "Then Marcus gets the note the next day saying she's finding herself and not to involve the police. In a way that makes things easier, so he doesn't. The only loose thread is what to do about the car."

"He was happy to lose whatever deposit had been paid, or eat the financial penalty imposed for crashing a hire car. It suited the label's narrative, to let the car be picked apart and whatever was left eventually crushed, so no one would know that Emefa was behind the wheel that night. If it ever got out that the car was driven headfirst into a tree, it would only stir up controversy about her long recovery. It could be labelled as an inciting incident, and that her reform was not strictly voluntary after all, but forced upon her as a hidden alternative to dangerous driving charges. And then there was her history with booze and drugs… the question would inevitably come up whether she'd been driving under the influence that night."

Charlie's phone buzzed with a text. She opened it and loaded a message, which she shared with Rebecca. Who tucked her lip in hard enough to dig her lip ring up into the soft palette of her mouth.

Ash had sent a screenshot of a text message conversation which had been posted on Anna's Facebook page:

SOPHIE 16.31:

You can't finish it I need u

16.31:

Soz. Just not working for me anymore x

SOPHIE 16.32:

I NEED you

16.32:

That's the problem. I don't need you. A break will be good.

SOPHIE 16.32:

you're dumping me! By fucking text!?

SOPHIE 16.32:

bitch

SOPHIE 16.36:

answer the phone

SOPHIE 18.22:

Anna please

SOPHIE 19.31:

pick up

Charlie put down the phone. "Well, that's one way to end things. I thought it was our generation who did everything by text message."

"Bit harsh to put it online, though," Becca said.

"It is, but maybe she's being cruel to be kind? There's no room for negotiation now, line in the sand drawn."

"What happens next?"

"Sophie's going to be upset, which means her behaviour is going to be less predictable. Hopefully, she'll have a little cry, then recommit to her marriage and all will be well with the world."

"Or she goes nuclear and looks for a rebound replacement."

"Mmmm." Charlie pondered the implications. "I guess we'll have to wait and see. Look, honestly, how's Clive getting on?"

"I wouldn't worry," Rebecca said. "He knows how to turn a laptop on and off now. A couple more weeks and I'll have him coding."

But they had plenty of worrying to do.

chapter
twenty-two

Seven Months Earlier

Emefa sat cross-legged on her bed.

She'd ignored the third call to dinner, and she knew that was the last time he was going to ask nicely. She was second-guessing herself as to whether she was fast enough, fit enough, and ultimately brave enough to challenge her captor. She felt strong. Months of home-cooked meals and clean living had helped, together with the forty minutes of punishing exercise he insisted she complete each day before they were able to set foot in the studio.

She got up off the bed and paced the room, stopping for a moment to look out through the barred and locked window. It was mid-summer, and the evenings remained light until nearly ten. She couldn't see much beyond the large trees, which stood like sentinels stationed on the other side of the walled garden.

Every time she looked down upon her domain, her eyes picked out the top of a sandstone church tower nestled at the bottom of the hill. She could make out parts of other buildings too—a slate roof here, a window there—but they were just momentary glimpses, stolen when the branches swung in the breeze. She could be anywhere and found herself wishing for autumn and then winter, hoping the hidden panorama would be revealed to her, one fallen leaf at a time.

She listened for the sound of approaching footsteps visualising how she would surprise him as he entered the room. She'd seen enough movies, seen enough clips on social media of slight girls overcoming much larger opponents. The key, it seemed, was to explode. Suddenly, violently, and with extreme prejudice. She needed to focus on two target areas. His groin and his eyes. With fists, feet, nails, and teeth, she would overpower him, grab the stun gun when he dropped it to the floor, and take back control of her life and her music career.

The kitchen door opened. Emefa heard the sound of the extractor fan. He was on his way. She estimated twenty-two seconds before he would appear in her doorway.

She rolled her shoulders and stretched her arms high above her head, preparing her muscles.

She was ready.

At least as ready as she'd ever be.

He appeared nineteen seconds later.

"I called you down for dinner," he said from the doorway.

"I don't feel up to it," she replied, placing one hand on her tummy. She was sure he would approach and try to comfort her. She groaned for good measure and made a show of wincing as she shifted position.

But he didn't come.

Emefa looked up. He was cradling something in a plaid blanket.

It moved.

He stepped into the room. "That's a shame, because there's someone I wanted to introduce you to."

That someone wriggled and a corner of the blanket fell to reveal a curly-haired puppy.

"Oh my God! It's adorable. Boy or girl?"

"Girl. Twelve weeks."

He handed her the puppy.

She smiled. Something she hadn't done in a long time. A little chortle escaped her lips before it broke into a full belly laugh. Fake illness forgotten, the pup licked her hand and ran in a circle on her lap.

"I was hoping you'd name her."

"Wait. She's yours? We're keeping her?"

"She's yours."

"Really? She's beautiful. I think she looks like a Leah."

She couldn't see if he was smiling, but his eyes were bright and sparkling. He clearly approved of Emefa's reaction and the proposed name. If he suspected she'd been not entirely honest about why she hadn't come down for dinner, then all, it seemed, was forgiven.

She realised it was a good thing he'd surprised her with Leah. She didn't know the first thing about fighting. She doubted she'd have landed one half-arsed punch before he would have completely overpowered her. And what then? Would her punishment have been limited to a bit of light electrocution before he served the starters, or would that attempted coup have been rewarded with something more brutal?

Emefa's world improved drastically the moment Leah came into her life. Having the puppy to occupy her meant she had reason to get up in the morning. She obsessed about what the dog was eating, how much she slept, exercised, and relieved herself. She noted the irony of her own situation, but the bond she felt with the dog was real and it helped her to shift focus away from her own hopeless situation.

Her reaction to the dog met with approval from her captor, and it was rewarded with a number of additional perks and benefits. Emefa found the patio doors out to the garden were now unlocked from early in the morning until they all retired at night. Emefa was free to go out to the garden wherever she pleased, and that relatively small concession went some way to making her feel like she was the mistress of her own destiny. Whilst there was no chance of Emefa walking Leah on the street, exercising with the dog in the garden did them both a world of good.

"What a difference a dog makes." He nodded approvingly as he weighed both dog and owner at their weekly assessment.

The little excitable bundle of fur had not just pulled Emefa out of her malaise, it had unlocked her creative juices and made her want to spend every waking hour in the studio.

chapter
twenty-three

Four Months Earlier

THE DAYS BECAME weeks and then months. She'd got used to the routine and the regime and resigned herself to it. Having Leah to focus on helped break the monotony. Leah was still a puppy and prone to eating chair legs, but was now fully house-trained. Emefa hadn't let on, in case it resulted in her freedom to go out into the garden whenever she pleased to be curtailed in some way.

It had been a slow start, but Emefa had to admit that they were getting somewhere with her music. What had begun as a battle of wills, trying to force inspiration whilst imprisoned by her producer, was now delivering results. She was literally singing for her supper and, quite frankly, enjoying it. They had six tracks locked, and the bare bones of five more in various states of undress. When completed, it would be enough for her comeback album. The material was good. Really good. She was still missing a title track for the album, but that would come, she was sure of it.

Despite the circumstances, she was happy to be writing the songs she wanted to write. He was there to bounce ideas off of and to try things out on, but he never overstepped his role as producer. He was honest about her lyrics, encouraging when she was despondent, and responsive to her suggestions regarding the backing track. He even fulfilled his promise to be her spirit guide wherever she veered towards trite or derivative. He was a skilled musician and competent sound engineer, and he genuinely allowed her to find her voice again. As much as it pained her to admit it, in terms of a professional partnership, it worked.

She'd resisted at first, but after months of clean living and productive days in the studio, she had begun to look back on her time before... that night. If she was honest, she hadn't been living her best life, despite the Insta posts to the contrary. Marcus had been steering her music in a direction she hadn't wanted it to go. Her life was micromanaged by an army of fixers, assistants, accountants, and tour managers. Ghostwriters had been brought in, without her consent, to *help* modify her lyrics to fit the market. She had, in a way, been a prisoner to the label. Maybe more subtle than a cattle prod, but the net result was the same.

"You've come a long way since that night in Liverpool," he said, pulling her from her thoughts. "Unrecognisable almost."

"Were you there? At the gig?"

He nodded, the disappointment showing in the way he couldn't keep eye contact with her.

"How bad was it?" Emefa asked as she rubbed the back of Leah's head with her knuckles.

"You really don't remember?"

"Honestly. No." Emefa could only recall snippets of her last gig. Feelings and snapshots rather than what could be called memories. "I remember going out on stage and the first track. Then nothing."

He put down his cutlery and folded his arms across his

chest. "It was awful. Management shouldn't have let you go out on stage."

"But they did."

"It went from bad to worse. They brought out a stool after the first track. You could barely stand up."

Moments in time forced their way up from her subconscious.

The blinding stage lights.

Tripping on a speaker

Scuffling with a stagehand who had to help her take the microphone out of the stand.

The boos from the crowd.

"You were angry about something. It came out in the way you sang. You kept looking off to the side of the stage. The drummer kept counting you in, but you phased out. It was like you were acting out a conversation in your head."

"How long was the set?"

"About forty minutes. But it was agonising. Between the random monologues and the pacing back and forth, even your most ardent fans lost patience. You managed about three songs."

"I'm sorry."

"Don't be. You were in a bad place. You needed help and I could see you weren't getting it from the record label."

"What happened then?"

"The crowd turned. They were jeering. You reacted… badly. Started shouting and swearing at them. Then the plastic cups started to fly. Security jumped up out of the pit and took you off the stage with you kicking, screaming, and roaring at the world."

Emefa pushed the plate of food away, her appetite having vanished. "Do they hate me?"

"Surprisingly, no. Your fans are… very loyal. No one was excusing the behaviour, but the narrative quickly painted you as a victim. The pressure, the gruelling tour dates, the need to perform. Ticket stubs to the Liverpool gig have been trading online for thousands of pounds. It's almost as if you're not a real fan if you weren't there for the breakdown."

"So, there's a way back?"

"With this album and this… attitude towards life? Of course. We'll be painting this as a rebirth, the phoenix from the ashes. A chance to reinvent and reconnect. Your fans will do the rest."

Emefa considered her dog, her captor, and the kitchen she was sitting in. She was too deep in her new matrix to still consider it as anything other than her new normal. What he was promising her resonated. She wanted that chance to make great music again. She wanted her fans to adore her, and she wanted to make amends.

"I've got an idea. Let's go back to the studio."

He shook his head. "Not now, it's late. You've barely eaten."

She scraped her chair back and dashed from the kitchen. Leah scuttled after her. Her captor was caught off guard, surprised by her sudden enthusiasm. He eyed the plates on the table, hesitating as he fought the urge to scrape away the food and tidy up, but was intrigued enough to follow.

Emefa urged him into the room, pulling out his chair so he could sit at the mixing desk.

He sat down and looked over at her. "Well?"

"Hit play," she said, grinning.

He did so, and they listened as the jaunty piano chords filled the room. Emefa tapped along with the beat and sang along to the lyrics.

"OK! I've got it. Go back to the top."

"Maybe we should revisit this in the morning. Fresh eyes and ears."

"Play it from the top!" Emefa demanded. She winced, the request coming out more like an order.

If he took exception to the insubordination, he hid it well

and obediently complied with the request. She was so ener-
gised he had to see this through. The intro bars played again
through the monitor speakers and both of their legs tapped
along to the beat.

"What if," Emefa reasoned, "we use the minor key
instead?"

He stared at the mixing desk, still listening as the lyrics
kicked in. "That wouldn't work. It's supposed to be uplifting
and—"

He looked over to Emefa, and despite the cloth mask, she
could see a smile forming.

"So, it juxtaposes what she's feeling about their relationship—"

"With a foreshadowing of what he's about to do."

"Exactly!"

He wheeled himself across to the keyboard stand,
stretched his fingers over the keys and experimented with the
chords. Emma dragged the microphone stand next to him and
they riffed through the song.

Forty-five minutes later, they had a completely new piano-
led intro with a powerful string arrangement. She'd re-
written the chorus, re-recorded the lyrics, and the song had
transformed from a bubble-gum pop song to a heart-rending
ballad.

"You're crying," he observed, concerned.

Emefa wiped at the tears flowing down her cheeks. "It's
beautiful."

He had to agree. His eye twitched, about to spill tears of
his own, "It's the greatest song you've ever recorded. I
love it."

"Really?"

"Yep. It's sublime. What are you going to call it?"

"It's the title track. Pink Is The New Black."

Caught up in the moment and the emotion, Emefa
embraced her kidnapper.

"Thank you," she blurted through tears. "I couldn't have done it without you. It's as much your song as mine."

At that, he shed a tear of his own.

chapter
twenty-four

CHARLIE OPERATED her business in the 21st century; everything had to be run with new technology. All their information came through app messages first, emails second, phone calls unwillingly, and whatever was left had to be sieved through the sluggish and bulky mail. Not that Clive minded.

He got the mail as part of the usual daily routine—sometimes twice a day if he noticed the postman or courier showing up a bit later than usual. The mail was always useful. It allowed the sending of delicate materials in a manner where they could not be committed to a digital footprint. Things that had to be touched and held and seen to be believed.

Clive came into Charlie's office waving a stack of paper. "Urgent letter, boss."

"From whom?" she asked. "All our bills are paperless."

"Anonymous. Hand-delivered," he said, "with 'urgent please read' on the envelope."

"That could be anything," she sighed, "from a sweepstakes entry to a takeout menu. We're on a lot of lists, as it happens. When you put an address out in an advertisement, people like to send stuff to it that isn't really helpful."

"I cut all that chaff out," Clive said as he settled the papers on her desk. "You can just ask to be taken off of lists."

"Uh-huh," she nodded. "And did you do that for us?"

"I've registered our discontent. They're dragging their feet on the paperwork," he said, "but it'll get done. In the meantime, I picked out all the most interesting money-off coupons and interesting adverts to be shared around in case anyone wants them."

"Thank you," she said, uncertainly. He left her to work with her already opened envelopes. The first one in the stack was a note from Marcus Durg of Dog's Hind Leg Records, sent via courier, with a top priority of keeping his identity discreet.

Charlie, it's your Top Dog client here. Had to send you this. It's a photocopy, but it's the real deal. We got a new demand from the kidnapper and a deadline. I'm gonna need you to sort this out before the 2nd of March. After that, we might need to get police involved. I'm talking SAS, Royal Marines, Delta Force if they're available, this is gonna be a massive breakdown and it'll cost us more in public image than it will in police mobilisation. Discretion is key here. I need to hear good news back.

That date was seven days away. She sighed. The added stress wasn't helping her find her deductive zen. She took out the other sheets from the envelope, a pressed and slightly faded copy of yet another ransom-style demand spread across two full pages.

From producer to producer,

There comes a time in every singer's life when they must seek out new inspiration and influence. The world is a stage, and Emefa belongs on it. Her newest single has been mastered. I hereby enclose a digitally water-marked version on compressed disk as a preview, but do not try to copy it or the data will be rendered worthless. It is for your ears only.

Emefa needs to fly. She needs sun and open air to further channel the spirits of summer before spring can arrive. You can understand the need to work ahead of what is offered. To sing songs of regrowth and flourishing, to escape the winter in which you held her and embrace spring, that cannot be done here in cold and dreary England.

You will arrange a private plane to fly us off of this island to a location which will remain undisclosed until the time of departure. It will require a pilot familiar with Mediterranean flight paths—that is all I will tell you. You will not follow or track us. After landing, you will release all of Emefa's bank accounts unto her through me and we will leave for her new musing grounds, where she will continue to work out of sight until she is well enough to perform again.

I am saving her career, and with it, her life. You cannot negotiate a higher position than that. I have enclosed the airport brochure where the flight must be fuelled and waiting at 7 on *the evening of Tuesday 2nd March. Or this will be her last single.*

She put the paper down and sighed. The kidnapper remained completely in control. He left Marcus cornered, and in that position, he found the nerve to actually go through with the total self-destruction of his branded image in the effort to protect his star player. Which was noble. He could just let the man go, and reap the benefits, but if he was willing to risk the international attention of apparent neglect for a contract, then she knew he was serious.

Even Marcus was now thinking it was time to bring in the authorities. Charlie wouldn't get paid if the police solved the case, and Emefa would likely disappear forever, or worse, if they failed. She took some photos of the letters and sent them to the group chat.

The Great E-Girl Caper, the secret missing persons case of the generation, now had a ticking clock. Charlie immediately diverted all of the agency's resources into locating the pop star.

Sophie wasn't getting any less gay and had thus far shown absolutely no interest whatsoever in playing away from home with a man. Charlie hoped now that things had cooled between Sophie and Anna, she'd remain holed up at home, feeling sorry for herself and behaving within the established rules of her marriage, which were hardly mainstream, but would deny Dave the pleasure of being proven right.

She poured through the letters that were sent to Marcus, Emefa's laborious social media cycle, and maps of all the Wirral, Liverpool, and North Wales where a body could be dragged from the banged-up car. It was her biggest case, a break that would launch her as high as she dared to go. She just had to solve it. Which was the issue.

The disappearance of Emefa was masterfully done. There

wasn't a trace of her anywhere. Imitators were spotted in the cities down south, cosplayers who flaunted Emefa's signature alternative looks in support of her triumphant return, or in protest against her sombre new style.

Marcus Durg made it clear that as long as Emefa was safe and well, he wouldn't mind the arrangement. But having her go missing was cutting into the label's profits, which was less and less about music sales and all about the merchandise, arena tours, and the sponsorship deals. Her face was the brand, and therefore the true revenue source—everything else was secondary. If she never sang another word in her life, she could still unlock millions in revenue by posing in designer gear on Insta, or fronting a TV campaign. But she couldn't shoot commercials, model accessories, or pose for billboard adverts if she was locked in a yoga retreat with a "wellbeing team."

That stuck out even more. Charlie started to connect patterns. In the end, she'd decided to go analogue with this one—a red-thread board dominated the wall of her office—so the whole team, but especially Clive, could track their progress.

Emefa's letters started out very cheerful, almost forced to sound positive, stating that she was seeking some kind of reprieve and recovery from her previous life of sin and excess. Which was a noble thing, if done for its own sake, but not when forced by a phantasmal hand. They also never mentioned a team until the song was nearly done. It indicated that the person controlling her writing insisted on not being revealed up to that point, as if to not confirm or deny whether she was alone or with a group. Something a solo actor would do to drive away suspicions and, more importantly, conflict.

Charlie was tapping her fingers on her desk, trying to manifest a clue she could act upon.

Clive interrupted her malaise with a knock at her door. "Boss?"

"Yes, Clive?"

"I've got something," he said. "Need to know how to present it. Can I request a meeting?"

"Uh, yeah, of course," she said.

"I need the whole team together on this," he said. He seemed excited.

She hoped it was news that was in some way related to the Emefa case, and not Clive announcing he'd just discovered how to jazz up his documents with WordArt or that he'd alphabetised all the utility bills.

She called everyone into the meeting-slash-interrogation room, where Clive was waiting with the laptop positioned in the most presentational way possible. He didn't know how to connect it to a projector or bigger monitor, so he just pushed it forward so everyone had to crowd around it to see his work. It was a wall of words, broken into three-word phrases, all sequentially taken from the lyrics of Emefa's return song.

"Mr. Powell," Clive began. "What does this look like to you?"

"Very good work," Ashley nodded. "You learned to type, and so many different words. We're very proud of you."

"Yes, thank you," Clive quickly dispersed. "But what *are* the words? What do they mean? If you saw this written by hand on a blank piece of paper and slipped under your bedroom door, what would you make of it?"

"That... someone got very confused after a night out," Ash said.

"It's the lyrics of Emefa's song," Becca commented. "Some of them. Not all of them."

"Indeed," Clive said. "This is the full array of all the strange and non sequitur phrases used by Emefa in her latest track, E-girl Unplugged. And while I was being tortured, listening to it for the umpteenth time, I picked up on something—namely this." He pointed to the screen, particularly to one word: trout. "Never much into fishing, was she?"

"You brought this up," Becca said, "but I just don't think it's that big a deal, honestly. They're just mock stanzas. I took it artistically, as sort of the chaos of her previous iteration in a lyrical form, and the follow-ups which blended them together into the rest of the song were part of the reformation, showing she was willing to meld her past into her present, rather than ignore it, no matter how messy it was." She spoke with confidence and pride in her answer.

"I'm hearing the words you're saying, Becca, but what the fuck?" Ash took a seat, massaging his temples.

Clive nodded, then turned to Charlie.

"Ms. Chan," he said, "give me three words. Nouns, non-proper, any three and without context."

"Uh," Charlie started. She struggled to think of anything random. She had trout on the brain. "Bass. Fiddle... Porcupine."

Clive nodded and turned to the computer. He leaned over the table and switched to an internet browser tab that showed a map. He typed in the three words, separated by periods, and the map loaded up a change of location. He zoomed out and soon a road came into view. Somewhere in the unmarked middle of Argentina. He tapped on the screen enough to make it slightly discoloured.

"You see that?" he said. "It's an app that launched a few years back called Any3Words. It's turned the whole world into a grid, each square is a couple metres across. Every spot on the planet where a human can stand or float. Registered them all to a combination of...?" He waited for them to fill in the answer, but the team was just confused.

"Wait," Becca said. "Plug in the words from her song."

Clive clapped his hands and worked, a bit slowly, to do exactly that, starting with the first set. *Rhinestone.Jelly.Deer*. The location: Tollerton, a small village in Yorkshire.

Becca pointed to the screen and addressed the other less-informed Emefa lightweights in the room. "That's her hometown! Where she was born! Where she grew up before auditioning for TalentStars!"

"And it's in the first verse of the song," he said. "I guessed Emefa was a bit of a fan of the app—and I was right. Turns out, she's even used it before. Give me a minute, I'll pull that up as well."

Clive opened a new tab and typed out, starting from *http://www*—the whole name of a blog which he'd committed to memory. He may not know how bookmarks or saved tabs worked, but he'd managed to break their case wide open. The rest of the team just didn't know it yet.

What he navigated to was a fan blog from years back called the EmTFK: the Emefa Tracker Fan Kolab. On it, page by page, were screenshots of social media posts she'd put up on Instagram, snaps of landscapes and buildings she was staying in, a couple with three-word codes.

"She deleted these, or her management team did, pretty quickly," Clive began, "after about an hour, they were gone. So, you wouldn't find them on her social channels now. And she only did this a few times, it turns out. Like she was playing a game with her fans, using this location app to tell them where she might appear for a small impromptu gig."

"I remember that now," Rebecca said. "I was just starting to get into her at the time and thought it was a weird thing to post."

"I'll ask Marcus what he knows," Charlie said. "It could have been a paid sponsorship that went unreported, and this was Emefa's way of making it a larger, more interactive experience."

"It gets better. Look what happens when we input this," Clive announced with far too much intonation, given that he was a one-finger typist.

Eventually, he had *Heather.Trout.Quarry*. The map changed locations and took them to Hawarden Airport. The whole team knew what they were looking at—locations of importance to Emefa, hidden within the lyrics.

"My man." Ash offered a high-five to Clive, but was left hanging.

"Incredible." Charlie beamed at Clive. "I'm very impressed."

The lyrical code that Emefa sent out to the internet's yawning chasm of disinterest was a chronicle of sorts, a list of locations that helped shape her as a woman and singer, together with some smaller venues she had played in her early years on the road to making it.

"Now," Becca said, impatiently, "do the last one. The very last one. The last line in the song."

Clive nodded sagely. "She's a crafty one," he said. "You gotta listen. Anyone can make a message worth hearing with the right backing track..." He typed in three words from the last line of the song: *Young.Tarnished.Rinsed*, and the map zoomed into St. Mary's and St. Helen's Church in Little Neston, Cheshire. Not ten minutes' drive from where the crashed Evoque was discovered. A clue thrown out into the void of the internet, hoping some genuine fan would pick up on it and find the trail she'd left behind.

And that fan was a technophobic 58-year-old man working the reception desk, who'd proven himself a detective just as well.

chapter
twenty-five

Two Months Earlier

Emefa sat cross-legged on one of the kitchen chairs, cradling a cup of tea. Her captor whistled through his mask as he loaded the last of the dishes from breakfast into the dishwasher, wiped the counter, and took a seat.

"You got your appetite back. That's good," he said.

She blew into her tea, releasing a plume of steam. "I'm feeling much better, thanks."

"So why the long face?"

Emefa looked over at him, considering her response. "It's just. I'd really like… No, it doesn't matter."

"Go on. What?"

"It's nothing, don't worry."

"Tell me. What can I do?" he asked.

"I need to use the computer."

He sighed. "You know that I can't do that."

"You can watch me," she said. "Make sure I don't do anything—I won't! I just… There's something I want to… reconnect with. Somewhere I want to see."

He paused. She could tell behind his cover that he was

deep in thought and wondering whether it was time to trust her. His heart won out.

"All right. I'll be watching. If you do something wrong, I'll stop you and the repercussions will be… serious."

"Okay." She nodded.

He led her into his den, next to the studio. It was where his desktop computer was situated. From there, he controlled the whole house, every camera and the remote locking systems that kept her indoors and under surveillance. He even had controls and monitors for the sauna and spare medical equipment for monitoring heart rates tucked away in a corner. He invited her to sit and do as she wanted, within his twisted version of reason.

She stretched her fingers over the keyboard and then wiggled the mouse to wake the screen. The settings were different from her usual setup. Super sensitive. The cursor raced across the page, and it took her a couple of goes to get it to settle over the search bar. She opened Google Maps and zoomed in over Yorkshire and the Northeast and started typing what looked like random names of Saints. *St. Michaels - St. Peters - St. Marys -*

"There was a church I visited when I was nine or ten," she explained. "It had the most amazing graveyard. Nothing fancy, no celebs buried there or anything, just local people who'd died. But it was… quite moving. I think it was the first time I became really conscious of death. You know? Like, that we only have a finite time on earth and then… nothing. I was just a kid, so I tried to reason what that would mean for me. No more television, no more homework, no more Lady Gaga, no more eggs, chips, and beans for dinner on a Thursday."

Emefa continued to type quickly - *St. Boniface - St. Pauls - St. Martins…* She scanned down the gallery of images and stopped. She poked her index finger at the screen, indicating one of the thumbnails.

"That's it!" She clicked on the image of St. Martin's

Church in Allerton Mauleverer and sixty images appeared of a derelict church—mouldy walls, broken stained glass, splintered pews, and a small, neatly tended graveyard.

"Doesn't look like much." Her captor leaned in closer to the screen, his mask brushing the lobe of her ear. She tried not to flinch.

"It's not. The image in my mind's eye is much prettier, to be honest. But I was right there." She pointed between two graves. "When I first knew I wanted to write songs."

He looked from Emefa to the screen and back again, beaming that she'd shared such a defining moment with him.

Emefa scrolled through the images, humming a tune. "I can't remember what the lyrics were. I thought they were very profound at the time. Something about crossing the veil into death. A blinding bright light and a welcoming bony hand to stroke your face." She laughed and looked at him. "A load of old crap really, teenage angst wrapped up in a Tolkien fantasy, but it set me on my path. I didn't—"

The doorbell rang. They both looked up at the small display on the wall. A delivery driver held a package. Emefa glanced at her captor before looking back at the computer monitor engrossed in an image of a gravestone. She zoomed in, trying to make out an inscription which had been worn smooth by the elements.

The man half stood, clearly debating with himself whether to answer the door.

"I think we should—"

He was cut off when the doorbell rang again. On the screen, the driver was crouching down, trying to look through the letterbox.

"Looks like a big parcel," Emefa said.

Decision made, he hopped up and hurried towards the front door. As he was leaving the den, he turned to Emefa, his gaze boring into her soul.

"Don't do anything you shouldn't with that computer. I'll know." And he hurried off down the hall.

Emefa didn't lose a second. She typed "Any3Words" in a new tab. The page loaded and she was presented with a search box, and she typed *Hawarden Airport*. This was the airport she was travelling toward when she'd been scared off the road. This was the airport she'd nearly reached the night of her gig in Liverpool. The Any3Words location of this airport was Heather.Trout.Quarry. She zoomed out on the map and there was the Wales/England border. She zoomed out again and she could see the Wirral Peninsula and Liverpool. She willed her brain to remember that fateful night. She'd been high. Off her face on a cocktail of smack and booze and whatever pills she'd managed to coax out of one of the Arena's electricians. The actual gig was still a blur, despite what she'd heard about that night from him. She just saw glimpses —

The stage lights burning circles into her retinas.

Dropping the mic and not being able to pick it up.

Jeers from the crowd.

Marcus pacing behind the array of speakers, looking across at her with both pity and disgust.

She couldn't remember being bundled off stage or getting into the car at all.

Then she was driving. The bright headlights behind her in the tunnel, giving way to dark country roads—trees and grass verges illuminated by her high beams.

But there's nothing quite like the terror of finding a stranger in your car and ploughing into a tree to sober up even the most frazzled of minds. She remembered the crash and hitting her head on the steering wheel. She'd been dazed, but she'd felt his hands on her as he'd helped her out of the car.

They had walked across the hard stubble of a harvested field. It had been so dark, he'd had to use the torch on his phone a few times to see the uneven ground in front of them. Then they followed a gravel path to a barn. There was a car there, a little electric vehicle. She didn't know which manufacturer. He'd helped her into the passenger seat, put on her seat belt, and they'd driven for no more than ten minutes.

If she could figure out the road she'd been on when she'd crashed, she might be able to figure out where she was now. She needed to think. What happened before the crash? What route had she taken? It was months ago, and it was as if the more she tried to remember, the further buried the recollections became.

"Oh, you stupid bitch!" she raged at herself, furious at her own ineptitude.

Opening another browser window, she typed *map*. As soon as the page loaded, she typed *current location*, and she had a name for her penitentiary. Little Neston. The map showed a red dotted line around a small village and a crisscross of roads.

It wasn't accurate enough to pinpoint the house, so she scanned the page for churches and clicked on one. A small pop-up appeared with some images. No. The next one. No. And then the third. St. Mary's and St. Helen's Church. The images confirmed it—the sandstone building, the crenellated tower, and the enormous lightning rod topped with a weathercock.

She switched to the other browser and typed in the name of the church. It returned three words. *Young. Tarnished. Rinsed*.

She snorted at the irony.

"...delivery for you. I just need to take a photo." Emefa looked up at the doorbell video to see the package being handed over and the driver taking out his phone. Damn it. She knew her time was up. She closed the active browser window and deleted the history for the last hour. She opened the tab with the images of St. Martin's Church and rapidly clicked on the images in the gallery to populate the history again. She let out a sigh.

"Feeling inspired?" his voice rang out from the doorway to the den.

Emefa turned and smiled her warmest smile as he adjusted the mask on his face. "Yes. Positively bursting with inspiration."

"Good. Then let's write some songs."

Emefa stood and joined him in the doorway. He glanced over at the computer before turning and leading her to the studio. She knew he'd check what she'd been up to later.

For the rest of that morning and most of the afternoon, she wrote like a woman possessed. He watched her with admiration as she filled page after page with drafts of verses and choruses. He brought her snacks and refilled her glass constantly, afraid that this waterfall of inspiration might suddenly dry up if she ran out of fuel.

If he'd bothered to look to see what she was writing, he might have been sorely disappointed. He left her to it, convinced this was genius at work.

Heather.Trout.Quarry. As much as it pained her, the best rhyme she could come up with was lorry. With lyrics like that it wouldn't be a good song, but maybe, just maybe, if someone figured out there were locations hidden in the lyrics, it might save her life.

chapter
twenty-six

CHARLIE WAS both pleased and vindicated that Clive was so quickly proving his worth within the agency. Granted, his technical know-how still left a lot to be desired, but that would come from further training and, if he continued to sit near Rebecca, osmosis. He had the nose of a detective and just the right level of stubbornness to scratch beyond the surface. His work deciphering the lyrics had been exceptional. She'd sent him out of the office with some errands about town to stretch his legs and try to get the damn song out of his head.

Ash had insisted on conducting a full audio-visual systems check before he was willing to sign out the van to Rebecca, who was chomping at the bit to go on a recce to Little Neston and free her idol from her lyrical bondage.

Their office was just busy enough to need someone up front, so Charlie asked Rebecca to sit at her former usual spot. She was the face of the company, the first person people saw and heard when they came in with a problem. Which was unfortunate when the person showing up was someone she didn't want to speak to.

Sergeant Jarvis walked in and slowed his pace as he approached the desk. Rebecca looked up at him with a glower and the room fell silent. It wasn't bustling before, but the refusal of speech somehow stood out far worse in the controlled, purposeful silence between her and her father.

"Hello, Rebecca," he said, finally daring to break the tension. She did not reply. "I'm glad to see you. Safe. Seeming well." Still no reply, and no intention at all to speak up. "Uh, I'm here on business, as it happens. For Ms. Chan, if she is in."

Rebecca could have turned around and traded places with Charlie, or just called for her, but she didn't. She was stuck in place out of a seething sense of obstinate rejection.

Her father took off his police cap and wrung it in his hands, then slapped it back on. He had his own anger to put forward in a polite, controlled manner.

"Rebecca," he said, with more authority than before, "if you won't come back home for my sake, think of your mother. She waits for you every day—sets a place at the table for you *every day* and has cried herself tired most nights knowing that you aren't coming back yet. It's not even the matter of not showing up. You're a grown woman. We respect your decisions. It's the not knowing that's got to her—to me as well. It's the avoidance and this... behaviour! You're a woman, grown, in body but not in attitude, it seems. We can't even know if there's something wrong or if you've just decided this is your new normal we have to get used to— silence. Avoidance. This... this abandonment."

Finally, the awkward lashing ended as Charlie ducked her head out of her office and saw the scene unfolding.

"Becca—"

Before Charlie could offer any kind of words of comfort or solace, Rebecca got up and walked past her father. He watched her go, rounding the corner and disappearing.

"Hello, Sergeant," Charlie greeted. "I'm sorry about that."

"No, no," he said, adjusting his cap in place. "I really didn't want to make a scene. She's just..." He sighed. "Well, you heard as much. I don't know how I can fix it. And she won't tell me."

Charlie nodded. Rebecca was especially sensitive when it came to her family. As friends and co-workers, the team was open to jokes at one another's expense, but they all had their lines. Dead dad jokes warranted swift disciplinary action from Charlie, crazy ex-girlfriend jokes were a touchy subject to Ash, and Rebecca met any talk about her father or family with a cold and emotionless silence. It was a weakness which Charlie assumed came from some kind of trauma, based on how drastically it changed her behaviour. But that was a case she wasn't prepared to investigate. Not without an invitation.

"I'll see what I can do," Charlie offered. And that was good enough for Sarge.

"How can we help?"

"The Cyber team is here."

"Sorry?" Charlie asked.

"The Security audit. Shall I show them in?"

Whilst the timing wasn't ideal, Charlie knew it was best to comply. "Of course!"

———

Whilst it was an hour Charlie could have really done with getting back, the Data Security audit was a breeze for the agency. The Inspectors commended Rebecca for her fastidious record-keeping and policy documentation, and couldn't find a single fault with her network architecture. They passed with flying colours and were even given a certificate for their troubles. As soon as the inspectors left. Rebecca and Charlie were on the move.

Rebecca drove the van along the country lanes of Wirral with a surety and purpose. She was grateful Charlie had just handed her the keys without a word, knowing how invested she was in locating Emefa. It was a bright but bitterly cold day, and it had taken a good ten minutes for the heater to kick in. Now they were both sweltering, and Rebecca struggled to unwrap her oversized scarf from around her neck and take off her winter gloves whilst holding the steering wheel.

As they entered the small village of Little Neston, Rebecca dropped her speed to an acceptable twenty miles per hour so as not to attract any unwanted attention. They cruised down the main road, past the barber's, sandwich shop, and post office, and then took a right along a tree-lined avenue.

"That's pretty." Rebecca pointed to a stone barn conversion with a very well-maintained front garden.

"They're all really nice," Charlie agreed. "Couldn't imagine living somewhere like this, though. It's so quiet. There's nothing to do."

"You don't need to go out if you live in a massive house. You could get your daily exercise just vacuuming all the bedrooms. I bet that one's got a cinema and a home gym."

"I need the city. People. Noise. Traffic... Life." Charlie shivered for dramatic effect.

"I'd love it. A little chocolate box cottage. Thatched roof, open fire—"

"Outside toilet!"

"Ewww. No, not that rustic."

A few more streets and cul-de-sacs later, they'd completed their tour in less than five minutes and had a good feel for the layout of the place.

"Moment of truth," Rebecca said as she swung the van down a narrow left turn and St Mary's and St Helen's Church loomed in front of them. The large sandstone building looked much more impressive in real life. They carried on past the imposing building a short distance and parked up at West Vale Park, which bordered the church graveyard.

Rebecca and Charlie wrapped up again and hopped out of the van. They linked arms, just two friends out for a winter stroll.

"I suppose it would be too easy if she's just sitting on the front pew working on her lyrics," Charlie said.

"Of course. She's more likely in the back helping the vicar light candles or baking cupcakes."

"Oh! What if it is the vicar?!" Rebecca wondered.

"Who says it isn't?" Charlie whispered as they stood in front of the building and looked up at the tower.

"Is that a lightning rod or a flagpole?" Charlie wondered.

"Doesn't matter really. It's so tall, if there is a storm, it's most certainly going to get zapped."

Charlie skipped up the stairs to the front door and twisted the handle. "Let's do this."

For the size of the village, it was a remarkably large church. Pristine stonework, a vaulted ceiling. The colours of the stained-glass windows popping thanks to the low sun.

"Wow," Rebecca was genuinely impressed.

Rebecca had never been one for religion—she got it, and she respected that for some it was important, but she'd made her peace with the fact that she was facing an afterlife of pain, suffering, and eternal damnation for all the pentagrams she'd doodled as a teenager. For Rebecca, it was all about the aesthetics. Whatever the meaning behind it, black magic certainly had the coolest iconography.

Their footsteps clicked and echoed off the stone slab floor as they did a circuit of the church, stopping to read the visitor information cards at each point of interest. Rebecca had been bingeing a TV show about Vikings, so was particularly impressed with the collection of rare Viking stones, as odd as that was to have them on display in a church.

"We should search the crypts," Rebecca said.

"We're all searching for something," a loud and clear voice announced from next to the altar. Rebecca and Charlie turned to see the vicar in a smart blue shirt and dog collar offer a little wave. "Peter Harkin. I'm the vicar here."

"Oh, hi, the door was open," Rebecca replied defensively. "I'm Rebecca, this is Charlie."

"God's door is always open," he beamed. "Well, to be fair, I have to keep it on the latch, at least during winter. You're a bit early for morning service."

"Oh. No. We're not here for the service. We were hoping to talk to you about something."

"There's always a listening ear, if you need one."

Rebecca side-eyed Charlie. They had agreed on a line of enquiry but not necessarily who asked what. Or when.

"We're looking for… an old school friend," Charlie offered. "She's gone missing. She mentioned this church once. I know it's a long shot, but I don't suppose you've had a new parishioner in the last year? Our age. Tall, blonde, quite a unique dress sense. Lots of tattoos."

"You could be describing most of my flock," Father Harkin replied deadpan.

"Really?" Rebecca was genuinely surprised.

"Sorry, no. My youngest parishioner is in her late fifties. I don't think there's a tattoo between them. Whilst I'd welcome an influx of new members, church just doesn't appeal to the youth." Father Harkin's face crossed with sadness. "Can't imagine why."

"No Wi-Fi," Charlie quipped.

"Probably right."

"Could we, err, see the crypt?" Rebecca asked.

"Don't have one. But I'd be happy to give you a tour and let you see the bell tower. Come on through."

He led them through the door next to the altar, which opened up into a wood-panelled corridor and more doors. Everything was painted either white or magnolia. The door immediately ahead was his office, which consisted of a desk, a couple of chairs, and a large bookcase brimming with leather-bound religious texts, and some dog-eared Colleen Hoover paperbacks.

"Do you have a computer, Father?"

"Not anymore. Had a burglary in 2015, and it was never replaced." He opened the remaining doors and let them poke their heads in—a storeroom with fold-up tables and chairs, a toilet, the sacristy with a selection of vestments and sacred objects, and behind the last, a wooden staircase.

Father Harkin was good to his word and led Rebecca and Charlie up the stairs. The temperature dropped considerably as they climbed. What Rebecca assumed were once windows had been boarded over, but they weren't fully sealed. There was a faint whistling sound as the wind blew through the louvred slats.

"Mind yourself on this last flight, it gets a bit narrow," Father Harkin called down.

Rebecca huffed and puffed her way up to the top floor.

"You need to start going to the gym instead of just paying for a membership," Charlie whispered into her ear before bounding up the last few stairs.

They were standing on a platform of sorts, above which was a large metal hook. Most noticeable was that the bell tower contained no bell.

"Isn't there supposed to be a bell?" Rebecca asked.

"Long gone, requisitioned in the war. But it does mean we can do this."

Father Harkin began to climb up a metal ladder pinned to the wall. He opened a trapdoor and flipped it up, before continuing his climb onto the roof. Rebecca and Charlie followed.

"Nice view." Charlie took it all in.

They could see for miles. To the west was the Dee Estuary and the hills and mountains of Wales, and to the south and east were the undulating hills of Cheshire.

Charlie engaged the vicar in small talk while Rebecca took shot after shot on her camera, less interested in what she could see from the top of the tower, and more interested in which houses had a view of the tower. There would be time to sort and sift through them back in the privacy of the van, but on initial appraisal, given the local topography, there were quite a few buildings overlooked by the tower. Rebecca and Charlie's search for which one might contain Emefa had only just begun.

They thanked Father Harkin for indulging them. If he suspected, just for a moment, that they were treating him as a possible suspect, even when he was offering them a slice of Mrs Harkin's gooseberry crumble, then he hadn't let on.

The church, they were convinced, was a point of reference, but not Emefa's actual location. It was time to do a bit of old-fashioned intelligence gathering and the best source of infor-mation was always dog walkers—happy to chat if you complimented their dog, full of local knowledge, and very quick to frown about the idea of gossiping, before recounting every titbit of scandal, hearsay, rumour, and suspicion they'd ever heard. Anyone who began a sentence with, *I shouldn't say anything, but…* was a private detective's best friend.

Rebecca and Charlie agreed to reconvene at the van in two hours, and went in search of the nosiest neighbours with the twitchiest curtains they could find. Charlie headed towards the coast, hoping to find a concentration of canines and their handlers bracing against the sea breeze. Becca headed for the playground in the park, hoping to find mums and tots in a talkative mood.

The park, however, was deserted. Thinking about it, Rebecca questioned who on earth would bring their toddler there in February. This wasn't a village for families. The youth had moved out the moment they were old enough to get a bus pass. Becca realised it was a village of pensioners and changed direction to head over towards the high street, which would be the most likely destination for anyone over sixty foolhardy enough to brave the bitter cold.

Rebecca was used to the quizzical looks—for some, it was

her tattoos, for others the piercings, the bright blue hair, or a combination.

"You'd be pretty if it wasn't for all that…stuff…on your face," an older gentleman had offered as unsolicited advice.

Rebecca nodded and turned away, choosing not to respond. Safe in the knowledge he'd be dead soon. Maybe even this month.

Just as she was turning back to meet with Charlie, she did get one intriguing piece of gossip, though, from a woman in her seventies who lived across the lane from a solitary, haunted-looking manor. Becca had been guiding the conversation towards music, which gave her the opportunity to show a picture of Emefa, explain that she was missing, and give her an excuse to play one of her songs.

"My grandniece loves her music," the lady said. "It's not my cup of tea, though."

"It's a taste you have to get used to." Becca nodded along.

"New music is always so confusing," the old lady remarked. "Some of it is good. It reminds me of older songs, ballads and the like. Simple music about love and longing. It stirs up the young girl living in my old heart."

"It's surprising how many different ways there are to sing about the same thing," Becca said, trying to stay polite.

"If Simon is still around, he might be worth talking to. Talented pianist as a young boy he was."

"Simon?"

She pointed past her shoulder to the house on the hill. "His family left him that house. He lost them a few years ago, the poor dear. He's had the run of it on his own ever since. And he's a good boy, he really is, but terribly shy. And it only got worse once he was left alone with his inheritance. Don't know if he still plays these days though."

"How alone?" Becca asked. "Does he take visitors, or go out much?"

"He used to," she said. "But not so much anymore. He

used to come over when he was a tot and play in my garden. He wanted to be an explorer, then a doctor, then a firefighter —a dream-filled young man he was. I haven't seen him in close to a year now."

"A year?" she asked.

"Oh, I see him around, occasionally," she clarified. "Getting groceries or a prescription. And then he often leaves town without returning for some length of time. I waved to him once, but I don't think he saw me." She sighed with disappointment.

"I'll see if I can get him in a talking mood," Becca said.

"It might do him good," the old lady claimed. "Nothing but us old folks around now. He needs to be with his own generation, and not languishing in the dark."

"Thank you for your time," Becca said in parting. She turned and faced the imposing house nestled at the top of the hill.

It was a big Georgian affair, broader and taller than the post-war detached properties that shared the same road. As tempted as she was, Rebecca couldn't very well hop the wall and fence in broad daylight and simply have a peek through the living room windows. Her second-best bet would be waiting on deliveries to see if someone came out, but that could take days. A proper isolationist probably stocked up weeks' worth of supplies, however healthy they were or weren't, and ate alone just to avoid the possibility of greeting someone at the door. It was a lifestyle she was quite familiar with.

Rebecca quickly walked away from the house, just in case there were any prying eyes in the windows. It might have been nonsense, it might have been made up, but it was the closest thing Rebecca had to a lead, no matter how flimsy. Glancing down the hill, she could see the top windows of many of the houses in the village. Above them all though, she could see the crenellated tower of the church. And if she could see it, anyone looking out of the window of that house could see it too.

She left with one suspicious location, an equally suspect individual, and an end of the trail. As far as she knew, Emefa was somewhere in town, possibly in that very house, being hidden away by dark forces bent on controlling her every word and movement. But they weren't the usual hands trained and seasoned in managing appearance and public image. She was enticed by an amateur with a grudge or a saviour complex. Emefa wanted her true fans to know about the little village, and not because it was her ideal retirement villa.

chapter
twenty-seven

Despite the hour, Clive and Ashley were there to greet the returning detectives when they arrived back at the office. Becca had posted a cryptic message on the group chat, which had hinted at their big news and intrigued Ash enough to ditch whatever plans he'd had for the night. Charlie and Becca were still wrapped up in their winter coats.

"Your lips match your hair," Ash said by way of greeting, placing the back of his hand on Becca's cheek and recoiling in mock horror.

"It's proper Baltic out there, just can't get warm," Charlie explained. "I love your van, Ash, but for the love of all that is holy, please sort out the heater. I'll pay."

They locked the office door, and the team assembled in the bullpen to go over their most important case. Charlie brought in her papers and Becca unloaded all of the equipment from the van to show hers. She had the digital presentation all prepared, with photos arranged in a straightforward clip-show of their day trip in the little nowhere village.

Ash winced when Becca ripped the memory card from his camera without turning it off first, and Clive kept his eyes mostly lidded the whole time and spoke quietly when it was his turn for greetings. He'd taken Charlie's recommendation to treat himself to a few tipples a little too literally and ended up indulging a bit too much. He was paying for it now.

"Right," Charlie began. "We've only got two days to make our report to the production company. So, Becca: the good news."

"I think I know where Emefa is," Becca immediately and happily declared. "I think she's here." She pulled up a picture of the house on the hill, framed ominously against a darkened midday sky of pure grey.

"She's dead then?" Clive asked. "That's a house people are taken to and killed."

"No, no," Becca said. "As long as she's still posting images of herself on social and there's a credible threat to her being taken out of the country, I have to believe she is alive and well, maybe even better off than she was originally, but our time to rescue her is running short."

"That's confirmed," Charlie said, waving her paper. "Marcus has asked the police to meet him at the airport, although he hasn't told them why. The person responsible is about to try to flee the country with her and get arrested in the attempt at the airport. That'll put a nasty mark on the music label, but they won't mind it as long as they get her back. But that also puts us out of a payday."

"So," Ash said, "we need to get her back immediately. Why'd you even come back here? You could've called us up and we could get it all done today!"

"Too risky," Charlie said. "We did a *tonne* of digging. Barely anyone living around there is even on the internet, wrong age demographic, so we had to go around inter-viewing and looking up land registry and parish council records to get the whole picture.

"So, this property? The haunted mansion?" Ashley asked.

Rebecca read from her notes. "It was once the Lord Lieu-tenant of Liverpool's hunting lodge, and was used as a summer retreat until the First World War kicked off and the local woods were felled. So no more cute, cuddly forest creatures ergo no more hunting. Which was fine, because getting on a bit, he hadn't used it for years. But the land needed new purpose so"—she switched to a slide showing the home in sepia tone with a posh chap sporting a mighty bushy moustache and a Pickelhaube helmet sitting atop a fine-looking steed—"it was bought by some Austrian horse breeders. After The War—" she looked at Clive.

"Wrong war," he said.

"Sentiments regarding *ze Germans* weren't great, understandably, and the family was politely coerced to sell the property, when it was then bought by the ancestors of the most recent owners. The two parents had their own business and kept good company with the locals and had a son named Simon who was sent away to boarding school as both parents were working. Then they died, and Simon inherited their fortune and the house, which he's lived in since."

"Wait," Ash said. "We're just skipping that whole tragedy? That sounds pretty important."

"It happened like ten years ago," she said. "Not a problem now."

"How old is this Simon?" Clive asked.

"Mid-twenties," she confirmed.

"Jesus," Clive sighed. "Lost his mum and dad that young and got a house out of it?"

"And went loony," Charlie continued. She swept through a few surveillance-style pictures in the slideshow to get to a picture of the two parents in an obituary from a sun-faded church pamphlet offering prayers and hymns to the congregation over their local loss.

Becca took up the narrative. "He then spent holidays with a family friend in Wales but continued at a different boarding school. He got into fights, was found engaging in the most unhelpful term—*ungentlemanly behaviour*—which is coded language for sexual harassment that gets covered up, so the rich boys don't get in trouble, and never graduated. He coerced his guardian to invest most of his trust fund in a record company, which then took off in a big way and made him rich. Well, richer. Guess. Which. One."

"Dog's Hind Leg," Charlie said. Becca snapped and pointed at the right answer.

"Because he saw a performer," she continued, "right here in Liverpool, where she made her debut."

"Emefa," Charlie said.

"And she signed with Dog's Hind Leg," Ash followed along, "so he put a good faith bet on her success. And—"

"He became obsessed with her," Becca concluded, "went to all of her shows regardless of where they were, and decided to take action. *He* was the one who followed her to her car wreck. Hell, he might have even caused it. That I can't prove, but I do know that she's in there, being forced to write and collaborate and sing against her will, while the rest of the world all sits out here thinking that she's in a rehab with a fancy little garden. Did you know that almost none of the flowers in her Insta posts are native to Britain? Turns out Simon's mum was a sponsor and patron at the Botanic Gardens, not one mile away from the house, who used her husband's good fortune to plant many exotic flowers in her own backyard."

Becca switched over to another picture, old but still in colour, of the suspect's house up close, with a great expanse of flowers across its grass and surrounded by tall, brick walls. It was part of an article regarding unique gardens in Britain's villages and the intense horticulture that went into them. Then, another picture, of the same angle from the other side of the walls, taken from afar and across the wide-open field. The gables along the roof and the windows were nearly iden-tical, as was the pattern at the top of the garden walls.

"This," she continued, switching to a side-by-side slide, "is what I've got."

On the left was one of Emefa's latest posts, and on the right were two pictures. One was of the flower itself, a dark indigo thing that looked like a kipper turned inside out, and a brief entry on Wikipedia listing its locality as somewhere in central Africa. That same flower was present, just in frame, on a blurry zoom-in she performed on the news clipping by the proud mother's ankle.

"That," Charlie said, "is an incredible...coincidence."

"It's this or a dungeon, or some Scottish castle. But the car wreck, the proximity to the village, the airfield— An Emefa superfan, with an unholy amount of cash, has her in that house and is producing songs that he thinks she should be writing. That's what's happened, and that's where we'll find her."

"Great detectives," Clive mentioned, "often have to put themselves in the heads of the criminals they chase. It's like method detecting. Doyle wrote Sherlock as a criminal who just happened to solve crimes in order for him to seem more brilliant than any man could be, because not every man can think like a lunatic."

"Yeah," Becca nodded.

"If you had all that money and time," Clive said, "would you do the same thing?"

Becca shrugged. "I think I'd get along well enough with Emefa that I wouldn't need to go straight to kidnapping."

"I'm willing to believe you," Charlie said, "but what matters now is what we do. And we need to do it fast, because in forty-eight hours I don't want to have to decide between keeping the lights on and keeping you lot gainfully employed. Because I will choose the lights. I don't like reading in the dark."

"No one would blame you, boss," Clive said.

"Okay." Ash clapped his hands. "So we need to get in, get Emefa out, and ideally, avoid Simon or he'll call the real cops and use his rich-boy influence to have us shot on the roadside like poor peasant dogs."

"Yes." Charlie nodded. "But we can't go to the police, or we lose the advantage of operating in private and the record label loses face. This needs tact and careful execution. Therefore, I am permitting us to be slightly more illegal than we usually try to be in making a proper plan."

"Nice," Ash said. "Can't wait to steal his credit card and buy a new car!"

"Less illegal than that," Charlie said. "The rescue can be conducted on the fringes of what *might* constitute legal, but after that, good behaviour only."

chapter
twenty-eight

SIMON PACED FRANTICALLY around the bathroom. His dark mask hung on a hook next to the shower. He avoided the mirror—it reminded him of his real face, pock-marked and pimply from his seemingly endless bout with puberty. He was still a young man, fair-skinned and thin-haired like his mother and father respectively, but his face was a war zone of grease and its unfortunate side effects. He was a monster, a scarred and demonic phantom of the mosh pit—but even so, he had his precious Emefa all to himself. Her voice belonged to him and him alone. Or so he thought.

He hoped her second song would be even more inspired, more poetic. *E-Girl Unplugged* was a statement. A line in the sand. The foundation for the new era of Emefa. The next track had to speak of the future. Something with more hope and an emphasis on rebuilding her past from the ground up, of starting anew. He didn't want to instruct her, but he certainly gave her as many hints as he could of what he expected. The next release should be the title track. A work of sublime genius she'd titled *Pink Is the New Black*. It encapsulated her musical roots and at the same time showed progression, self-awareness and growth, not to mention it was just a damn good tune.

"Why?" he growled. He bent over the sink and ran water on his face until some was forced up his nose and he coughed it out. "Why?" he moaned. He took a soggy towel and rubbed it hard across his face. Some of his pimples ruptured, causing scarring and even the chance of recurring whitehead intrusions later on, but he didn't care. He just soaked the blood-speckled rag again and watched as his face went from red to streaky red. "Why?!" he shouted. He slapped his hand on the mirror and panted.

With no one around him for years, Simon never had the chance to bounce his ideas off of anyone else. If he did, they would have surely told him how insane he was and got him some help. And then he would have had to live somewhere else, or under supervision, which was completely uncool. He was a creative, rich, and incredibly lucky man who could make his own fortune and future. He didn't need his parents' legacy; he just needed their money. The light he was reaching for was something brighter and stronger than what they could have provided.

Simon dried himself off and slipped on his mask. It clung to the spots on his face that were still slightly moist from skin, blood, and dermal pus. He returned to being the dark and featureless producer, the shape of the man who had helped raise Emefa from the dead.

———

Meanwhile, Emefa sat in the recording studio on a plush chair and stared up at the wires that snaked out of the ceiling and powered the array of consoles, amps, instruments, and lights. She had long given up on thoughts of suicide, knowing the brackets supporting the wires were too weak to suspend anything substantial, but she didn't give up on thoughts of using them to strangle him.

After nearly a year, all the novelty and mystery of her

survival had worn off. All that remained was the annoyance and drudgery of being forced to work all day, every day. She never had a chance to play the way she liked. The whole other half of diva life, being in the spotlight and partying with the rich, beautiful, and famous, was missing and made the work itself meaningless.

Her first song, *E-Girl Unplugged,* was a guided set of instructions on how to find her, or at least get close. If someone managed to decipher the code, they could rescue her. Or so she still hoped. Everything else was just a long string of waiting, watching Simon use her phone to upload pictures to her social media profiles, playing the role of tame pet, and impotent escape plots. At least she had Leah. The one ray of sunshine in her bleak world. She held the dog close, and it nuzzled into the crook of her arm as it tried to get comfortable on her lap.

Simon returned to the studio and walked right past her, and sat in front of the mixing desk. "Your label has received the album," he said. "They love it. A return to form. They've agreed to release the songs in the order I—we—suggested."

"But I thought *you* were going to distribute it. Cut out the middleman and all that?"

"An oversight. If we try, the label will just throw a copyright infringement notice every time a track drops and the platforms will pull it. No exposure, no plays, no royalties, whilst you're still under contract."

"And they're happy with this arrangement?"

"They want your music; they're not going to do anything to rock the boat."

"But they don't want me," she mused.

"I think it's a matter of keeping the money train on track. Don't take it personally. It's a seedy business, and you're best out of it.

"Okay," she said. "What's next?"

She'd learned how to push Simon around without getting punished. When it came to work, especially hers, Simon was a rabid perfectionist with poor social skills. He had a vision in his head, which he couldn't quite explain properly. He got tongue-tied and frustrated easily when trying to direct her, but as long as she made it known that the immediate results were all his idea and that she needed his counsel, she knew she could avoid his stun baton.

"I've arranged for us to leave the country," he said. "It's just… no good here."

"Leave?"

"Yes," he said. "By tomorrow, I'll have all our things packed. There will be a plane waiting. And if they defy us, or try to trick us, they will not be receiving the master recording of the album or the gift of another song from you again."

Emefa ignored his threat, though she still believed that he meant it deep down, and got up to clap cheerfully instead. "Where will we go?"

"Somewhere wide open," he said. "Somewhere closer to nature. Away from the cities of the world. A place where we can find the true root of music together, which will help you connect to your lost inspirations."

"That sounds perfect," she said. Just the thought of leaving was exciting, but if it had to be with him, she would rather stay put in the haunted mansion. Her input wasn't necessary. Simon already had their plans put together, like always. But her rebellious spirit never died, it just slumbered, waiting for a moment to take advantage. "I was just growing used to this place—the little I've seen of it. Can I spend some time in the garden one last time? I'll take Leah out for a wee."

Simon rubbed a hand over his face. "You… should stay in your room," he said. "I'll deal with the flowers. Like I should have done a long time ago."

"You aren't going to get rid of them, are you?" she asked.

"I am," he said. "You don't need them anymore. They aren't natural. They're all plants that have no business being here, planted by a… person who cared for them too much."

"Well," she said, "what if I'd like one or two of them? Can't I take them with me? I can plant them where we land. To settle roots into my new life. Something familiar for Leah, wherever we end up next."

"Hmm," he contemplated. "Perhaps." He pressed a button, which unlocked the studio door. She left and waited for him to leave as well. She'd been punished for moving around too freely before, but she could sense that Simon was distracted. She wanted to twist the knife and take advantage of his distress.

"Are they sending a car?" she asked.

"No," he said. "I'm taking you there. I can't trust anyone else with you until we are gone."

"Is it the car… I came here in?"

"Yes, yes," he nodded. "It'll get us there. The plane will be chartered, and it should get us out of the country where we can negotiate a more high-scale transfer."

"Really?" she asked, hopefully. "But— Will you be okay abandoning your car? And your house?"

He placed a gentle hand on her shoulder. "Having you is all that matters."

Emefa learned not to show her repulsion. She acted through the pain and maintained eye contact. She smiled hopefully at him like she was a puppy lovingly controlled by a doting owner. She looked over to the front door, the most forbidden object in the house with its many locks, and then over to the carpet-lined hall that led to the garage.

"Not to be rude," she said, "but the last time we were in a car together, well… How can I be sure it will be safer than my last rental?"

"Of course it is," Simon said. "I've driven it routinely

while you slept, to get supplies and commute our messages to the label."

"Can I see it?" she pleaded in a low, sultry tone. "You know, I grew up around cars. Dad let me tinker with the engine. Replacing spark plugs, oil changes, and stuff. They were a big part of my inspiration, especially for 'Ride Me Round the Track.'"

"Hmm," he hummed, once more in deep thought. "It's an EV, it's just a motor and a battery, really. Not an awful lot to look at."

"Please?"

He took her by the hand and led her over to the garage. It was her first time seeing the space, along with the sliver of light that cracked through the garage door. She approached the dinky little EV hatchback with something bordering genuine reverence. Having been trapped indoors for the best part of a year, the thought of just going for a drive was both exhilarating and terrifying. She vowed there and then, if she were to ever escape, she'd never complain of being stuck in traffic ever again.

She sat in the driver's seat for a few minutes toying with the steering wheel and then popped the bonnet to take a look at the inner-workings. She had never thought about going electric before but would now seriously consider it. After enough time had passed to convince Simon her curiosity was genuine and now sated, she turned to the garage door that led out into the open.

"Simon," she said, "won't people miss you? If they find out who you were all this time, they might come looking— and get worried! The neighbours nearby, have you told them where you'll be?"

"They don't need to know," he said, "and they won't know I'm gone until we're gone forever."

"Isn't that cruel?" she asked. "Didn't you grow up here?"

He turned away. "That doesn't mean I have any love for

this place. It's stifling. The smell of the old who are dead set in their ways like posts in the field has been the backdrop of my life for long enough."

"But I've never seen it," she said. She moved over and pointed her hand to the door opening button. She turned to him with pleading eyes. "Am I leaving behind a place that I never even knew?"

"Wai—" He reached out to stop her, then paused. She could see he wanted to believe she was still searching for her inspiration. She'd deliberately used the language of home and leaving, of her roots and resettling—it was all a bit much, a bit on the nose if she was honest, but if they really were leaving tomorrow, what did she have to lose?

He was happy, but also curious, about what she could find out front that wasn't readily available for her to explore in the sealed garden. Emefa continued a pleading, understanding look and really drilled the guilt of her enclosure into him at their final hour. Just like she used to with her previous handlers. After days, or even just hours, under their watch and instruction, she always managed to puppy-dog her way out on the town to have her own kind of fun.

Simon stepped forward, took her hand in his, and they pressed the button together. The door slowly opened up. She stood near him, pressed slightly into his chest, to show a willingness to stay close even as freedom crept up along the chain track overhead. He walked her forward until she was just in the light, a step away from being properly outside.

It was a cookie-cutter nowhere village street, just like she'd seen on the map. A place that even had 'little' in the name. No signs of industry or metropolitan civilisation. Nothing caught her eye, and there were certainly no passersby. It was, however, her one chance to appear in public. Maybe it would be her last and so she wanted that moment to last as long as possible.

Emefa turned and reached for Simon's hand. She smiled

and laughed with childlike gaiety and tried to swing him to-and-fro in a dance. He didn't understand why, but seeing her that happy after so long was worth celebrating. He danced with her, his face a blur of a slipped-on mask, just a shadow and a diva dancing in a driveway to nothing.

chapter
twenty-nine

It was time to get things moving. Cases didn't solve themselves. If they did, no one would pay for an accidental conclusion. Or, more likely, the unsolved cases handled in private would be sent upstream to the police and their superior resources.

Charlie Chan & Co. Detective Agency couldn't sit on their laurels forever, waiting for good fortune to come their way. And Emefa couldn't wait another day to be rescued—if the letter was to be believed, they had less than twelve hours before she would be whisked out of the country and very much out of their jurisdiction.

Rebecca clicked her fingers, "Check it out, peeps, another connection."

They gathered around her workstation. In front of them, filling the large monitor, was a pixelated photo of a smiling, spotty teen.

"Trust-fund boy Simon Deenhurst has been a shut-in since his parents died but before that—" She minimised the image and brought up an abandoned and locked-out Facebook page of a much younger Simon Deenhurst with a profile picture of a band logo. "He was a fan of Daisy Decay."

"And the significance?" Clive asked.

"It's a punk group," Becca said snidely.

Rebecca clicked a different tab, a very old web page showing a directory of Liverpool venues. She scanned down the list with the mouse pointer and then clicked on a link to the Krazyhouse, which had since closed down and reopened under a new name years ago. The web page advertised a few things, including sign-ups for open-mic nights and a list of local bands playing on Tuesday nights. Becca scrolled down to a date in September and highlighted the text—*Daisy Decay. Emo and pop-punk. Free Entry*. The entry showed a low-res photo of the group, the same logo, and listed the names of the band members. She highlighted one of the names: Rose Pinscher.

"That's Emefa's real name," she said. "That was when she was just starting out and got her first big break. After that, she took on a stage name, Emefa. She did a few more gigs on a personal tour, ran into Marcus at Dog's Hind Leg Records, skip a bit, and now she's being held hostage by one of her oldest fans and most financially able stalkers, in a creepy mansion behind two layers of private security."

"That's a heady claim," Clive said. "We haven't actually had eyes on her."

"It's literally the only place she could be," Becca contested. "You pointed it out yourself—the 3Word thing. She doesn't know where she is, but she can see that church from wherever she's being kept. That house, in that village, is the only house where anyone who's even so much as *heard* of Emefa is currently living. If he's not a suspect, then I guess I've just been learning wrong for the past year and a half I've had this job, and my woman's intuition isn't worth the blood it costs me every month."

Clive grimaced, which Becca took with a bit of pride.

"Are you sure?" Charlie asked, wanting in her heart of hearts to green-light the operation.

"One hundred percent."

They'd pulled an all-nighter in the office, checking and double-checking every web search, fan conspiracy theory and their own suppositions. They had tried to find fault with, or a contradiction to, their strongly held belief that Emefa was alive and being held against her will in the home of one Simon Deenhurst of Radcliffe Road, Little Neston. Their belief had only been reinforced.

The red eyes around the room, not to mention the ever-shortening tempers, were evidence enough that Charlie had pushed her team as much as she could. The last few hours had become almost intolerable.

Charlie felt all eyes on her. It would be great if they were right. Although circumstantial, all evidence certainly pointed in one direction.

In an ideal world, they'd set up surveillance, sit on the property day and night, and collect the kind of proof they usually provided their clients to justify any next steps. But they didn't have the luxury of time.

Charlie needed to make a call. It wasn't her ego holding her back, but a fear of failure —she wanted to see out at least a full year in business and her employees to thrive with her. Breaking into a random person's house, suspicious or other-wise, in search of a delinquent e-girl living a clandestine life off the grid, could be the end of the business she'd worked so hard to build. But only if they were wrong.

If they were right, the police and their client would have to acknowledge their part in the arrest and subsequent conviction of a very dangerous and disturbed criminal, who had evaded the long arm of the law for too long. That was the trade-off of the razor-edged coin flip.

Charlie needed to make sure it landed heads.

"All right," Charlie started, "but if we're wrong and we break and enter the wrong house, the police will shut us down. Agency finished. So, I'll ask again. Are you all sure?"

Becca, Ash, and Clive all held Charlie's gaze. "Absolutely," they said in unison.

"OK, logistics," Charlie addressed the group. "I'm with Clive. I'll feel most comfortable if we get eyes on Emefa. However, I'll settle for proof that Simon is still residing at the property. For all we know, he hasn't been seen for nearly a year because he left the UK behind and is running a Scuba shop in Koh Samui. We've still got a few hours before we need to charge in like the cavalry. Let's see what we can see."

"To the Batmobile," Ash announced.

"Give up, you knob," Becca replied, nabbing the van keys from his hand and running for the door.

They arrived in Little Neston just after nine in the morning, which gave the team plenty of time to check the exterior of the house and the surrounding fields for a place where they could park and have a clear view without being obvious.

Becca managed to squeeze the van into a small space under a tree near a children's play park, which they knew from experience would be very quiet. The van hardly fit in the lanes, which were designed for much smaller cars built before the 70s, and there was a house in the way, but as long as their target didn't hang up their clothes to freeze-dry outside, Ash had a clean line of sight to the front of the house with a powerful 30x optical zoom digital telescope.

For her cover story, Becca made sure that the first five young families she encountered in the park all knew she was an online journalist highlighting the local area's historic vintage and pride and the rest of the team were there to capture additional photos and B-roll in case the local news was interested in running the piece. It also gave her an excuse to take pictures whenever she wanted of whatever she wanted with the cover story of doing it to show off the town's rustic charms and old-time livery.

Rebecca was almost too happy to lie to people, especially those who gave her a suspicious once-over but didn't have the courage to say anything about her piercings, tats or, especially for this stakeout in honour of Emefa, her shocking pink hair. The one person she couldn't lie to was Charlie, out of respect and the very real terror of losing her salary. Anyone else was fair game, even the sweetest old ladies who promised to bring her biscuits and invite her for tea if the notion ever struck her fancy. Anything to get what she wanted, and she wanted to get in that house.

Clive, pretending to be interested in buying property in the area, confirmed with a couple who had walked down from Simon's road that the owner of that particular double-fronted Georgian property was rarely seen. No car left or entered, no deliveries, no visitors. It really did look abandoned.

Ash and Charlie held hands and took a casual stroll over a field towards what would be the rear wall of Simon's garden on the lookout for signs from Emefa's visual diary, uncommon flora that might have spread beyond the enclosed garden space and propagated itself in the weedy outlying grass of the private meadow. A rare plant, or even a familiar petal from the idol's Insta, would be proof enough to take back to the team and instigate a rescue. One of them just needed some actual evidence and they could return, head high, hands wringing with excitement, with a just cause for intrusion.

As the team munched on their shop-bought sandwiches, Rebecca finally got it. Squatting in the back of the van with her eye to a telescopic lens, she saw the electric garage door slowly rise. Nothing happened for a moment, then she held her breath when she saw Emefa walk out of the garage and appear on the front drive. Simon joined her, and the two of them danced.

They had eyes on Emefa.

Rebecca took shot after shot with the camera.

"We've got her!" Rebecca whooped from her hiding spot.

chapter
thirty

THE MOMENT finally arrived for the big sting to go down. For private detectives, proving or disproving a hypothesis through good old-fashioned surveillance and evidence gathering was only half of the coin that made the job appealing. The other half was staging daring rescues of absconded public darlings held in gilded cages against their will to perform for the sick fantasies of depraved maniacs.

Granted, it was a much rarer side of the coin to land on, but when it came up, it was like magic. The operation was underway, and it had a name: *Punk's Not Dead*. Becca's idea.

Charlie, Ash, and Becca climbed out of the van to stretch their limbs and to give Clive a bit of privacy while he changed his clothes. They were in the cosy little hamlet of scattered houses and spotty Wi-Fi signals. Little Neston was a quintessentially English village just a couple of miles west of Emefa's crash site. Charlie walked everyone to the temporary base camp at the play park to go over the plan, get them prepared, and to go over their roles and assignments.

"Right," Charlie began. She had a selection of Rebecca's photos that encircled the property from as many angles as she could get. Some were taken from the cover of brush, others under the veil of night, touched up and bloomed accordingly to match the approximate shading of the daytime lighting. Charlie motioned to her map strategically as she went on.

"Clive will be here at the front door making an unholy ruckus, which Simon won't be able to ignore. Meanwhile, the rest of us will use this path here to get to the boundary wall. We'll scale it to get access to the garden—here, where the tree just barely crests over the wall."

"Since when did we have these?" Ash asked. He picked up one of the grappling hooks. It was a rock-climbing ice pick attached to a garish pink and fluorescent yellow length of knotted rope. The ideal, modernised take on a grappling hook. "Where's the, uh, shootie bit that makes it go?"

"It's here," Becca said, poking his shoulder. "You need to oil it up first or it gets clogged with flab."

"You don't want a wide shoulder profile," Ash said. "I have to stay svelte. If I can't fit through the alleyway without turning to the side, how'm I supposed to carry off a crushed velvet three-piece suit in a chase, huh?"

"Why would you want a velvet suit?" Charlie asked.

"To look good in," he said. "Strength is a worthy sacrifice for fashion, boss. So is speed and, to a limit, health."

"I get it, you're avoiding a potentially embarrassing situation with humour," Becca said. "If you can't throw it, then just let Charlie do it. She's got those honed arms."

"And I think I'm the only one who can rope-climb up a wall," she added. "How are you two getting in?"

"Oh, I'll do it," Rebecca said. "With sheer desperation, rage, and passion. I'll peddle my way up and over, don't worry."

"And I'll remain here offering plenty of moral support," Ash said. "I'll pitch over some water bottles to keep you hydrated."

"We'll *all*," Charlie persisted, turning to a printout of a Google satellite image of the garden from a couple of years ago, "wind up around here, near the tree. From there, we're at the house, but he'll have the whole place secured. There are cameras all over the front of the house, so we can assume that's true at the back, so it's up to Clive to keep his focus elsewhere. Now, our best guess is that she's being held in this upstairs rear bedroom, as it would give her direct line of sight to the church."

"I have a feeling," Ash said, "he's not gonna be entertained by Clive for very long."

"I think he will," Rebecca said. "Long enough for one of us—namely me—to get up to the window and break in. Whether or not Emefa's there, once we're in, we can stay in until we find her and get her out."

"This is a…" Ash began. "It's shaping up to be a… uh…" He snapped his fingers. "Movie where characters are trapped inside a house together… with a bad guy. Not *Home Alone*. That's the first one I thought of, but it's not that."

The back doors of the van swung open. The group was initially shocked to see a stranger in their midst wearing a postman's uniform with a few errant stains across the shoulder. He was a grey-haired, slumping, almost deranged-looking figure until he stepped up and looked at them past his unkempt fringe.

"How do I look?" Clive asked.

"You're supposed to say trick or treat when you knock on a door like that," Ash said. "Jeez, you scrub-down well."

"Many thanks," he said. "You see enough drunks on the job, you end up half-pissed around them. Just channelling some of the finest floor-polishers I've had to work around."

"And you remember your lines?" Charlie asked.

He nodded. "Just keep asking for Darren. Yell and rant for a bit until the boy gets cross."

Rebecca clapped her hands. "We're ready. Let's get up there and save a pop star!"

"Lock and load!" Ash cheered.

The detectives got back in the van, and bravely seated

themselves in proper positions and rolled out. They dropped Clive off at the end of Simon's street so he could make a convincingly long, trawling approach towards the house clutching a small box.

Ash parked the van up against a low sandstone wall. It was a good sixty metres away from the garden wall, up a hill, and totally exposed with no cover to speak of, but once their diversion was in place, they would be clear to go running and panting and even grappling up the wall without pause.

Clive walked up the paved drive on cue and pressed the video doorbell.

———

Simon only opened the door to people with packages, and if they were left on the doorstep, he never let them sit there for long, especially if they were things that he needed for his studio or to keep Emefa happy.

Even on their last day there, he didn't want to miss a delivery and end up having repeated attempts making it clear no one was home. No one could know what he'd done, or they would cut off his finances. Not until he had the guarantees he needed from Dog's Hind Leg Records, including an estate agent to properly flip and sell the house and legitimise his move forever.

All of Simon's plans were changed when a seemingly blind-drunk man came to his door with a cardboard box that had a dented corner.

"Sorry, lad," Clive slurred. "Got a package 'ere, it was already damaged at the depot. I didn't drop it or nothin'."

"Uh… okay," Simon said through the door. He cracked it open just a bit and tried to hide his unmasked face in the dark. He glanced over his shoulder, up the stairs. Emefa was locked in her room. He never wanted her to see him without his mask on. It would break the illusion, and remind her that he was a person instead of a symbol of her rebirth.

"Is Darren in?"

"What?" Simon snapped.

"Oi, Darren!" Clive shouted, leaning his head into the hall. Simon pressed the door in, but Clive shouldered it open a little more. "Darren! You in, mate?"

"Stop that!" Simon protested. "He's not—Darren—no one called Darren lives here."

"What?" Clive said. "Yes, he does. I 'aven't had a pint with 'im in ages. He sick or something?"

"He's gone," Simon said. "He…"

He couldn't say it. Not to strangers. A combination of his shyness and ruined self-image made it impossible to talk to anyone about his dead parents. It's what drove him away from the community in the first place, where everyone knew his parents, but none of them had cared to learn about him.

"He ain't back yet?" Clive asked. "What's he up to nowadays? He was a right laugh at school, he was. Dug up a mole with his bare hands in the playing fields, he did! I saw him do it. Called him Mole-man Daz! You know old Mole-man— He tell you that story much, does he?" He laughed like he was half-cut after a morning on the whiskey.

"I'm sorry," Simon said. "He's not around anymore. Do— do you need my signature or something?"

"Agggh," Clive grunted. He patted himself down for a second and even reached through his legs to feel his pockets on the other side of his trousers. "Ah—forgot me pen. I need to get it, it's in the van."

"Just wait here," Simon said. "I'll get a pen. I'll come back. I'll sign for it. Okay?"

"Yeah, alright," Clive nodded. "Hey, is you Darren's son? You is, right?"

Simon didn't answer. He quickly shut the door, locked the handle, and pressed his hands to his head as he paced around. His first move was to run into the living room and pick a shotgun off of a decorative rack. Then he searched through some drawers for two shells and loaded the barrels.

He wasn't about to let neighbourly trivia stand in his way. He had plans for the day and no drunk would ruin them...

chapter
thirty-one

GETTING to the garden wall was easy. Swinging the grappling hooks was easy. Surprisingly, climbing up was not as hard as suspected. Getting down, however, was. Charlie made it look easy. Rebecca struggled and took a face full of cypress fir when she overcompensated for the small border and launched herself deep into the garden. Ash, despite his earlier protestations, scooted up the wall quickly and straddled the apex long enough to pull up his rope, and then fed it down the opposite way. He tried climbing back down, but the hook slid out of place, and he fell the remainder of the way. He landed on the soft, recently turned dirt of a former flower patch.

"Oh, God," Rebecca said.

The garden was destroyed. Everything but the tree was torn up, tossed, weeded, cut, mulched, buried or otherwise removed. The plants that remained looked like weeds. She bent down and recognised one of the crushed flowers from Emefa's recent Insta posts.

"We're just in time. He's probably planning on burning the place down for insurance money or something. Don't touch any more flowers. They're part of the evidence."

"Too late," Ash said as he pulled some affectionate

clematis vine off his trouser leg. "Don't worry. I'll bring some seeds home. You can find them next time I use the toilet, because they're up my arse right now."

"Shush," Charlie insisted. She slowly crouch-walked over to the back door and silently tested the handle. As predicted, it was locked. She put her ear up to it to try and interpret how things were going from the other side. She could still hear Clive occasionally belt out an odd word or two from the open door on the other side of the house. Charlie took out a small leather pouch, which she unrolled to reveal a large selection of lock picks.

"Naughty, naughty," Ash whispered.

"I'm going up," Rebecca said. She approached the space under the upper-storey window and waved Ash over. They both observed the situation together, but it looked a bit hopeless. There was no grating or iron latticework like there was in the old historic photo. Just a sheer, barren wall of pleated wood painted white. Nothing to clutch or climb up by hand.

"I can try throwing you up," Ash offered. "Might not work, but it'd be funny to try."

"Wait," Rebecca said. She scurried back to the wall to recover Ash's grappling hook. She looked up higher to the roof gable and saw a decorative railing over the window that stuck out. An old iron fixture that was never removed, just sturdy enough to look stable. Rebecca looped the rope, pulled back her arm, and sent it up.

The small hook lightly hit the siding and fell back down. She tried again, and it fell again, landing over Ash's shoulder.

"Ow, that hurt," he whinged.

"You try it," she offered.

"You need to swing with your hips," he said. He tried to make an example of it, gave it an earnest underhand cowboy-style lasso toss, but didn't even get halfway. "Okay, for real this time, though." On his second attempt, he sent it up high and tugged at the remaining lead to make it snare on the contact point. He tugged hard on it to test the sturdiness and nodded to himself.

"Way to go," Rebecca said. "You can now wear assless chaps with pride."

"All chaps are assless," Ash said. "That's part of the design. It's like saying sleeveless vest."

"Hold it steady," Charlie spat. "In your mouth, if you can't keep quiet."

Rebecca started to climb with fervour, one hand over the other, all the way up to the window. She quickly pulled out a screwdriver and jammed it into the sill to pry it loose. The nails on the outside were old and misshapen. They splintered the wood as she hoisted the window up a few millimetres with sheer force. Once it had a small amount of give, she swapped to her other, larger tool.

Emefa, meanwhile, was inside and heard the minor commotion from both directions. Leah, also alerted by the commotion and Emefa's reaction, began to run in circles around her feet. She heard someone shouting at the front door, hoping it was a paparazzi trying to squirm their way in to get pictures of her—right now, if they asked, she'd pose nude for them if it got her out of there.

Behind her, she heard something attacking the window frame, which raised her suspicion more, as old wood began to crack and splinter. Then the window, which was once a tanta-lising mockery of her limited freedom, was open to the world outside. The first fresh air in nearly a year flooded the room, and was then immediately blocked by the figure of a girl entering with a crowbar in her hand.

Rebecca put a finger to her lips and slowly reached the floor, checked herself for any splinters or scrapes from the gnarled nail-lined windowsill, and looked up in fascination. Before her, was the literal idol of her dreams, the one and only Emefa. No makeup, clean and clear skin, her natural roots were showing—this was Rose Pinscher, the woman behind the act. But it still caused Rebecca to gasp hard and hold back her desire to let out a squeal.

"Who are you?" Emefa asked.

"Uhhhhh," Rebecca began. "A— a fan. But also—"

"Are you here to rescue me?" she asked.

Rebecca stood up and seized the once-in-a-lifetime opportunity. She reached out, took Emefa's hand, and shook it.

"Yes. I'm here to rescue you."

"Thank fuck," Emefa sighed. "I'll sign your fucking throat from the inside if you can get me out of this loon's house."

"I—we can work that out," Rebecca said. "I actually have a tattoo, based on the art from your second album. It's on my—"

Emefa slapped Rebecca's mouth shut and turned toward the door. They both heard the thudding of footsteps approaching. Rebecca immediately ducked and rolled under the bed while Emefa reached over and tried to force the window down with her fingertips. She got it mostly closed, drew the curtains and launched herself through the air to land on her bed. Leah jumped up to join her. The lock tumbled and Simon entered. Emefa turned and was shocked to see he had a shotgun in his hand.

"We're leaving," he said.

"All right." She nodded and gulped. "My... things?"

"We'll have *new* things," he said. "But I need to get rid of an... old problem first. Get dressed, stay in here. Don't come out, no matter what."

Emefa nodded obediently. He left and locked her back in the room. Once he was gone, Rebecca rolled back out from under the bed and picked herself up.

"That sounded," she said, "like an old, shitty lock."

She whipped out her handy lock-picking kit, strictly for practice and entertainment purposes and never to be used in real-world situations, according to the manual.

Emefa went to the bed and unscrewed one of the posts

from a corner to hold on to as a makeshift club. Something she'd been considering using for many months but was terrified she'd mess it up on the first swing and be punished severely for it. Emboldened by the presence of her would-be rescuer, she was ready to go out fighting.

"Cute dog, by the way." Rebecca smiled as Leah's tail rhythmically thumped the floor with nervous energy.

"Thanks. Are you the only one here?" she asked.

"Nope," Rebecca said. She tumbled the lock and twisted the door open. "I'm with Charlie Chan & Co. Detective Agency."

"Are you Charlie or Chan?" Emefa asked.

Rebecca averted her eyes and slowly opened the door.

Downstairs, Simon was ready to end the stalemate he had with his visitor. Postman or no, he wouldn't be in the country long enough to suffer the consequences of a wandering drunk. The garden was freshly tossed and replotted. What was one more dirt mound in the graven grounds? He was committed to his idea. He felt his sweat squeeze against the sheer fabric of his mask. It trickled down and soaked the whole thing until he could barely breathe. He reached for the door and cracked it open, just a little, to talk.

"Sir," Simon said, his voice renewed with confidence. "Darren isn't here. Please leave the package on the step and walk away."

"There's a procedure we got to go through, lad," Clive slurred. "You gotta honour that procedure—Darren knows! He oughta've taught you about that by now. Didn't your father ever teach you to—"

Simon held up the gun. He started to aim it through the sliver of the door.

Clive broke his character immediately. He dropped the box, pushed forward, and pressed his open palm against the barrel of the gun, levering it away from his body against the door frame. Simon lost control but retained his finger's position on the trigger. With nothing else to do, he fired.

The whole agency was thrown into action. Charlie, having no luck with the deadlock on the kitchen door, took a garden rock and smashed the backdoor handle off, then kicked the door open once the lock tumbled out of its socket. Ash ran in after her and picked up some dishes from the nearby sink to throw, while Charlie ran toward the front door. Rebecca and Emefa came from upstairs. Emefa lagged far behind, dragging her bedpost, while Rebecca crept forward to peer around corners.

In the front hall, Clive was stuck in a struggle for control of the gun. He wasn't hit, but Simon was resisting hard. Clive got the gun to aim up and was twisting Simon's arm from the grip. Simon's only option was to let go or sprain himself to keep his finger on the trigger—the basics of military close-quarters combat.

What Simon lacked in practical training, he made up for in his raw, almost intuitive counteraction. He let himself drop down, spun against Clive's force, and tried to twist the gun barrel closer to Clive's head.

Clive couldn't support the weight of the man by the rifle alone, so he ducked down as well to avoid becoming higher than the barrel. They were on the ground when Charlie appeared. She couldn't dodge bullets. She had to wait until the gun was no longer waving around before she went in.

"Get him!" Emefa screeched. "Shoot him!"

Simon thought it was Emefa instructing him. It spurred him to take a chance and rid himself of the intruder for her sake—for theirs. He reached up to pull the trigger, but Clive worked his thick hand down, trapping Simon's finger behind the trigger, stuck tight like he was wearing a ring a size too small. Simon released his grip, spun on his back, and threw his legs at Clive to kick him away. Then he took out his baton and delivered a zap to Clive's shoulder, which sent the older man into a seizing fit.

Charlie moved in. She charged and delivered a flying knee-tackle to Simon's chest. It sent him back against the door, which swung hard into the wall with him still on it. The gun skittered across the floor, but he held on tight to the baton.

Clive managed to recover and roll away just as Charlie came in with another kick to Simon's face. Simon swung his head away from it, took the glancing blow, and rolled to recover, losing his face mask in the process. It was a trained manoeuvre, to minimise the impact by moving in the same direction as the blow. He was good. And still armed.

"Wash your dishes, loser!" Ash shouted. He threw a cup like a cricket ball past Charlie and hit Simon in the arm.

It distracted Simon enough for Charlie to reach over and grab the arm wielding the baton. She positioned herself for a hip throw, then braced, and brought Simon down and forward as she split her legs to toss him onto his side. His arm was twisted nearly to breaking at the joint and he dropped the baton. Charlie kicked it away, then wound up her leg and kicked him in the chin.

"You're under citizen's arrest," she declared, "for the kidnapping and false imprisonment of Rose Pinscher, AKA Emefa!"

The group was overjoyed. None more so than Emefa, who ran down the stairs to the scene.

Simon saw her approaching and reached up to her. He tried to tell her to run—save herself—to continue the legacy and their work together. That he always loved and believed in her, and now she didn't need him. She could be free.

Emefa growled and delivered a running punt-kick to his bollocks. Charlie backed away as Emefa rolled Simon over and stomped on him over and over in the dick and balls while snarling all the hottest, most raging profanities that the group had ever heard. It was like she'd been saving up an album's worth of the most raunchy and wrathful lyrics for a whole year, just in case she had the chance to sing her true feelings to him.

Simon cried. He heard the true sound of Emefa's inspiration, and it was not at all what he'd wanted. It was a song about how happy she was to kick him in the balls.

chapter
thirty-two

Five minutes later, the police arrived. Despite reports of gunshots, it had taken a while for the authorities to show up, mainly due to Little Neston being somewhat of a jurisdictional black hole—straddling the border of Merseyside and Cheshire, but also a stone's throw from the Badlands of Wales.

First, the local PCSO came to investigate the gunshot without any weapons of his own, just a friendly neighbourhood check-in, assuming it was teens messing around with fireworks. Then the real cops came and tripled the village's population in an instant. There was a major breaking story involved, so tonnes of reporters and freelance gawkers also filed into town, but thanks to the narrow roads, the police were able to control them and keep them far from the scene.

Simon was formally arrested, cuffed, and placed in the back of a squad car. Every square inch of the house was evidence, including, at Rebecca's insistence, the ruined flower beds out back. She already had a full report ready to hand over of her observations and findings, all legally done, and the rest of the team was pleasantly tolerated for their hand in the matter. Charlie Chan & Co. Detective Agency won the day and saved the girl. All was right with the world.

Emefa sat on the porch, her first time really out in the open in months. Her toes were curled with anxiety. Her breathing was shivering and erratic as the evening came on. Leah rested on her lap as Emefa absently dragged her fingers through the dog's fur. Rebecca sat next to her, nervously at first, then tried to be open and warm enough to start up a conversation.

"So," she began, "that must've fucking sucked, huh?"

"Yeah," Emefa nodded. "Well… yeah. It sucked. It was just like being at work, constantly. And he did shock me sometimes but, like…. I don't know. I guess I'm still having Stockholm Syndrome for him or whatever. I feel like just going back upstairs to bed and sleeping this all off."

"You can probably just take the house," Rebecca said. "This guy's gonna get everything seized."

"Nah, he's crazy," Emefa said as she lit up a cigarette she'd bummed from a policeman. "And it's a shame. If he used some acne cream, he'd be kind of cute. I never saw his face until just now."

"That's creepy."

"He was fucking terrifying at first," Emefa admitted. "But now… I mean, I don't like what he did, but there was never any hate in it. I never felt, like, totally unsafe. He was just another producer trying to make something out of my talent."

"Your real producer was the one who wanted you back," Rebecca said. "He wasn't about to let some crazy Stan keep you all to himself."

Emefa scoffed. "Marcus *would* hire out just to find me. Whatever. You guys did a good job, though. Especially that Asian chick. She's a badass."

"That's my boss," Rebecca said. "Charlie Chan."

"Catchy name." Emefa stubbed out the cigarette on the patio, clearly not enjoying the taste after so long without.

"Talking about names," Rebecca desperately wanted to keep the conversation going. "I mean, if we're talking about naming sense, it was your lyrics that led us here. I listened to it, like, a hundred times, but didn't notice. It was Clive there who figured it out and caught onto the meaning."

"Sorry," Emefa smirked. "Can't believe I made you put up with that shit."

"No, it's— it's good," Becca said. "Really. It's new, it's different, but it's still way you. And it's amazing you could make something that good under so much pressure, even against your will. It's like, that's true talent. Like, even if you wanted to fail, you couldn't because your song-making heart can't be stopped."

"Pfft!" Emefa spat into her cup of tea. "I'm sorry, sweetheart. That's fucking cringe as shit."

"What?"

"I'm just, like, a fronter," she admitted. "I got hired for my vocals. Marcus is the one who came up with the whole e-girl aesthetic and the public persona, ghosts wrote all my songs—most of my songs. I wrote, like, two per album, or a B-side track when I wasn't feeling it that much. But now that I've got this amazing trauma to put behind me and talk about, I can go on the talk show circuit for, like, a fucking *decade* non-stop. And I got soooo good at acting because of that loser, you have no idea. You thought I was a good performer before? I can work this into a career in a second. Hollywood beckons, baby, just you wait."

Rebecca was at a loss for words. The Emefa she thought she knew, and was excited to meet, was gone. She wasn't even gone from the apparent hardships or torn up from the frustration and change brought on by her harrowing situation. She was never there at all. It was always an act, even the act of it being an act. She was never the spoiled brat rebel child of Dog's Hind Leg Records. She was a perfectly well-trained show horse, whose talent just happened to be showing off as a punk in idol clothing.

"Anyway, Becky," Emefa said as she stood up and

stretched. "I'll be sure to give a shout-out to your Scooby-Gang when I start my tour on the chat shows. It'll be worth a shitload more from me than from a PR agency. Thanks for being a fan!" She sauntered off into the yard and down the walkway toward the police. Leah looked up at Rebecca and then followed.

"Uh—yeah," Becca said. "Thanks for…" She couldn't even return the compliment for Emefa being an idol, because no thanks were necessary for her. She was just doing her *job*. Rebecca reclined and sighed. She was in a slump of defeat, until Clive came up and sat near her.

"You all right, hon?" he asked.

"Are you?" she asked. "You didn't get your ear shot off, did you?"

"My tinnitus came back a bit," he said, "but it'll drown out sooner or later. I've had it since the war. Not my first time handling a gun from the wrong end."

"Yeah?" she said. "Well, let's hope it's the last."

"It always could be," he said. "You get an autograph?"

"No," Becca sighed. "Not sure I want one now, to be honest."

"That's the thing with musicians, they say never meet your idols," he said. "It's all made up. The simpler the story, the harder it is to construct. That's why KISS was so popular back in the day. They were manufactured and proud of it. Went crazy with their backstories because they knew it didn't matter."

"Yeah," she nodded. "They keep changing the lyrics, but it's all the same song…"

Clive stayed with her and let her be as the sun set over the quiet village, which was, thanks to them, no longer quiet. The strobes of blue mixed with the sky of orange and purple to layer a harmonic hue of colours high up into the night sky…

chapter
thirty-three

AFTER THE HIGH of cracking open the Emefa case, it was back to the mundane for the staff of the agency. Work persisted and droned and dragged Charlie's feet and the Phillips case was shackled to her like a ball and chain. She needed a major break in that to feel better. At the very least it would be some income to rely on while they waited for the Dog's Hind Leg 'finder's fee' to clear. Good favours only got so far. She didn't want a life debt with the electric company.

Charlie's phone buzzed on the desk, rotating slightly with the vibrations. It was Ash. She swiped to accept the call.

"What's happening?" Charlie asked expectantly.

"Absolutely bugger all. She's been in all day. Curtains are drawn. And I'm frozen to the marrow." Ash chattered his teeth to drive the last point home.

"Told you to wear long johns."

"There are lines I won't cross, even for you." Ash joked, then shivered for real.

Charlie tutted, "You could be dying of hypothermia, and we wouldn't know until it was too late."

"At least my frozen corpse won't be discovered wearing long johns. I couldn't live it down, even in a morgue. Please, can I go home?"

"Sorry. Two more hours. Clive's relieving you at seven."

"If I make it until tha—" Charlie heard Ash shifting in his seat and the echo of his fingers tapping on his phone. "Hang on. Status update on Anna Cartwright's Facebook page. She's off to The Pit. For *fun and frolics*, apparently, and she's tagged Leslie Redding."

"But not Sophie?"

"Nope." Charlie heard Ash switch the phone from speaker, and place it back against his ear. "But I think Sophie's just spotted the same update. A light's gone on in the front bedroom."

"Ok, you stay on Sophie. I'll head over to The Pit. Stay in contact."

"Will do, boss."

———

The Pit, as the name suggested, was a student hangout. The club was filled with angsty and discordant rock, played by university students who wanted an honest break in an industry that was more interesting, if not more harrowing, than whatever profession they were studying for. They did fancy coffee and cheap booze, combining the mellow setting of a Seattle-style coffee shop with the saucy libations of a proper grunge club. The crowd was mostly students around Charlie's age or younger, legal drinkers as well as a few underage sixth-formers, sporting bumfluff above their top lips, who wanted to hang out with the cooler crowd and listen to whatever was playing.

Charlie knew from their research that it was also a property where Leslie Redding, yet again, had free rein. She owned the ground floor and the office space above. In this case, she wasn't the licensee named over the door, just the landlord.

Charlie wore a scarf over her head and more makeup than

she'd normally apply. It was enough to convince a casual onlooker that she was Middle Eastern or North African rather than East Asian. She stood out in many places as looking foreign. Liverpool, compared to most cities, has always been diverse thanks to its maritime history, but there is still a contingent that would raise an eyebrow and remember seeing someone who looked unfamiliar in their favourite haunts. Usually older, wealthier white women had issues with that. Leslie Redding might be one of them.

Charlie sat near a group, blending in, listening to the music, until Leslie got up from across the room. She was looking at her phone when she left, probably responding to the signal of some third party. Charlie quietly and slowly followed her outside and around the corner, into a street-facing alley lined with bushes that were part of the local décor, like a garden walk between two asphalt roads.

And who else was there to meet her but Anna Cartwright, the lady-pal and known fling-haver with Sophie Phillips? The *trifecta of cougars*, as Ash had dubbed them, seemed to have stronger ties than Charlie knew. She never expected the two extras in her case to have business together. Anna had been a paralegal until she got married, then she divorced and became an accountant. She was a fairly plain woman, who lived with her sexuality openly rather than hiding it, or adapting to it, like Sophie did. She was out and proud, without a ring holding her back.

Charlie kept her distance until both women were gone into the artificial brush of the garden walk. Then prepared herself to go stealth. She took off her shoes, revealing padded soles stuck to her feet, silent even on broken glass and thick enough to protect from the same razor tinsel underfoot. Her clothes were already muted and dark-toned, and her headscarf helped to hide her bright skin. She became a ninja in an instant, with two thick mid-heel pumps as her weapons, which she tied together by their laces into a leathery nunchucks so she could arm herself with her phone in the off-hand. She prowled ahead until she heard the sounds of the two women exchanging information.

Via their mouths. And saliva.

It was, unmistakably, a make-out session between two well-off middle-aged women, neither of whom was Sophie. Charlie wondered if this was also something normal and expected and, more to the point, if this was the reason Sophie had not been making the most of Dave's sojourns abroad. The text exchange between Anna and Sophie that Anna put online would certainly explain Sophie's duvet day today. Whilst Leslie was a married woman, Anna had no one to answer to but herself. But there was nothing in her notes about her having such an open playbook.

It wasn't David who was being cheated on unexpectedly. It was Sophie. Leslie Redding was in the clear for shady dealings for the time being, but she was instrumental in bringing down the house of lust around a person of significant interest. A person who needed to know the truth…

Charlie hid from sight and angled her phone just so, to take a hidden video of the two ladies. They were unintentionally courteous enough to turn one another over against the wall between two bushes as they mercilessly snogged with the thump of unadjusted bass just through the wall. Charlie only took a few seconds' worth of footage then retracted her phone, placed her pumps back on her feet, and made her way back into the bar.

Charlie had seen enough and was ready to head off. She offered her raffle ticket to the young man at the cloakroom. As he went to fetch her coat, Anna and Leslie entered the bar, laughing and joking. Leslie reached over and tucked some errant hairs behind Anna's ear. Anyone observing them would agree they made a really attractive couple, and would surmise they were clearly in love, or lust. Unfortunately, one of those observers was Sophie, who stood frozen to the spot, mouth open, trying to make sense of the scene.

"What the actual fuck?" she spat at Anna.

"Sophie!" Anna instinctively detached herself from Leslie and put on her best smile, but it didn't wash.

"I think I'll let you two have a moment," Leslie said as she strutted past Sophie and out of the bar.

"I thought... I mean, I..." Sophie's face and shoulders dropped.

Charlie watched the defeat wash over her body. Anna and Sophie just looked at each other and, without another word, Sophie turned and left.

"Here you go," the cloakroom attendant said to Charlie as he pushed her coat into her shoulder, clearly fed up with waiting for her to notice he'd been offering it to her for some time.

Charlie tipped the attendant, put on her coat, and hovered by the bar for another minute before she left through the same main doors. A short flash of headlights alerted her to a familiar grey van across the road and she headed over to Ashley.

"Why didn't you tell me Sophie was on the move?"

"Check your messages," Ash replied.

Charlie did as she slipped into the passenger seat and realised he had. Repeatedly. She'd switched her phone to silent and missed the warning.

chapter
thirty-four

To tell, or not to tell, Dave. That was Charlie's dilemma as she sat at her desk early the next morning. She had hard video evidence of Anna Cartwright, Sophie Phillips' girl-friend, having an affair with married estate agent Leslie Redding. Charlie, along with Sophie, had witnessed this transgression, and anyone observing the stand-off in the bar immediately after was under no illusion about Sophie's opinion of this new world order.

Charlie could hold tight and observe what happened next. If she was lucky, Sophie would be appalled, heartbroken, and run into David's arms with regret, keen to swear fealty to him once again. Their marriage would be saved, her wandering eye would be healed once and for all, and Charlie would probably get a bonus.

The flip side of the coin was that Sophie was now likely feeling hurt, alone, and would be seeking out companionship. Possibly with another woman, or possibly not of the same-sex variety, but with someone younger, and altogether more male. Sophie was known to be receptive to such flirting in the past. If Sophie acted on that impulse, and Charlie caught her, she could at least bring that proof back to David. She would ruin a marriage, motivated by the spite and paranoia of a jealous, horny husband and get paid exactly what she was due. Her main decision was whether the extra pay was a hair worth splitting.

She didn't have a chance to make the decision when her phone rang, and Mr. Phillips was on the other end of the line.

"It's me, Dave," he said. "David Phil—"

"Hello, Mr. Phillips, thanks for returning my call," she said. "I just wanted to clarify something. You were aware that Sophie and Anna had a physical and sexual relationship in the past?"

He was quiet for a bit, as if he was shifting uncomfortably from the remark. "Well, yes. Just aware. I don't— It's not like I'm involved or anything."

"Is that door open for any woman," Charlie asked, "as long as it's a woman? Have you given her carte blanche to add any other parties into her extramarital affairs, so long as they are not men?"

"It's… just been Anna, since we both know her. I can trust her. I can't say I'm jumping for joy over the situation. But I came to terms with it a long time ago. Maybe I'm naïve, but I just see it as harmless fun."

"And is Anna," Charlie continued, "well known to… *do* whomever she pleases? Or is she dedicated to Sophie? Are those the terms of their arrangement?"

"Uh… I suppose?" he said. "Why do you ask?"

"I think the situation's changed between Sophie and Anna," Charlie admitted. "I think they've cooled things off, and I just wanted to understand what constitutes an affair in your eyes."

"I mean— Here's the thing, right? Do you have any evidence she was cheating with a man?"

"None," Charlie said. "She's been under 24/7 surveillance. I have collected a substantial profile of her character, of her actions, and have confirmed that she has been alone, or with Anna, during your time abroad. She has not once in my investigation, nor under surveillance, taken the advances of any man, young or old, nor has she gone to a home besides your own, nor taken any man inside with her."

He sighed and went quiet. Charlie's tone was assertive and factual, and she spoke with as much clarity as she could to ensure the words reached him. She could hear the fabric of his clothing rustling against the phone as he rubbed his head. She was telling him that the entire reason he hired her was all in his head, that he was wrong, and that he should expect a bill when he arrived.

"Right," he said. "So, I actually flew into Manchester this morning, but she doesn't think I'm coming back until tomorrow afternoon. So, she'll think she's got the night to herself. I think she'll use the opportunity to meet up with someone. And then I'll be there to catch her, and so will you, and she'll know she's had it then!"

"David," Charlie said, "this… I don't think this plan will work."

"What's not going to work about it?" he asked. "If she thinks she's got one more night to play, she might just do that, you know?"

Charlie was convinced that Mr. Phillips' paranoia was, in fact, an elaborate fantasy wherein he wanted to cause his wife to cheat on him as some sort of gratification, or *ex post facto* justification for his own wandering eye. If it did happen, he would let it, and then probably use it as an excuse for his own past or future infidelity.

That was not part of Charlie's business model. Playing spy for some middle-aged romantic triangle was one thing. She didn't want to accidentally produce private extra-marital therapy sessions.

"I'll tell her," he said again, "that I'm coming home Tuesday. And you follow her Monday, to see what she does. I'll set up some cameras in the house while she's out and about this afternoon, and then we'll have it all on video. I'll suddenly arrive home a day earlier than she thought and catch her. I need you there, and the video footage, otherwise it will be *he said, she said* in court."

"And if you have this proof? What then?"

"If she cheats on me with a man," he said, "I'm getting a divorce, simple as that. I'll have all your evidence to show to the judge. It'll go in my favour, and you'll be paid."

"You know you can just get a no-fault divorce now; I don't see the need for evidence. If you no longer want to be married, maybe the right thing to do is to have that conversation with Sophie."

"I do want to be married! But only if I can be sure it's an exclusive arrangement. You can help prove or disprove that."

Charlie thought long and hard about talking to Dave about trust, or in his case, lack of, but they now had a deadline. It was make or break tonight. Then she'd be shot of him.

"I'm sending your invoice today," she said. "That's part of our contract, which a judge would uphold long before you set foot in a divorce court."

"Uh—okay then," he timidly agreed. "See you soon."

"Fine," Charlie said, her frustration showing. "Ash will have the camera equipment ready for you. Pop into the office at lunchtime. You'll follow his instructions to the letter. Once they're in place, you're to stay away from the house, and our offices, for that matter. We'll be watching Sophie and the house. If she brings someone back tonight, I'll... I will call you and we can—We will monitor the situation from afar as necessary."

"Right, okay," he agreed. "This is a good plan, Ms Chan. It's just like a caper movie. It'll work."

"If you insist. But come tomorrow morning, Mr Phillips, we will no longer be working together."

"Agreed."

He hung up, apparently giddy at the prospect of catching a strange man in bed with his wife, which led Charlie to cover her face and scream. Clive heard her from the reception desk and got up to check on her. She met him at the door.

"Trouble, boss?" he asked.

She looked up at him with tired eyes, like she'd stayed up all night on a call that lasted all of ten minutes. "Where's Ash, do you know?"

"Due in at lunchtime." Clive flipped open a schedule book and tapped next to the entry he made for everyone's work-week. "Says, 'Paper mill.'"

"Of course, and Becca's on leave." Charlie groaned. She clapped her hands and stood up straight. "Right then. It'll be up to us."

"Us, boss?" he said.

"Clive," she said, "we are nearing the final, pathetic end of the Phillips case, but before that, we need to make some preparations. Sophie will recognise me, so I'll need you to put on your best going-out clothes and get ready for your first true detective mission."

"No offence, boss," he said, "but I've been doing proper detective work already. Even just by filing—"

"Let's call it spy work, then," she said. "The new, modern way of detective work: dressing up, blending in, and lying your pretty head off."

"Ah, like my little cameo as a drunk postman." He smiled at the prospect. "What are you looking for, broody, moody Moore, or a bit of Connery panache? I can go as far as Bros-nan, but I can't do Craig."

"What?"

"He was great, but the action... and my bones—"

"Whichever wore a suit and walked around with a hidden camera."

"That's very Moore. Do I need a handle? A codename?"

"We'll figure that out later," she said.

She was glad he was eager, but worried that he was a bit overly so. A lot was riding on, frankly, just blind luck. Their client needed Sophie Phillips to be lonely enough, desperate enough, and stupid enough to take a marriage-wrecking plunge the night before he returned from a business trip. Charlie believed it wouldn't happen, that Sophie Phillips was too headstrong and cemented in her own selfish but harmless ways. Hopefully, after tonight, she could prove it to Dave once and for all.

chapter
thirty-five

THE AGENCY HAD a long-standing contract with Rishi Khan, a local paper mill owner on the Dock Road, to watch over their premises, which had been previously targeted by arsonists. Ashley had drawn the short straw, thanks to Clive's fastidious scheduling. He was assigned to more or less babysit the mill and act as a fire safety officer, armed only with verbal warnings, good hair, and loose morals.

Having done so many lates, earlies, nights, and weekend overtime recently, he absolutely couldn't be bothered with it. He'd also matched on Tinder with someone this week and, after a quick message exchange, had bagged himself a hot date. He looked across to Becca trying to guess her mood and the likelihood she'd bow to his will. Or failing that, bribery. He approached her with a printout of their weekly schedule.

"You need to take this for me," he said. "I can't be doing another all-nighter for Rishi. I'll fall asleep."

"So, vote him out," she remarked.

"The paper man!" he corrected. She scoffed. "You know how he is— You've done this before."

"Yeah, once," she affirmed. "And that was enough. Honestly, this is *literally* what we hired Clive to do."

"Yeah, but he's not been cleared for solo work in the field

yet, and he's down to help Charlie tonight," Ash complained. "And we'd need to introduce him to Rishi's family, and his life, and the mill, and well, everything— I'd rather just do the job than that."

"What's the issue? You just want to vent at me? You can't wait until you get there to cry into the reams of kitchen roll that he has in stock? It's very absorbent."

Ash wrung his fingers. He was frustrated, but kept himself well-contained and reasoned. He had to tell the truth and risk his hopes on Rebecca's tide-like sympathies.

"I have a date."

"I hope she likes the smell of freshly milled paper," she remarked. "If she can endure that, then you've got a keeper."

"I'm not bringing her to the mill," he said.

"Why not?"

"Because that's not what dates are. That's work!"

"Yeah! You have a job!"

"I just need this once," he swore. "Please."

Rebecca realised what he was asking. He got on one knee with his hands clasped for dramatic effect. She stood over him, arms crossed in a stoic huff, tapping her tongue stud against the back of her teeth.

"Please," he begged. "Swap with me."

"Oh, Lord," she sighed. "Is this gonna happen every time you get swiped to the right?"

"N—" he almost denied, but had to bite his tongue. Being honest was a commitment that he couldn't duck out of halfway through his earnest plea for help. "I've been talking to this woman for a few days, yeah? She wants to meet up in person. It's the only chance I'll get for a while, you know?"

"Unless you wait, until, I don't know, the weekend maybe?"

"I can't. She's, err, married."

Rebecca glowered down at him. "And she's how old?"

"She's forty-two," he said. "But looks a lot younger."

"Okay," Rebecca sighed. "So, you want me to assist you in corrupting a married woman, and this somehow supersedes protecting a paranoid local businessman from potential arsonists?"

"Yeah, exactly that," he said. "What'll it take?"

"You're not even going to accept a no." She sighed. "Willing to leave a staple—a fixture—a *minority-owned* successful business exposed to arsonists and vandals and street urchins throwing poo at the windows, just so you can cop a feel with a MILF."

"You're objectifying!" he said. "C'mon, you know it's been too long. You miss old Rishi, don't you?"

"I literally do not remember what he looks like," she said. "You say Rishi, and there's only one face that pops into my head."

"That's not his fault," Ashley protested. "What'd you need? You must need something. I mean it, though. Can you think of something I can do to make it up to you? Just hold it over me for a while, I promise, as long as I'm able to, I'll honour it."

She tilted her lips in thought.

Ashley checked the time on his phone, which was running out. "I'll help you hook up."

"As if I'd let you," she snapped.

"I got more experience with what girls like," he boasted.

Rebecca rolled her entire head back and swung it around with a groan. "My price for this… It's gonna be worse than you could possibly imagine."

"You'll do it?" he exclaimed.

"It's gonna be *bad*."

Ashley's excitement faded just slightly, but he was still more grateful than he was afraid of what grim fate awaited him. He shook her hands in delight. "Say hi to Rishi for me, yeah?"

"Yeah," she said. "I'll tell him you got hurt taking down a

fire-starter prowling around on the early shift. See if it gets us a better hourly rate."

"Just tell him I hurt my face," he said. "He knows that's my real meal ticket. He'll be full of sympathy."

"Knock, knock," Dave said as he entered the office.

Ash realised he had work to do and fist-bumped Becca. "Come on in," Ash responded with a cheery smile. He led Dave to their store room, fitted with floor-to-ceiling racking and all manner of audio/visual and electronic equipment.

"We don't normally lend out this stuff. I want you to pinky promise you'll look after it as though it was your new-born daughter."

"Yes, of course."

Ash gave Dave a detailed crash course in discreet camera surveillance. In terms of equipment he didn't give Dave the agency's crown jewels, but their 'spare' stuff was still top of the range. Dave left soon after with an impressive haul of cameras, wires, transmitters and the knowledge of how to use them. Ash said a silent prayer as he showed Dave out, hoping that at least half the stuff would make it back intact.

The remainder of the afternoon passed without incident. Ash left to get changed in preparation for his meet-up with the potential Mrs Powell, while Becca got herself prepared for a long night in a rank old mill with an overbearing client. It was one of the simplest jobs, but also very mundane and degrading. She decided to dedicate her time on the job to thinking up the most ridiculous, embarrassing, and demeaning task for Ashley to complete as payment. She drove out to the paper mill with a big smile.

chapter
thirty-six

THE DETECTIVES that made up Charlie Chan & Co. Detective
Agency weren't on the clock non-stop just because their
suspects and tracking targets were always up to something.
Their job wasn't in crime prevention. That was a different sort
of work, which they performed sparingly and usually for
favours instead of payment. When their time at work was
over, their time in life resumed and they indulged in each of
their own passive hobbies and habits.

Charlie attended a mixed-gender jiu-jitsu class to expand
her repertoire of personal combat skills as a way to hone her
body, centre her mind, and remain ahead of the competition.

Rebecca dodged her parents by couch surfing with friends
or went on dates in secret, until the morning, when she would
come back angry and bitter and ready for vengeance, which
she funnelled into her work as motivation.

Clive was a borderline retiree, and just watched the telly
all evening with his wife when work wasn't on his mind. He
was also fastidious and held a strong work ethic, so he spent
his time working on his IT literacy and wasn't averse to
coming in at the crack of dawn to run a vacuum and duster
over the office a few times a week.

Ash, meanwhile, was Liverpool's great Tinder filter, and

he'd matched and subsequently arranged a date with someone he was very keen to meet. He was a solid right-swipe for most of the ladies seeking hookups across the city. His profile was professionally structured. It was a skill that he'd even contemplated selling as a coaching package to lonely chaps who wanted a leg up on the far better-looking men who took their profile pictures with a toilet in the mirror's reflection, and still reeled in more requests than they needed. Ash's hobby, aside from fashion, was using his fashion sense to win at the dating game.

Ash also got a lot of attention from men, mainly due to his bold sartorial choices on a night out. As one would-be suitor noted, he was simply too well-dressed to be straight.

Ash's biggest gripe with app dates was not knowing if the other party would A) look remotely like their photo and B) actually show up. It was always a gamble to see if an accepted meeting would actually happen, or if the girl would make different plans and *forget* to announce them to the other men who set aside a time and place for her.

Ash was used to rejection. He'd long since developed past the point of getting his blood pressure up over a simple miscommunication or missed connection. Not every dodge was malicious. Sometimes it was just bad timing.

Which was why Ash planned his meetups in places that weren't too expensive but not too trashy, like Zanzibar. It was a bar-cum-club that had taken residence in a former bank.

The owners had clearly thought long and hard about the trendy look they were trying to achieve, but the budget hadn't stretched to decent lighting—the whole place seemingly illuminated by a single 20-watt bulb. They didn't serve anything on draught, just fancy bottled beers, wine by the expensive glass, and a menu of cocktails as long as his arm. And leg.

A local band—one of hundreds—was playing some

smooth alt-rock in the corner while Ash enjoyed a relative distance from their noise in a booth.

He checked his phone again, at least once per minute, for any updates from his absentee date or emergencies from work. Nothing from either. He didn't want to be *that* lonely guy scanning his phone at the far end of a bar for too long, so he put it away and inspected the scene. If the girl he'd arranged to meet didn't show, maybe another opportunity would present itself. There was a sizeable crowd. Plenty of girl groups around, as well as some couples. All the ones alone were guys like him.

Ash was skilled with people. It was what he brought, aside from an apt hand at disguises and glam-ups, to the team. Rebecca was a computer hacker, a *digital* hacker. He was *analogue*, and could get a read on someone at a glance and gaslight them into telling him truths they were otherwise sworn to protect.

Then his date arrived. Ash was more about girls his age, or reasonably younger. But thanks to spending the past few weeks investigating the Philipps case, he'd found himself thinking more and more about older ladies—in Ashley's lexicon, that meant thirty and over. Older women had a charm about them, which was unmistakable and often hard to resist. And they had keener eyes for fashion as well. The prospect of exploring his recent fixation intrigued and excited him, and he breathed an audible sigh of relief that she'd come.

Leslie Redding sashayed towards Ash with a wry smirk and wiggle in her hips. She was a successful businesswoman who helped those with access to cash find corners of the city centre ripe for development. To him, she was a potential lynchpin holding together the delicate framework of a complicated and city-shaking case of adultery—and, if he played his cards right, his first cougar.

"Evening," Ash casually greeted, as he stood to kiss her cheek. She rubbed his biceps as she took a seat.

"Good evening to you, too," she said. She held his gaze as she adjusted her dress, a test to see if he would look at her chest. He did.

Ashley had read a considerable amount of background information on Leslie, thanks mainly to Becca's incredible skills. So it was understandable that visions of her dilapidated, poor old husband walking his yappy dog flashed through his mind, but Ash stayed calm. His face was a facade, a part of his outfit, and he could keep it one way even while feeling another. He could sit on a drawing pin and not twitch an eyebrow for the entire evening if needed. He could never be caught lying, but could always pick out a liar.

"So, Ash? Real name or moniker?"

"Short for Ashley," he replied with confidence, just a hint of allure. He had a name that was strange for men and was proud of it.

She interpreted that confidence positively and made a signalling move. She straightened her back to raise her head and look at him at an angle—no longer head-on and face-to-face but in a sort of chase-ready manner. She was a reverse flirter. She wanted him to reel her in, and he obliged.

Because he couldn't help himself.

"I'm glad you came," he said, remaining casual.

"It's nice here," she said. "Haven't been for ages, thought it was an interesting choice for a date…" Her eyes drifted a little past him, over to where the music came from.

"They playing your song?" he asked.

"Oh, no," she confirmed. "Made me nostalgic. I was in a band in sixth form. Coming to places like this makes me think I can sap some of the youth off these strangers and get back to those days for a while."

Ash feigned a nervous look. "Did you swipe right because you want to sap my youth?"

She smirked at his playfulness. "I'm considering it. But I get the feeling it's a mutual curiosity. We both know you could set your filter plus or minus three years and never work your way through the results."

"I could… but where would the fun be in that?"

"It's good to have fun, but people need to set themselves on a path early and stick to it. You blink and twenty years have gone. That's a lesson you kids aren't going to learn," she said.

"I already learned it," he said. "Not at uni."

"Oh, pardon me," she said. "I assumed you were a student."

"I'm a working man about town," he confirmed. "A… photographer. Not a thing that needs a degree but always needs to be done well. You work for yourself?"

"Yes," she said.

"And do you party?"

She smirked. "Not often."

"And the partners you look for," he asked, pointing to a group of students dancing near the band, "could you teach them… a lesson or two, about life and love?"

"I don't have the time to teach what needs to be learned," she mused, as if she'd thought of the line and practised saying it many times in other flirtatious exchanges.

Ash already knew she was disloyal to her husband. No reason to pry into that, but rather exploit what loyalties she did have outside of work or home.

"Just how much experience do you look for on a…CV?" he asked.

"Is your own business not doing so well?" she asked. "Are you working it out of the back of your car?"

"The back of my house, more like," he said. "Aren't all the most successful start-ups born in a garage?"

"That might not be so true," she said.

He'd pushed just the right button, engaged her as a professional and, despite her reluctance, as one who thrived on sharing her *experience* with others. She took a slim plastic wallet out of her bra and slipped a business card out of it.

"My oh my— Ah, property," he said with a slight chuckle. "That's not what I was expecting."

"Really?" she asked. "What did you think I worked in?"

"Honestly?" he said. "Being in a band, scoping local talent —I thought I was talking to a producer of some kind. Someone who highlights the shining stars in the night sky of Liverpool."

She piqued an eyebrow at his take. A lucky stroke or a perfect read, either way, Ash felt like he had an in. And he took that in to talk some more, flirt a lot, and learn a little. If Charlie found out that he'd hooked up with a target from an investigation, he decided at that moment that it was better to beg for forgiveness than ask for permission.

chapter
thirty-seven

CHARLIE AND CLIVE pulled up across the street from the Ivory Staircase. With Ash supposedly tied up at the paper mill and Becca enjoying a rare night off, Charlie was unable to mount her usual full-scale stakeout with a complete team and equipped mobile surveillance lab. It was time to break in the newbie.

"How do I look?" Clive asked.

He stood semi-hunched in the back and then capitulated to going down on a knee. His suit was grey, but distinguished and gentlemanly. Not the dark and daring tuxedo he had hoped for, but it was what they could get from a charity shop in his size that afternoon. Ash managed to flair it up as best he could with a new hem, distinct gold threading along the pockets to draw the eyes to Mr Aston's old soldier frame, and a paisley cravat in place of a tie.

It also served to distract from the coronation decor on his lapel, which housed a tiny wireless camera, thumb-sized but well-hidden and pressed all the way through to the inner lining of his collar. His pants were neatly pleated but widened out at the bottom like he'd come from church in the 70s, to party in the 80s, and the entire ensemble was capped off with freshly shined wingtip shoes.

His hair was greased back and coloured a tone darker than usual to hide the greys, but not all of it, which gave a sort of fade from the top down to his sideburns. Ash had tried to touch him up with a bit of foundation to hide his wrinkles, but that was a step too far for a man who'd been in a war.

Charlie checked her phone, which had the video feed from his camera. It was cast at a wide panoramic angle that she could modify and control at will. When she saw herself, she adjusted based on the angle he was at.

"You look great," she said. "Turn a little to your left." The camera swivelled with Clive. "Right there—that's your dead-ahead. So, when you hear me say dead ahead, I want you to turn like this so I can get a look."

"Got it," he said. He memorised the position where his hips and legs and shoulders all locked together. "Any other keywords?"

"For you," she said, "if you need a fast out, have to go, or if you've completely lost sight of her leaving the building but you're tied up in a talk, or caught off guard, just say, 'This music's too loud' and I'll swing by to pick you up."

"Seems fitting," he said. "I might just say that anyway— don't come on the first signal, wait for a second."

"If you lose track of her," she continued, "go to the bar and I'll retrace the footage. If you spot her, say 'I need a drink' and head for her."

"Right," he said.

"Your mission is to observe, not to engage," Charlie explained. "Hopefully she'll have a few drinks, an uneventful night, and return home incident free. We'll then be able to give David the good news. He'll be surprised, I'm sure, that she didn't actually cheat on him like he thought she would and will demand proof, which we will have, that she has remained loyal and honest to him despite the circumstances."

"So, this is to prove her innocence," Clive said, "and we're still getting paid for it?"

"Yes."

"And everybody wins," he confirmed.

"Everybody goes back to normal."

"What if," he said, "she does get flirty? Finds a lad who loosens her up with some drinks and slips out with his hand around her shoulder and a glint in his eye?"

"Then you will need to enact plan B," she said, "which will be intercepting said lad, acting like a drunk London tourist looking for the studio where the Beatles met, and scare her off to head home alone. She'll reconcile with David and be glad to have him, ergo a happy marriage, and I'll pick you up before anyone gets hurt."

"Except the chap who throws a punch at me," he said. "And me, if I hit back. I'll lie down if that happens. My code word will be 'Take me to the hospital, please.'"

"Let's make plan A work," Charlie said. "Are you ready?"

"Do we have a high-five thing?" Clive asked with his hand out. "Or is it just yes and go?"

Charlie pointed at the door. Clive hopped out of the van, adjusted his suit, and sauntered down the street to get in line for the club. It was a quiet night, and being a man, he was passed over once or twice before getting in. Once he was inside, he smoothly operated his way across the floor toward the main stage, in search of Sophie. He held his hand up to his ear and tapped on the earpiece, flesh-toned and hard to spot in the dark.

"This music *is* too loud, you know," he muttered. "And that's my free one."

"Can you find her on the ground floor?" Charlie asked. Her voice was clear, but compared to the noise it was hard to hear without him pressing his whole palm against the side of his head to cup his ear. He passed it off as an adjustment of his hair and swept it back to look around again for some company. And he found some. Most of the single ladies that weren't on the dance floor, together in large groups, were taking up space around the bar, distant from one another.

Sophie was alone, as suspected. Her girlfriends had betrayed her, and she was clearly struggling to recalibrate to her new situation. Her husband was on his way home to ruin whatever fun she might have been having while he was gone. Leslie, who'd helped her get into the VIP room before and was now in a *something* with Anna, was absent and unresponsive, meaning she couldn't even enjoy her last night out in relative luxury. She was positioned at the bar, leaning in. She wore a sleek red dress with plenty of tied-up holes along the side and thin, strappy stockings that hugged her toned legs down to her high-heeled feet.

"I've got my eye on a prize," he said.

Charlie interpreted his message and confirmed it on her camera.

"Target in sight," she said. "Move in."

"Aye, aye," he affirmed.

He made his way up to the bar, spotting some glances under the ruffled curls of a few other women who were a few drinks down, making him look a few years younger. He kept his chest centred at Sophie, which made him miss the oncoming traffic just off to his right side.

"Sorry mate," a man said.

Clive turned around and was about to move away with a courteous bow, when he felt something wet hit his jacket. Just a splash of a drink the young man was carrying.

"No worries," Clive said. "It's crowded here. Could happen to anyone."

"Still, my apologies," the man said. He was a cheerful man, dark skin and slightly unshaved scalp, in a long sleeve shirt and waistcoat. "Having a good night?" he asked.

"Really good," Clive said, slicking his hair back again. "Figured I'd see what all the fuss is about. I heard the Beatles played here once, may as well cross this off my bucket list."

"Everyone's come in and out of here," he said. "Townsend and Frankie too."

"Well, they aren't showing that local pride now," Clive said, minding the music in the air. "Cheers, mate."

"Cheers," he said, and walked on up to the bar and sat next to Sophie, who was very glad to see him.

Clive hung back and walked away in a side-step to keep his camera on them just long enough for Charlie to call in.

"Clive?" she said.

"We're in luck, boss," Clive said as he turned to talk to no one. "I can drink through the rest of my shift in—"

"I know that man," she said. "Keep your distance."

"Right," Clive said.

Ordering a drink, he took it to a dark corner and turned on his security guard mode. He kept his eyes on the player who was holding Sophie's attention and was clearly familiar not just with the bartender but with his mark as well.

Charlie rubbed her forehead in the van, somewhere between upset and confused about how Dion kept showing up when she least expected and least wanted to see him. If anyone was going to prove David right, it'd be him…

chapter
thirty-eight

Ash watched as their Uber pulled away, then turned to look at Leslie Redding's double-fronted detached house.

"Second thoughts?" Leslie asked.

"Not at all."

"Come on in, it's freezing."

Leslie was about as far away from Ash's usual type as you could get. Given that recently his usual type was usually saying no, or worse, ghosting him when he did swipe right, he just needed a little boost of confidence to get back in the saddle, and feel good about himself again.

Besides, it was for research, or at least that's what he told himself, and that excuse made up for whatever mistakes he ended up helping her make tonight.

He adjusted his shirt cuffs, took a deep breath, and followed her through the front door into the expansive hall.

"This man a friend of yours?" Ash asked, pointing to one of many photos of her with her husband in their younger years. He seemed to look the same despite how young she was in the ascending chronology of photos displayed on the wall.

"Sort of," she said. She held out her hand to show her wedding ring properly. "But he's not here anymore…"

"I'm not an accessory to something, am I?" Ash asked. "I'm no good with alibis on the fly. I need a script."

"No, no," she said. "He's alive. Staying with his mother while we work things out. Even if he were here, he's not what I'd call suitable company for the evening."

"Aha," Ash nodded.

Ash placed his house keys and phone on the sideboard in the hall, signalling his attention was wholly and completely on his date for the night. He took a dramatic breath in and looked at her.

"I gotta say, doing this makes me feel like kind of the bad guy. Taking a woman like you away from a man like that…" He made a move and put his hands on her shoulders. "But good girls like bad boys, don't they?"

"We do," she said with an excited laugh.

She pulled him in, and they kissed their way to her bedroom, taking breaks to catch their balance against the wall and awkwardly undress. When they got to the master suite, she pushed Ash onto the bed with some force, which left him a bit stunned. She eyed his bare chest with clear desire.

"Take a breather," she said with a lustful sigh. "I need to get out of my work clothes and… get to *work*."

"Sounds like we'll be busy all night," Ash said.

"Make yourself comfortable."

She winked at him, shut the door to her bathroom, and tumbled the lock. A moment later, the shower began to flow. Ash estimated that she would be in there for at least ten minutes to clean up fully and slip into something more in line with high-society infidelity, like a Satanist robe or a druidic animal hide. He'd seen it all and not done much. His line usually went up to bondage, and if it required that he spend time suspended in the air by belts and hinges, he opted out and went home in a cab.

He had more to do than lie back and think of England. He got up and quietly moved around the room to look for clues.

Feeling literally and figuratively naked as he padded around in nothing more than a tight pair of boxer jocks. He was after some sort of connection to David Phillips. The chances of Leslie having this evidence, if indeed it existed, were slight, but Ash wasn't one to leave a stone unturned, and this stone wanted to party.

He went from dresser to drawer, wardrobe to vanity unit, looking for something she might keep hidden where her husband wouldn't search. He had a feeling that of all the rooms in the house, Mr Redding probably used the bedroom the least. He had the posture of a man who slept in a recliner night after night.

The outlook was poor. Ash didn't want to risk looking like a thief or a snoop by not being in the bedroom once she came out and was ready, but he had to take the chance and find something like an office.

He went downstairs in a rush and tried to find the kitchen first. It would be his excuse—had to get his energy up, it was his routine, whatever would work on her. He took a crusty chilled bagel out of the fridge and held onto it as a prop for his alibi while he found his way into a closed-off and dark alcove just under the stairs. There was a cold computer on a desk and rows of filing cabinets. It looked like a sad hovel of an office, which meant it probably belonged to Mr Redding, or was a shared space that just happened to suit him more than her.

Ash scanned every paper he could find, searching one desk drawer after another, until he found something. The bottom drawer of a dented and scratched metal filing cabinet. It wasn't locked, but it was stiff and resisted his first attempt to open it. Inside were meticulously labelled dividers, each folder marked with a building name or address. Ash's eye caught the names of Leslie's properties—The Ivory Staircase, The Mariner's Arms, Seagram Building—recognising them from Rebecca's background check. But behind those folders were many more... All of them were properties belonging to David Phillips.

Leslie was collecting a vast amount of material about commercial property owned by a competitor. But for what exactly, Ash wasn't sure. He fingered through the other folders in the cabinet drawer and found much more than he expected. Folders with copies of receipts, leases, land registry reports, and land searches filled each one. The minutes of City Council meetings, Planning Permission documents, Buildings' Control certificates along with a selection of flash drives he assumed would contain more documentation or photographs.

Just a cursory glance at the documents relating to a property on London Road showed Dave had intentionally bypassed credit checks so someone could get a lease when they really shouldn't have. If Leslie's intention was to blackmail Dave, she could make a fair penny.

Ash pulled out another folder. The first page was a photocopy of a Change of Use application form for the building that now hosted Ends Meat—the restaurant Charlie had tailed Sophie to—handwritten notes filled all the blank space. Names of the City Council members and Building Regs staff and, next to them, amounts of money. £20k here, £15k there. It seemed the going rate to get planning permission for turning a dormant office building into a restaurant wouldn't leave much change from sixty grand.

Ash continued his search through the stacks of papers and found a pattern, a manifesto of sorts. He scanned all the documents, not as individual acts of blackmail and leverage but in the aggregate—and quickly realised how they all linked—and his formerly tense, flight-ready muscles went limp. She was hoarding a treasure trove of evidence from people who, in one way or another, had aided and abetted illicit land and building purchases.

Dave was knee-deep in the muck of a real estate scam that

had clearly inflated commercial property values across Liverpool City Centre. Apparently, Dave and a cabal of offshore holding companies would buy all the properties at suboptimal prices and then sit on them to force a shortage. They were all the same, every folder. But there was a twist. Leslie, rather than being the quintessential estate agent, happy to rip people off and earn a commission no matter the human cost, was in fact in possession of a significant body of evidence that could expose the whole thing.

"The whole point of planning permission is to stop this from happening," Ash muttered.

"That's exactly where the trouble tends to start," Leslie replied.

Ash turned, red-handed, to a leather-bound handcuff-holding dominatrix blocking his only way out. And she looked angry. Not play angry. An angry with no safe words.

"All right, wait," Ash began as she heel-clicked towards him. "This looks bad and I'm gonna be honest—you're a hero for this."

"Oh, I'm no hero," she said. She lifted the handle of a heavy-looking leather whip up to his throat. "I'm a *baaad girl*."

"I'm sure you are," he nodded. "But... I—I'm a private detective. That's all this is. I was gonna put all this back and forget it—it's not my case."

"You one of their mutts, then?"

"Hey, I'm on your side, okay? You—you get yours. I'm just not here for it."

"You gonna bark for your master, little doggie?"

"Okay, let's walk that kind of talk back to the bedroom where it belongs, okay? I'm not—"

She cracked the whip hard enough to slam the cabinet door shut. The wind off the swing hit Ash's naked chest skin and perked his nipples up like terrified diamonds.

"I'm on a case," he admitted, desperate to save himself, or

at least get her to hold back a little. "Sophie Phillips. You know her. I'm investigating whether she's cheating on her husband with a man."

"And what's it to you?" she demanded.

"A paycheck," he chuckled.

She stepped back, eyes wide and disbelieving. Ash thought he was free and loosened up a little. Then she got defensive—almost scared.

"You're him, aren't you?" she asked fretfully. "The Wedding Veil Killer!"

"The what?"

"You're after me," she said, arming herself with the whip in both hands, "and then you'll go after her! Aren't you!"

"That's insane! Why would—"

She leaned forward with a grunt and swung her whip down like it was ten times the real weight. The leather-barbed tail clapped against Ash's shoulder and froze him in place. His voice squeaked out at first and then burst into a manly yell.

"I need to lock you up," she said, grabbing her cuffs again, "for the good of all womankind!"

She grunted and lunged to wrangle his hand and slapped one of the wrist cuffs around it, then latched it immediately to the nearest thing—a handle on one of the filing cabinet drawers. Ash was locked down and at her mercy, and she proved how lacking in mercy she was by smacking his arse through his boxer jocks with the handle of her whip a few times with ferocious golf club swings. Ash took the blows and gripped his hand hard from the pain.

"Not so hot now, are you?" she shouted.

"My arse is hotter than a kitchen fire," he said. He caught his breath and picked up the bagel. "Speaking of—you might think you've caught me now, but take care when you make a cup of tea." He wiggled the bagel over his shoulder and cackled with his best *evil serial killer straight off a daytime soap opera* laugh.

And she believed him. What had he done to her kettle? To her kitchen?!

Nothing, but it got her to run out of the room and check. Ash had already clocked how flimsy the filing cabinet handles were when he'd almost pulled one clean off earlier, in his haste to look inside. With a sudden, violent pull, he jerked his cuffed wrist away from the drawer and the handle ripped free. The pain in his wrist as the cuffs chafed his skin was just slightly worse than the echoing sting in his backside.

Wearing nothing more than his underwear and a pair of fluffy handcuffs dangling from his wrist, he made a run for the front door. Retrieving his keys and phone, he was out of the torture house before Leslie could get dressed to chase him. Not his smoothest exit, but a viable one. And he left richer in knowledge as he jogged through the suburbs of Liverpool in his undies, ignoring the car horns and the lascivious cat calls from a bunch of girls who slowed down in their Ford Focus to admire his physique.

Leslie was a justice-driven real estate crime fighter with a kink for punishing evil in or out of bed. If they'd met under different circumstances, they'd probably get along quite well at night. Moreover, she wasn't involved in Sophie's romantic life. Rather, she was using Sophie to get to Dave. Ash needed to update the team. He also needed some new clothes to go with his underpants, because tonight's ensemble was lost in action…

chapter
thirty-nine

"NICE NIGHT FOR A WALK," Clive said in passing to the bouncer on the front door. And to Charlie. It wasn't one of their agreed phrases, but the meaning was clear. He was on the move, after his target, but not by her side. This was quickly confirmed when she observed Sophie coming out, snuggling into the shoulder of her escort for the night: Dion.

"Keep this distance," Charlie instructed. She was in the van, juggling between the camera on her phone and starting the engine of the van. "I'm heading over."

"You said you know this bloke?" he whispered. He waited for a response and kept his eyes and ears open for an approaching van across the road.

"What was that?" Charlie asked over the sound of the van's rumbling engine.

Clive took a brief detour into an alley and spoke more clearly. "You know him?" Then he walked back out and kept his pace, but with a bit of distance added on.

"Sort of," she explained. "We've crossed paths... in there, before, as a matter of fact. He's got a taste for older women."

"Easy pickup then," Clive said. "Call David and tell him to get ready."

"No, Clive—you need to stop him."

"Eh?" he said. "Isn't the whole point—?"

"Just trust me on this," Charlie said. "Call it a hunch, but I think we need to shut this one down."

"All right," he said.

Clive pulled off the cravat and pulled his shirttails out of his trousers, preparing to play the role of wandering drunk, but then recalled that he'd spoken to the man just minutes before. Acting like a belligerent stranger wouldn't pass. Their exchange had been brief, but would still be fresh in his memory. Clive followed them to the car park, where Sophie got up close and personal with Dion. Clive hid around a corner and watched.

"What's happening?" Charlie asked.

"We're at the car park up the road," Clive said. "I'll narrate for you."

"Okay. I'm almost there."

"They're talking."

"Good."

"She's making a move!"

"Quick, interrupt them—"

"No. No, he rebuffed her."

"What?"

"I think she's had quite a few drinks. She staggered, and he caught her. She's laughing now. He looks concerned. She looks like she's playing it off."

Charlie beeped her horn, urging a black cab that blocked the road to move on. She grew frustrated with the two passengers as they stood at the driver's window and fumbled in their pockets for some cash.

"Wait— Hold on." Clive continued to watch. "He's walking her to a different car."

Charlie's phone rang. She glanced at the screen; it was Dave.

"Hold on, I'm getting a phone call."

"I'll keep watch."

Charlie put Clive on hold and accepted the call from David.

"Hello?"

"Hello, Ms Chan," David said, very close to the receiver. He was hidden away as planned in what sounded to Charlie like the inside of a wardrobe. "Is Sophie on her way yet?"

"Ye—possibly," she said.

"With a man?"

"There… is a man with her."

"Really?"

He sounded weirdly excited by the prospect. "I'm actually trying to monitor the situation right now and I can't while I'm on the phone. Can I call you back?"

"All right, all right," he said. "Let them show up. I'm holed up at a friend's place, just round the corner. Ring when you're at the house."

She hung up quickly and got connected with Clive again. She swore at herself for losing the video feed from Clive's camera. She was good at plenty of things, but not all at once. She really needed Ash to run the audio-visual tech, whilst she directed the team. Turned out, all the kit in the van wasn't as important as who was in it.

"Clive, you there?" she asked.

"They're on the move," he reported. "Coming out of the car park in a black BMW 1 series."

"I'm swinging by," she said. "I've a good idea where they're going. We need to get eyes there, fast."

"I'm at the kerb," he said. "Slow down and I'll get in."

"You'd better," she said. She got to the car park entrance and saw Clive on the pavement. She slowed down, while he ran up beside the van and pawed the door handle. She unlocked it, and he jumped in, sliding the door shut behind him.

"What happened?" she asked.

"Looked like he was helping her out," he explained. "'Oh,

you shouldn't be driving, I'll take you home.' That sort of thing."

"Why didn't you stop them?" she asked.

"We bumped into each other at the bar," he explained. "Would've been hard to handle that exchange."

"Right," she said. "And I've met him before, too."

"So now we need to change our faces up," he remarked. "That's the one thing I'd rather not do."

"Roger Moore wore makeup," she said. "Don't be a sissy."

Charlie cut some corners and blitzed the wrong way up some one-way streets to reach the Phillips' house ahead of the 2017-plated hatchback carrying the lady of the manor. Clive got out and hid around the corner to observe, while Charlie looped around to avoid detection and parked up on the opposite side of the street. She kept her eyes focused on the rearview mirror and waited for the target vehicle to turn up the street.

A few minutes later, Dion approached and pulled in along the kerb. Clive leaned around the walled corner and watched. Dion helped Sophie out, chatted with her a bit, then extended his hand and invited her to go on ahead. She tugged at his shirt, begging him to join her, but he wouldn't relent. Chivalry, it seemed, wasn't completely dead and buried.

"Looks like she's going in alone," Clive said.

Charlie sighed with relief. Over not watching Dion go into a strange woman's house to further immolate her marital relationship, or just because the alternative would have been more stressful, she didn't know. She was just glad the night seemed to be over.

They continued to watch as Sophie took out a napkin and pen from her handbag and, using the car's roof, wrote something on it, then wetted a corner with a kiss and folded it over like a crude seal. She handed it to him and hip-swayed her way up the paved path, through the open gate, and disappeared into her house.

Dion watched her enter and remained standing there until the door shut.

He walked back towards his car with a spring in his step and pointed his key fob at his car.

Bleep. Bleep. The car unlocked.

Charlie and Clive watched as Dion got into the driver's seat. One hand on the steering wheel, he leant forward as if to start the ignition.

But he paused, then reached down below their line of sight and retrieved the napkin.

A moment later, he was out of the car and walking towards Sophie's front door.

"Shit," Charlie said and pulled out her phone.

She clicked the call button and put the phone to her ear.

"We're outside the house."

"On my way," Dave replied.

chapter
forty

CHARLIE FLICKED on the bank of monitors in the back of the van.

"I was really hoping we wouldn't need all this," Charlie said, as she positioned herself in front of the array of audio-visual equipment in the back of the van.

One by one, black-and-white images appeared on each screen, showing various rooms in the Phillips' house. Dave had followed Ashley's instructions to the letter and set up the cameras correctly. Clive and Charlie now had the unenviable task of watching Sophie's infidelity in high fidelity.

"OK. Credit where credit's due, he's done a good job positioning the cameras. We've got video, but we're not going to be able to hear anything."

A terse rap of knuckles announced the arrival of a new team member.

Clive slid the door open to find Dave's eager face peering in.

"Jump in, close the door."

Clive scooted over to the driver's seat and indicated the empty folding camping chair he'd just vacated. "Take a pew. They're in the kitchen."

Dave craned his neck to look at the four screens partially

blocked by Charlie's head. His bedroom. The guest room, the landing, and the kitchen, in which Sophie was clinking glasses of Prosecco with a tall, dark stranger.

"I'm sorry," Charlie offered.

"Don't be. This is what I've been imagining. It's—It's almost a relief to know I wasn't going mad," Dave replied matter-of-factly. "Who is he?"

"Goes by the name of Dion. Regular at the Ivory Staircase," Clive offered. "That's where he, err, met your wife tonight."

"What's he like then?"

"Young, fit, and strong," Clive said as Dave flexed what, in a good light, could be generously described as his biceps.

Charlie glanced down at Dave's leg, which was jigging up and down.

"Dave, you seem a little on edge. You don't have to be here. We can send you the recordings."

Dave glanced from Charlie to Clive and back again, all the while chewing frantically on his gum like a raver at a late-90s Cream night. "Just. You know. Trying to deal with the fact that the wife has brought another fella home."

"You have intent. We can end this now," Charlie tried one last time to save her client from humiliation.

"If I'm wrong, I'll pay anyway. You've done nothing but great work in assisting me, but I need to know. I have to know. If she sends him away with nothing more than a–a peck on the cheek for giving her a lift home, then we're done."

Charlie held Dave's gaze for a moment longer than was comfortable for them both. She got it. She really did. It was a difficult thing to witness. But Dave's whole demeanour, his sweaty brow, and the fact that it was absolutely freezing outside, led her to believe he'd snorted a line or two. Brilliant. A coked-up cuckold who's spoiling to play superhero was not what she wanted to deal with tonight.

Charlie turned back to the screens. The needlessly long and impatient battle to catch a bored housewife cheating behind her husband's back with someone other than their pre-agreed cheating partner was about to end. She concentrated on the strict factual matter of what was underway and suppressed her dark worry that they could be unwittingly watching the Wedding Veil Killer in action. There was a cheating housewife about to be caught and a strangely paranoid husband, both wanting and not wanting to watch the definitive moment.

Sophie and Dion left the kitchen. All four screens were showing empty rooms, as the amorous couple, they all assumed, were ascending the stairs.

"I chose a good spot in the bedroom," David said. "Right between our wedding picture and a picture of us moving into the house. It's somewhere she'd never look."

"Great thinking, and sorry again," Charlie said.

David leaned forward to get a better view of the bedroom monitor. Charlie looked over to Clive, who kept himself primed to intervene should their troubled client become a liability.

"Should be arriving at the master bedroom soon," Clive offered.

Still, the monitors remained devoid of life. No movement was detected in the kitchen, living room, on the landing, or in the master bedroom. No one else was around. Charlie didn't like the delay. It felt like they were being led astray somehow.

"There they are," David said.

Charlie looked up. The pair entered the bedroom. The camera provided a full view of the room, all the way to the half-open walk-in wardrobe and ensuite bathroom. Clive put his binoculars away and sat tight in the driver's seat.

They all watched as Sophie entered first, giddy and excited. She must have kicked off her heels downstairs, because Dion seemed much taller as he held her hand and followed her into the room.

"Showtime."

To David's apparent excitement, a kiss between his wife and another man happened on his very own bed. He gasped in a bit of shock, but not disgust, and continued watching.

Charlie also watched the screen, but started to drift away. It was a fairly mundane scene as far as scandalous content was concerned. Their clothes hadn't even come off yet.

After some minutes of making out, the pair split apart and started talking. They couldn't hear what was said, but it ended with Sophie smiling and walking away from the camera's view.

"That's her walk-in wardrobe," David said. "She must be getting changed."

"Should we go in yet?" Clive asked. "It's starting to look like—"

"No," David said. "No, it's not enough. I've looked into this. A lot. Right now, it's not quite adultery as written in the law, and in fact, this could be construed as an invasion. Which would mean this fella's facing criminal charges if we brought in the police now, Sophie might change her story and say she was forced into it. I can't have that."

"There needs to be very apparent verbal and physical consent expressed for this to be considered adultery," Charlie said. "There are more ways out of that kind of claim than there are into it."

"There's really only one way into it," Clive said. "It's not going to be pleasant. To watch, I mean."

"But it's important we do," David said.

Charlie watched Dion as he undressed one piece of clothing at a time. First his jacket, then his waistcoat, and finally his shirt. His naked torso was in stunningly good shape. He looked like a man who could run miles and lift stones. A healthy lifestyle advocate, with the proof of advantage sauntering into view not soon after.

Sophie appeared wearing something unexpected, causing David to mumble in confusion, and caused Charlie to sit straight up.

A wedding dress.

"Shit. Call the police," Charlie said.

"Wha— Are you sure?" he asked. "Is this… courtroom worthy?"

"Yes." She nodded.

"Oh, she hasn't looked at that in years," he said. "It's a bit tight around her waist now—"

"Shut up and call the police. Now!"

This time Dave did what he was asked. He took out his phone and dialled 999 as they continued to watch the screen.

Dion looked her over, inspected her, and even posed her with hands together like she was holding a bouquet. The whole time, she looked like she was enjoying herself. Then he had her lift her dress up so he could peek at what was underneath. She twirled for him and went back into the wardrobe.

While she was gone, he paced around and inspected the room. He kept his pants on and his top garments at the ready nearby, all neatly piled and ready to throw on like he was just about to head out. He wasn't doing the prep work expected of a swinging playboy in the den of a lioness for the night. At the very least, Charlie expected to see the shape of his butt through some boxer briefs, but he remained trousers-on down to his shoes.

And he kept wringing his hands, like he was nervous. Or testing his grip.

"Is the front door unlocked?" Charlie asked. "If the police don't get here, we will have to go in."

"Wait a moment," David said. "This— It could just be like a— I don't know, a consultation? Are you sure this bloke is all he's supposed to be? He's not some poof designer obsessed with clothing, like?"

"Clive," Charlie said, "can you run up and make sure the doors aren't locked?"

"Just run up?" he asked.

She nodded urgently.

"Right. Mate, you got your keys?"

"Uh, sure," he said. "But don't—"

David had his hand in his pocket to fish his keys out, but stopped. He was distracted when Sophie reappeared wearing her wedding underwear —stockings, brassiere, white lace pants, and on top of her head, she wore her old wedding veil crumpled from the drawer it was tucked into, now spread over her hair. Dion moved toward her and pulled her closer to the bed. He lowered the veil down over her face. She looked uncertain, but still enthralled. Dion's back was to the camera, just enough to block out most of Sophie's figure as he lowered her gently onto the bed.

"What's happening?" David asked.

"Keys, now," Charlie demanded.

Clive climbed back and forced them out of David's pocket and exited the van.

Charlie sprung up and followed him out.

"What—?" David exclaimed, as he found himself alone in the van.

David couldn't take his eyes off the live feed. Sophie was fully underneath Dion, her arms reaching around his torso. Her legs gently writhed from the motions. Then his arms went higher, her legs moved slower, her arms clutched at the duvet cover, and then reached up to cling to his back with gripping fingers.

"All right," David said. "I suppose that's e— What's she doing?"

———

Charlie ran across the street after Clive. He was ahead of her, but half as fast. He got to the front door and unlocked it just as she caught up and sprinted past him.

"Boss!" Clive called out.

Charlie didn't wait for him, or for backup. She flew up the stairs, two steps at a time, and burst into the room to the sound of a creaking mattress and breathless, groaning agony.

But it wasn't the scene she had been expecting.

Sophie was straddling Dion and had the wedding veil wrapped tight around his neck. His legs were twitching as she choked him. Sophie was pulling up with all of her strength ensuring the full force of her efforts were centred on his carotid artery. Enough that Charlie could tell no blood or oxygen was getting to Dion's brain. It was a wonder he wasn't completely unconscious already. He'd be dead in seconds.

Sophie turned just enough to notice her. Her eyes were wide and glinting with an evil sort of intent. Like Charlie was interrupting something very dear to her that couldn't be excused or explained. An animalistic glare of a merciless hound defending the meal it had snared with its own vicious teeth.

Charlie was face to face with the Wedding Veil Killer, the stalker and serial murderer of adulterous married women across the Northwest, who happened to be in the process of killing a man.

Charlie ran forward and planted her foot just in range to throw a powerful roundhouse kick into Sophie's ribs. Charlie felt like she kicked a tree trunk—standard training—but it was enough to topple Sophie off of her target, and she fell to the floor along with an empty syringe, no doubt used to level the playing field and counter Dion's physical superiority with a powerful dose of Diazepam. Dion, unable to move, tried to suck in oxygen, while Sophie scrambled up and launched herself forward to tackle Charlie by her shins. Charlie braced her arms to stop Sophie from advancing and jabbed her in the spot between her shoulder and neck.

Sophie rolled off her and sprung to her feet, trying to stomp on Charlie's head. Charlie rolled out of the way and watched as Sophie escaped into the hall. She got up and sprinted after her, planning her route to intercept.

Sophie jumped down the stairs, almost the whole way, an athletic and intimidating feat that Charlie couldn't copy. She ran down the stairs as fast as she dared.

Sophie, in nothing but racy white lingerie, was crossing the foyer to the door, about to escape outside where her options to flee were limitless, when she was stopped. Something flew through the air, meeting her face and knocking her to the ground. She landed on her back an instant before a thick phone book landed next to her with a thud.

Clive hopped out of hiding from the doorway leading to the living room, retrieving the Yellow Pages from where it had fallen to the floor.

"Always comes in handy," he said, then went over and apprehended Sophie with some makeshift cuffs made of plastic zip-ties, one around the wrists and one around the ankles.

Sophie flopped like a fish briefly, then realised her predicament entirely. When Charlie reached her, her expression was flat. Glaring at nothing, her eyes were devoid of any light or thought or deeper meaning, dead like a wolf's eyes, watching its hunt being dragged off by nosy hunters with rifles.

David ran in soon after and came to a sudden stop in the doorway as he looked down at his wife being restrained by Clive.

Fearing the worst, Charlie was about to race back up to the master bedroom to check on Dion, when she saw him taking tentative steps down the stairs, one hand gingerly rubbing his bruised throat. The Wedding Veil Killer had been stopped before her next victim could be taken. And that would-be victim was a barefoot and bare-chested Adonis of a man.

"Right, boss," Clive said. "Police are on their way."

"And an ambulance," she called.

"Naturally," he said. "Not the case we took, was it?"

"No," she said. "Not at all."

Clive smiled up at her from where he sat beside Sophie.

Charlie knew she shouldn't smile with a scantily clad serial killer lying prone on the floor and her confused client trying to make sense of what he'd witnessed, but she couldn't help herself. They'd done the impossible and outdone themselves in every way. By morning, Merseyside Police would be releasing a statement that an arrest had been made in relation to the Wedding Veil murders, that a fiend of the modern ages had been apprehended. Courtesy of Charlie Chan & Co Detective Agency...

chapter
forty-one

THE DOORS OF CHARLIE CHAN & Co. Detective Agency finally opened after an impromptu, well-earned and restful, management-imposed duvet day. Crime never slept, but after putting down the region's most high-profile kidnapper and ensuring one of the UK's only female serial killers was behind bars, Charlie thought she and her team had earned a little break, even if it was just a day. She celebrated the reopening bright and early, at about the same time that Clive arrived, and they both entered the familiar office space.

The same one as before. No improvements or interior designer intervention, just the same old former beauty spa, but with the air of victory and good feelings hanging in the air. She'd just noticed that the bank account for the business got hit with the deposit from Dog's Hind Leg Records, more than the agency had earned collectively in the last six months. It was enough money that threats against not being able to pay out her employees wouldn't fly anymore, because she absolutely could.

Charlie went into her office and started her day with a courtesy call to check up on her client, Dave Phillips, who, she imagined, had gone through a tumultuous thirty-six hours since Sophie's arrest. He'd suspected his wife of

257

playing away from home whenever he went on business trips abroad. The truth regarding her other secret life was far more sinister.

Four women had been brutally murdered, and Dion was in hospital due to the injuries he'd sustained when she'd tried to kill him.

Why Sophie had made herself judge, jury, and executioner of cheating wives, when she had taken a female lover for years, was beyond Charlie. She hoped it would all come out in the trial. She was just pleased the danger had been removed from the streets, and that was a closure, of sorts.

Following the debrief from Ashley, it was clear that Dave was just a phone call from being behind bars himself. As to when the long arm of the law would come down on his shoulders, that was dependent on when Leslie decided to dynamite the foundations of his illicit property portfolio.

Bribery, corruption, and racketeering would just be the first course of the charges he'd be facing. But she wasn't being paid to investigate Dave, and she shouldn't know about Leslie's damning collection of evidence, so that wouldn't be a topic she'd be covering on the call.

She cleared her throat, unsure quite how to prepare for such a conversation, and just decided to hit the call button.

"Hello, Mr. Phillips," she began. "It's Charlie."

"Hey," he said.

"I just wanted to see how you're doing?"

He sighed. It wasn't his usual pathetic, glum sigh, but a hopeful one. "You know what, I'm actually a little bit relieved. Like someone's taken a huge weight off."

"Are the police looking after you?"

"Now they know I wasn't an accomplice or something." Dave paused, still processing the events of the last few days, weeks and months. "It doesn't feel real at all. You think you know someone."

"It's fair to say you instinctively knew something was amiss. What will you do?"

"Need to sell up. Press has been camped outside for days. Neighbours aren't talking to me. It's an opportunity, I suppose. Haven't quite got my head around it all."

"Well, if I can offer any advice, don't rush any decisions. Take your time," Charlie said. "I'm sorry the secret we uncovered wasn't what any of us were expecting. As for our fee— Given the circumstances—"

"I already sent it," he said, "International transfer from my Brussels account. So, it might not clear until tomorrow morning. But you don't need to worry. We had a contract."

Charlie was genuinely surprised. Since she'd taken on the case, a little part of her had been worried Dave had been racking up the hours with no real intention of paying up unless they'd turned up the proof that Sophie had been having an affair. Another one. With a man. She'd mentally prepared herself for having to pursue him in the Small Claims Court to recover her costs.

Now that Dave was, unbeknownst to him, likely facing a lengthy incarceration and the high probability that most, if not all, of his assets would be seized, she really had given up hope of seeing a penny. Waiving their fee had seemed like the decent thing to do and would have saved her from being disappointed that she'd been right all along. She was pleased to be wrong.

"I appreciate it. And I'm sorry."

"Yeah. Me too," Dave replied. "I'll see you."

Dave ended the call and Charlie exhaled.

She had one more call to make. It seemed a lifetime ago she'd run into Dion in Noise & Friction. They'd danced, they'd exchanged a few words and, for the first time in a long time, she'd actually, genuinely, been attracted to a guy. Whilst there was a casual arrogance to him, he had the physique and the charm to pull it off. She'd been enjoying herself and although she never mixed business with pleasure, she had let herself think, *What if he just kissed me?* as he'd leaned into her ear to make his apologies. She'd be lying if she hadn't felt a pang of jealousy when she'd been fobbed off for his true targets that night—Sophie and Anna—leaving Charlie with a lingering regret of a path not taken.

Charlie found his profile online and clicked through to Contact. She tapped the number into her phone and took a deep breath as it began to ring.

"Dion's phone," a bright, cheerful Trinidadian voice replied.

"Oh. Hi. This is Charlie. I was hoping to check up on Dion."

"He's not quite up for talking yet, but he's recovering just fine."

"That's good to hear. Well, if you could tell him I—"

"Police told me I have you to thank for my son still being with us. God bless you, child. I don't have the words to express how grateful I am." Dion's mum's voice began to shake.

"That's quite alright, Mrs Joseph. I'm glad he's on the mend."

"Doctors said he had a partially collapsed windpipe, hard to heal up, but with a neck brace and lots of mommy's home cooking, he should be alright again in no time."

"That's wonderful to hear," Charlie said. "I'm… glad things weren't worse."

"I'll tell him you called. I've no doubt he'll want to speak with you himself, when he can."

"Have the police let you know when it will go to Crown Court?"

"Not yet," she said. "They want to interview him, to check a few things, but the solicitor says your videos will be enough to secure a conviction. She's on her way to prison. For a long, long time."

"Great," Charlie said. "Maybe we'll see each other at court."

"Yeah," she said. "It's strange to make friends on the telephone, but sometimes it works out quite well."

As morning became lunchtime and then afternoon, it was clear to the whole team that Charlie's agency was now well and truly on the map. Before, work had been somewhat tidal, ebbing and flowing with what seemed to be the phases of the moon. More often than not, there had been long periods of rest where the team burned through the goodwill and good pay of their last job to wait for the next big thing.

However, something unusual was afoot at the agency. The phones hadn't stopped ringing. People were calling from all over the country, even internationally, to give their attention and time to the detectives who'd rescued Emefa and put the Wedding Veil Killer behind bars. Not all of them were job requests. Clive ended up learning about quite a few new crank call techniques and YouTube gotchas from the youth as a result.

"Don't," Ash tutted when he saw Charlie pick up her phone, about to dial Sergeant Jarvis for the third time that morning to try and get an update on both Simon and Sophie.

Simon was on remand in Walton, awaiting trial and was likely facing a very lengthy sentence. Charlie knew she was being paranoid, but after so many suspects had danced and weaved their way around the justice system, she couldn't help feeling a little on edge that their evidence, or Emefa's own testimony, somehow would be insufficient to secure a conviction. She dropped the phone back on the desk and put up her hands in surrender.

Sophie was on remand in HMP Styal and the body of evidence against her was growing and growing. A positive DNA match placed her in the bedroom of Janet Bambridge, her third victim, without an alibi. Charlie's own video footage of the events at the Philipps' household had led to charges of attempted murder. Forensics would be re-examining the first two murder scenes in the hope that something was missed the first time around.

Charlie prayed to her ancestors that there would be enough to throw away the key. She'd call Sarge later to check that there'd been no change, when there wasn't a team of professional investigators watching her every move, ready to mock her paranoia.

After her rescue, Emefa immediately went into a sort of public resurgence as a mix of her old and new self. The restrained and artistic Emefa that Simon tried to cultivate and rear, was used as the front for the real Emefa to speak through about her honest and sincere opinions of the pop-idol world. Namely how it sucks, and she hates it and wants to move on to acting. How learning to lie to, and play along with, her captor was what had kept her safe and sane for the best part of a year. The frankness about widely regarded industry secrets was a breath of fresh air for her fans, who were glad to see her back in one form or another.

And in her first major interview, which was viewed online so many times that the record label's pay-walled streaming app crashed several times, she mentioned Charlie Chan & Co. Detective Agency in Liverpool, and how a group of her fans led the charge to rescue her by decoding the secrets in her first song as a hostage. That name drop did more marketing than they could have ever done.

Though, it wasn't without issues.

"Hello?" Clive answered the phone for the fiftieth time that morning. "Can you say again? You're looking for Dee—what? Dee's what? Nuts? What kind? Almonds? I think you've got the wrong number, sorry mate." He hung up. "Is a nut bandit really worth ringing up about?"

The phone rang again before he could catch his breath, or before Rebecca could teach him what mockery was being had at his expense. She also had her hands full with answering emails, texts, working the social media pages, and live updating their new blog with the long-form tale of Operation Punk's Not Dead from her heroic perspective.

Ashley sauntered into Charlie's office with a casual knock on the open door.

"Well done, boss," he said. "Your stock value has just shot up. You're getting noticed, for all the right reasons. And that's no mean feat."

Charlie nodded, accepting the praise from her first employee and knowing that she would need to have words with Ashley about his unauthorised date night with Leslie at some point. But not today.

She wanted to cheer and laugh and joke with the rest of the team. She wanted to give them all a rousing speech about how this was the first day of the rest of their lives. She should be popping open the champagne and ordering in lunch. Of course, she was pleased with the prestige the two latest collars brought her business, her friends, and herself. She did what she did for the sake of the common good of stopping a terrible evil. But she was also doing it for someone else. She reached into her pocket and felt the ornate jade mahjong tile. All that fame had to lead to something.

Hopefully, someday, it would lead to him...

epilogue

It was another night at work for Ash. This time, however, he was under a new obligation to go it alone. Clive had dinner with an old platoon pal who was in town, Charlie was busy helping her mum get settled into her new apartment, and Rebecca called in her favour from two weeks ago when he'd begged her to cover for him.

So, he was on a stakeout. Alone.

The job—a suspicious company director was concerned that his star salesman was ripping him off by using the company credit card to impress his wife, but claiming he was wining-and-dining clients. He needed photographic evidence to prove no such clients were present.

Ash was in the back of the van and had a camera fixed on a window table at a restaurant up the street, only occasionally blocked by a passing vehicle. It was focused on the salesman in question, as he tucked in to his five-star appetiser. He was with his wife at a table for two. It was clear from the outset no clients or prospects were joining them. While the camera recorded, Ash lounged back in the driver seat so far that he was nearly horizontal.

Someone tapped at the back door, which startled Ash so much that he fell backwards and hit the floor. He feared the worst. It could have been a nosy neighbour, a vile teen with hands full of spray paint or blades to do his tyres, or a cop, who'd never heard of their agency or the specific laws relating to recording in public, looking to make an easy arrest. He crawled over and cracked open the door to see who it was.

"What are you doing here?"

"What?" Rebecca asked. "I can't come hang out with a friend from work?"

She held up a small bag of clinking, chilly bottles. Ash assessed her mood, her tone, and the beer she'd brought. He raised his seat upright and invited her into the van, but remained suspicious even as he reached for one of the drinks she was sure to hand over. She didn't, immediately. She just held them up and smiled.

"Is that all you're here for, really?" he asked.

She shrugged. "Yeah, actually. I was more bored than I thought, so why drink alone when I can drink with a friend?"

Ash looked again at the bottles. "It's zero percent beer. Is it really drinking at all?"

"You're on duty, and in charge of a motor vehicle. And I don't really like beer."

"Fair enough. What about the favour, though?" he asked. "You're not gonna turn around and get me to cover again next week, are you?"

"Nope," she said. "We're already even."

"Nice," he said.

She offered him a bottle. They clinked and glugged back their pretend beers.

The next half hour passed uneventfully. The couple followed their tempura prawn starter with a generous selection of maki and teriyaki chicken, which left Ash feeling both jealous and hungry.

"You sort out things with Sarge?"

Rebecca took a sip of her beer. "Yep."

"Oh, come on. That's all you're gonna share? I don't know if I should be welcoming your dad into our office, or knocking him out for upsetting you."

"That's sweet," Rebecca admitted. "But please don't fight him. Anyway, he'd probably win and you wouldn't be able to deal with the humiliation."

"I'd risk that for my bestie." He clinked the bottom of his bottle on the top of hers and grinned as the froth rose up the neck and cascaded all over her top and leggings.

"You're a knob."

"Stop objectifying me!" Ash grinned, then reached into the glove compartment for a box of tissues and handed them over.

Rebecca dabbed at the wet spots, but it was a lost cause and she gave up. "It was stupid really. He wanted me to 'dress normal' in the house. I wouldn't do it, and it turned into something bigger."

"You've been living out of the back of your car for weeks because your dad wanted you to wear a frock?"

"When you say it *like that*, I know it doesn't capture the nuance. But I needed to make a statement; I'm not his little girl anymore. I needed him to accept me for who I am, not who he expects me to be. We had it out last night. It got… emotional. We're good now."

"Glad to hear it," Ash looked Rebecca up and down. "I can't imagine which part of the ensemble offended him most."

"Piss off."

They opened another bottle each and watched the evening antics of scousers on a night out.

"Come on. You show me yours and I'll show you mine," Rebecca offered with a wicked grin.

"Excuse me?"

"Tinder. What y' got?"

Ash side-eyed Becca, still not sure of her motives, but was

too intrigued to miss the opportunity. He whipped out his phone and started swiping through profiles. He turned the screen to Becca.

"You," Ash said, "would like *her*."

He showed her the image of a girl who posed in a black strappy corset with thick shoulder straps, bright blue tattoos on either shoulder, neon blue raver hair, and a split lip with a huge piercing through it.

"Why would I like her?" Rebecca asked. "She probably knows some good places for concerts, though. I might like her music but—"

"That's a start," Ash said.

"What about him?" Becca pointed to her own Tinder app. There was a very strong-looking man with a not-so-strong-looking jaw that was blatantly a different tone from the rest of his body. "People should have to pass some sort of test before they're allowed to install Photoshop." She giggled.

"The poor guy." He shook his head. "He's probably thinking, why won't anyone swipe on me? Bro, most of that picture ain't even you!"

"He needs you," she said, pushing the phone into his face.

"Yeah," he said, "as a friend. No one's on here looking for friends."

"Not with that attitude they aren't," she said.

"What about this chick?" he said, offering her another girl to ogle.

Rebecca shrugged and swiped left on Ash's behalf.

Ash recoiled and pulled his phone away from Rebecca. "Hey! No touchy! I might have swiped right for her."

"No, you wouldn't."

"Yeah, you're right, I wouldn't."

Ash looked down again at his screen and swiped another potential wife into the long grass of rejection, then paused. His eyes and mouth did their best impression of the shocked emoji.

"What is it?" Becca asked.

Ash hid his phone from her and looked at it again, just to be sure. It wasn't a scandalous picture at all. Not for Tinder. He was more shocked than anything.

"Don't freak out," he said. "You know how we, sometimes, make fake accounts?"

"Yeah?" she said.

"And we *don't* use our real names and professions?" he added.

"Y-yeah?"

"Well..." He turned his phone to Becca. She mirrored his expression when she saw it.

Charlie Chan, 23, in a beige pantsuit with glasses, smiling like she was posing for a company *meet the team* photo. Her personal information was there as well, her schooling and interests and her position as CEO & Lead Investigator at a detective agency—all public for the Tinder user base to find and judge.

"Home girl's got game." Ash swiped through the gallery of Charlie's profile shots.

They were so fixated on finding Charlie's Tinder profile that they missed the moment when their stakeout target asked the waiters to pull another table next to theirs and they were joined by another two couples. That case would have to wait.

Adi Flynn

JOIN THE MAILING LIST

WWW.ADIFLYNN.COM/MAILING-LIST

JOIN TODAY

BINGE THE SERIES NOW

READ THE NEXT
CHARLIE CHAN
CRIME THRILLER

SCAN TO CONTINUE

BAL
KON
media

A CHARLIE CHAN CRIME THRILLER

#BOOKTOK MADE ME DO IT

ADI FLYNN

#booktok made me
do it

In the pulsating heart of Liverpool, Charlie Chan and her vibrant team of Gen-Z detectives are plunged into a new, darkly viral terror.

Inspired by the murders in a #BookTok bestseller, a malevolent killer paints the city red with copycat slayings, signing each kill with a hashtag. The team must go deep into the TikTok phenomenon to prevent more innocent readers from becoming a victim of these brutal crimes.

Charlie Chan & Co. navigate the treacherous waters of fame, passion, and social media fandom, to battle a killer who remains one step ahead. As the body count rises, they are confronted with a chilling question: How many lives will be extinguished in the quest to stop a murderer who carves a legacy through virtual trends and historical terror?

prologue

It was a quiet evening across Liverpool. It would be another week until payday. Disposable income had long been disposed of—credit cards were maxed, sofa cushions searched, and children's piggy banks raided for all but pennies. The good, the bad, and the beautiful were hunkered down indoors, in forced hibernation, until they could afford to come out again and play.

It was on nights like this that the click-clack of a lone female hurrying home after a late shift echoed on foggy streets. It was the kind of night that nocturnal wildlife rummaged in bins and alley cats fought. The kind of night where Gothic horrors and Victorian mysteries abound. A night prime for evildoing and murder. A night just like the ones so vividly described in the twenty-weeks-at-number-one Young Adult bestseller *Teenhunter*.

The alt-history retelling of Jack the Ripper had become a #BookTok sensation, taking the UK, Australia, and the more literate parts of the US by storm. Each scene was so viscerally detailed that even those least acquainted with their own imaginations could feel the terror emanate off the pages, and coat their sweating hands.

One such reader was so deeply enraptured with the book

that they were covered in much of their own blood and hung halfway out of their bedroom window. They were a fan with a TikTok account dedicated to lauding the book and vehemently defending its rising success against haters. They'd fought the good fight, but there were always bigger fans online.

A cloaked figure stood in the super-fan's room, their apparel deliberately mirroring the design of the killer's wardrobe in the novel. An old-style navy blue nautical peacoat hid an elaborate mirage of different clothing, with each fluttering angle offering a glimpse of a patchwork ensemble to confuse any potential witnesses, and confound the investigating officers, who would, no doubt, be pouring over the scene in a matter of hours. Some parts of the suit beneath were pinstriped, others patterned with paisley decoration, and still others glimmered with faux satin. A kaleidoscope of false identities, just like the eponymous killer wore.

The real-life killer opened the victim's copy of the book and flipped to an early passage. Partway through chapter three, where the crime scene was revealed, and the mystery began in earnest. They checked the scene around them for the details. The body was hanging out the window, with bloodletting from signature wounds. That part was done. Blood on the bedspread where the murder had taken place was cleaned up, and the fragments of stained cloth were cut out and stashed in the killer's inner coat pockets.

The killer looked around the room. It was nothing like the room described in the novel. It was too modern. There were neither LED spotlights nor electrical sockets in a tenement building in Victorian London. They weren't even in London. The skyline that the corpse beheld as their soul left the confines of this mortal plane—another crucial scene from the book—was impossible without the great clock tower in the distance to catch the rays of light that would reflect heat and begin to decay the body before investigators arrived.

The breakage in the window, likewise, wasn't right. Windows back then were made of proper glass. These modern, double-paned windows had tempered glass—built for safety—not impossible to break, but when it does, it shatters into tiny fragments. The toothy appearance the killer was going for, as if the house had grown a set of fanged jaws with which to profanely gnash the body to pieces, couldn't be replicated. The stubby glass edges around the body resembled molars rather than incisors, more likely to ground and chew than bite.

The last part of the scene required assembly. The killer took a scrap of a cut-up baby's bonnet and slipped it into the book, marking the page of the death scene being imitated. The bonnet was just a doll's costume, but it was close enough. Approximation seemed to be the only recourse for emulating such a fantastical scene. The only actual gaslight fantasy around was the delusion of house heating prices staying low.

The killer found a spot on the victim's desk, swept the unfinished homework assignment to the side, and placed the book on a holder. A lamp in the corner was pulled over and swivelled to provide dramatic backlighting, so only the foil-embossed letters of the cover, *Teenhunter*, were illuminated. The killer then arranged the finishing touches, made up of items from the victim's own drawers.

First, a doily, old-fashioned enough to look like it came out of the right era, but with a hidden tag holding washing instructions and a warning not to use near open flames on the underside. It slid in under the book to hide the holder. Then a vase, intentionally broken. It looked handmade. The shard of glass which made the killer's impromptu knife was smooth instead of bloody sharp, but that detail didn't show up on camera. Then a glove, one the victim wore, which the killer delicately held in their own gloved hand.

The killer left a smudge of the deceased's blood across the leather's backside and moved it into place, just enough to see the missing fingertips. The macabre diorama complete, a short video was recorded of the ensemble. With one last look at the victim, immobile with their stomach cut deep into the serrated glass of their bedroom window, the killer left the room as silently as they'd entered.

It was a perfect night for a murder, in and out of fiction...

about the author

Adi Flynn always wanted to be a private eye—devouring everything from Victoria Mars to Magnum P.I., Sherlock to Strike, and reading all the hard-boiled noir he could get his hands on—but that didn't happen…

So, instead, he lives vicariously through his characters who, quite frankly, are far better at it than he would have been.

www.adiflynn.com
  @adiflynn_books

BALKON
media

Printed in Great Britain
by Amazon

57547028R00169